CAPTIVA MEMORIES

CAPTIVA ISLAND SERIES
BOOK THREE

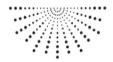

ANNIE CABOT

CABOT PUBLISHING GROUP

Copyright © 2022 by Annie Cabot

All rights reserved.

No part of this book may be reproduced in any form or by any electronic or mechanical means, including information storage and retrieval systems, without written permission from the author, except for the use of brief quotations in a book review.

ISBN ebook, 978-1-7377321-4-3

ISBN paperback, 978-1-7377321-5-0

Cover Design by Marianne Nowicki, Premade Ebook Cover Shop

For the latest information on new book releases and special giveaways, click here to be added to my list.

❦ Created with Vellum

A FEW WORDS...

This story was inspired by actual events. It is, however, a work of fiction and therefore should not be taken as actual fact.
There are two important and sensitive topics in this book that need to be addressed.
The first is military wounded and limb amputation specifically.
I've done the best research that I can on these topics as I've not had first-hand exposure to either subject. I hope you will let me know if there are any errors in my depiction of these issues.
The second is suicide.
This is another sensitive topic that I'm not personally touched by. However, it's important to state that if you or someone you know is thinking about suicide, please get help.

You can reach out to:
https://samaritanshope.org/
They are there to prevent suicide and provide hope.

PROLOGUE

Christopher Wheeler watched his mother lift his seabag and place it in the corner of the room. Maggie leaned the crutches against the nightstand so that he could easily reach for them from the bed. He admired the cozy atmosphere of the place, but this room, especially with a chair near the window, appealed to him. *A perfect place to hide.*

His mother had taken great care to help him settle into his new home. The Key Lime Garden Inn, although a traveler's destination, would serve his desire to enjoy his surroundings while staying invisible. Any interest in him would fade as soon as the guests went about their vacation. A corner chair provided a perfect spot for him to look out the window and watch the butterflies swoop in and out of the bush, and he could hear the ocean waves crashing against the sand.

The awkwardness that hung over them started the minute his mother met him at the airport. Christopher wondered how long before he would wear out his welcome. Perhaps he should have had a Plan B if this arrangement failed.

He could tell that his mother didn't know how to talk to him, and that suited him fine because he didn't want to talk anyway.

She and her new husband, Paolo Moretti, had built a ramp for wheelchair access when they took over the inn. Such things were required for establishments these days. He imagined that his mother had no idea at the time that one day her youngest son would have need of it.

"Would you like to take a tour of the place? I know you must be tired, but I'd love to show you around."

"Not right now, Mom. I am tired. I'd like to take a nap if that's all right with you."

"Of course."

Maggie turned down the bed and then lowered the shades. "We get lots of sun here. You'll need to keep the shades down if you want to sleep in the middle of the day."

Christopher smiled and nodded. "That's fine."

She stood in the doorway, unsure of what to do or say next.

"Do you need help getting into the bed?"

"No."

The second he answered her, he regretted it. He sounded angry, and he was, but none of this was her fault.

"I'm sorry, Mom. I can manage on my own."

She looked lost. He could see her needing something more to do for him.

"Mom, you're going to have to get used to this. Being in this wheelchair isn't a temporary thing. I'm sure I'll probably fall now and then, and you can't always be there to pick me up. Do you think you can stop hovering?"

"I'm sorry, Christopher. I didn't mean to hover. I understand what you're saying. This is all so new. I'm not sure when to help and when to leave you be."

"I know."

He could tell that she heard his words but was a long way from accepting his situation. That made two of them.

"I've got to run over to Chelsea's for a bit. If you need anything at all, send me a text."

Christopher held up his cell phone and wiggled it. "If it makes you feel any better, I'll put it right next to the bed."

His mother closed the door behind her as she left, and he immediately wheeled his chair to the window instead of getting into the bed. The garden looked beautiful and abundant with flowers and vegetables. He could see his stepfather, Paolo, cutting the grass.

Looking down at his legs, he cringed. They had amputated his right leg just above the knee; his pants folded under what remained. No matter how many times he played the day of the bombing over in his mind, he couldn't make the leap from laying on the ground to sitting in a wheelchair. Piecing together what he remembered with what he was told proved almost impossible. Too many days and nights passed before he found himself under his mother's care once again.

He wheeled himself back near the nightstand and pulled one crutch close. Standing on his left leg, he leaned onto it. He pushed the wheelchair out of the way and sat on the bed.

What seemed like a small maneuver drained him quickly. These were the moments that frustrated him. He'd ran marathons and jumped out of airplanes. Now, he couldn't get onto his bed without concentrated effort.

Realization set in fast—that was before. Before he lost his closest friend in the world. The day that ended everything for him and began a new life that would expect much of him. It would demand that he believe in a future filled with joy and happiness and would insist he get on-board with living.

Except he didn't know how and felt no desire to try. The days following post-op were a blur. Surgeons, nurses, occupational therapists, physical therapists, and social workers, each involved with his care and rehabilitation annoyed him and so, he did little to assist in his recovery.

His lack of interest in a prosthetic device fitting, kept him firmly in his wheelchair most days, and although he'd met with a psychiatrist a few times, he hated those sessions and dismissed the man after four appointments.

With very little interest in healing, he struggled to get out of bed every morning. His family's love and support meant the world to him, but he couldn't forgive himself for being alive when so many of his friends were dead.

That pain tortured him every minute of every day. Now, living on Captiva Island, he planned to lay low and keep his suffering confined to his room as much as possible.

He placed the crutch up against the other and lay back on the bed. He longed to be back in Iraq. He wanted to fight those who killed his brothers and sisters. The military had become his home, the soldiers, his family. Now all he had left of that life were memories.

He stared at the ceiling, feeling untethered and alone. It would take a miracle to bring him out of this darkness. If he could only sleep. Maybe when he next opened his eyes, that miracle would come. The only problem was that he didn't believe in miracles. He didn't believe in anything anymore.

He reached inside his shirt and pulled out the dog tags that hung around his neck. Everyone had a set—one to stay with the body for identification, and one to be sent back to the family in the event of death. Christopher wiped the tears that fell with the sleeve of his shirt. He never knew what happened to his friend Nick, only that he'd been killed in the blast.

For now, finding out what happened to him was the one thing that gave him purpose. As soon as he was able, he made a promise to himself that he would visit Nick's family and tell them all that he had promised to. He'd explain it all, and then, whatever happened after that, he didn't much care.

CHAPTER ONE

*B*ecca Powell locked the door to Powell Water Sports and threw the keys into her backpack. Getting on her bike, she decided to ride to the Key Lime Garden Inn.

The inn was only a few blocks from the store and although the sun had just set in the sky, she didn't yet need to turn on the bike's headlight. Weaving along the sidewalk path, her heart raced in anticipation. All she wanted to do was look in the window in the off chance that she might see him.

Once she reached the inn, she walked her bike along the shell-covered driveway and then parked it up against the bike rack. If anyone noticed her she would simply explain that she'd lost her sunglasses and wanted to see if she'd left them inside when she cleaned the rooms that morning.

The lights were on, and she could see a few guests relaxing in the living room. Two people were outside on the porch, enjoying their wine and the cool night air. Lights were on in the carriage house too, which meant that either Maggie Wheeler-Moretti or her husband Paolo were home.

Careful not to make too much noise, she figured her best bet was to go inside and take her chances. She could see the chefs,

Riley, and Grace, putting out the breakfast settings in the dining room. Before long, they too, would leave and the inn would be quiet except for the voices on the porch.

She hadn't thought beyond seeing him, but now, facing the window, reality hit. What would she say to him? It had been ten years since she last saw Christopher Wheeler, and for all she knew, he probably didn't remember her.

She pictured his face as if it were yesterday. His light brown hair was long on top to the point that it flipped over his eyes when it got wet. Back then, she'd made fun of him and in response he'd pull her underwater, pretending to drown her.

Nothing about their first meeting gave her a hint that they would spend every minute of the summer constantly by each other's side.

Always up for a game of volleyball, her best friend Stacie and Stacie's brother Kyle set up a net, and before long, a group of kids joined them.

Christopher was on the opposing team, and as they played, he impressed Becca with his athletic ability. She decided to find out more about him so that they'd include him in any future games.

"Stacie, who is that guy? He's really good."

"I know. His name is Christopher Wheeler. He's here on vacation with his family. I wish he were here for the whole summer. We could use a good player on our team."

Becca agreed. "I know what you mean. I'm getting tired of losing."

As soon as their game was over, Becca walked up to Christopher. Her emerald eyes met his and when she couldn't think of anything to say, she said, "Nice game."

He nodded and then walked away.

As it happened, the Wheeler family stayed on Captiva Island for five weeks. Their father would return to Massachusetts for work, but their mother, Maggie, and her children remained behind.

Becca loved a challenge and decided that five weeks was plenty of time to get to know Christopher. The day after the game, she saw him on the beach once again. Never shy, she plopped down on his blanket and started talking.

"Hi. I'm Becca."

She could tell that he didn't want to talk, but that didn't stop her.

"You're Christopher, right?"

He nodded. "How do you know my name?"

"My friend Stacie's brother knows you. You play volleyball really well. Do you play any other sports?"

"Yeah, I play football back home."

"Where's home?"

"Andover, Massachusetts. How about you? Where are you from?"

"I'm an islander, born and raised. I have three annoying brothers too. My family owns Powell Water Sports, do you know it?"

"Yeah, I know it. My brother Michael went in there yesterday."

"What did he buy?"

Christopher shrugged. "Nothing. He said everything was too expensive."

Becca laughed. She couldn't tell if he was teasing her or was serious. Either way, she liked the way he talked. She didn't know Massachusetts very well, but if Andover was anywhere near Boston, then that explained his accent. Lots of tourists came to Captiva from Boston, and she could recognize a Bostonian the minute they opened their mouth.

Christopher and Becca talked for hours about everything and nothing in particular. Becca loved to run and so every morning she'd get up early and hit the beach. She'd talked him into joining her and soon they became inseparable.

Each day when Becca finished working at the store, she

would run to the beach where he'd be waiting for her. If they weren't running, they were biking, swimming, water-skiing and occasionally, collecting seashells. They'd run to the Mucky Duck for sandwiches and then ride their bikes along the various paths leading into Sanibel.

They had an unspoken competition between them. Everything they did seemed like another opportunity to win or lose. If they had to bike somewhere, she'd pedal as hard as she could to move ahead of him.

If they played volleyball, she insisted they be on opposite teams so she could say she beat him. It became a game to her but one that she took seriously. When he asked her why it was so important to her that she win, all she would say was, "I don't play to lose."

Becca asked for more time off from work and her parents indulged her. Their only girl, she had never been interested in any boy until Christopher Wheeler came to the island.

Her parents knew how short-lived summer romances were and prepared themselves for tears and pouting when it was over. Every now and then, her father would remind her that she had responsibilities at the store, but he'd say it with a knowing smile. Her mother explained to him that she was still a child and should be allowed to enjoy her friends.

Becca wasn't dumb. She knew what everyone was thinking—that summer romances never last. Even if the memory of a first kiss lingers, the realities of life take over the minute Labor Day rolls around. By Christmas, you might even find yourself in love with someone new.

But that didn't happen for Becca. Christopher Wheeler dominated her thoughts all through the months of September, October, and November. She'd spent countless hours trying to figure out how she could get to Andover, Massachusetts from Florida. She'd struggled with schoolwork because she'd been daydreaming about him. When she failed Algebra, her parents became concerned.

Becca and Christopher stayed in touch through email and texts but after a few months, all communication suddenly stopped. When he didn't answer her by January, she gave up. Christopher Wheeler would forever be nothing more than a childhood memory—something to be put away in a box for the attic like her roller skates and Beanie Babies.

When the Wheelers returned to the island the following summer, Becca did her best to stay as far away from Christopher as possible. But it was no use. The island was small, and her family's business made it impossible to avoid the Wheelers completely. She needn't have worried though. Christopher never stopped into the shop or asked for her. She'd assumed that he had moved on with another girl and forgotten all about their friendship.

Years passed and, for Becca, the memory of Christopher Wheeler had become a happy one. It warmed her heart to remember her first kiss and the boy who stole her heart. She had long ago lost any anger toward him and saw their romance for what it was—a sweet young puppy love to be remembered and treasured.

When Becca heard the news that Maggie Wheeler was buying the Key Lime Garden Inn property, she investigated further. *What were the chances that it would be Christopher's mother? Could it be that his family decided to move to the island permanently?*

Eventually, Becca started working part-time at the inn, not to get information on Christopher, but rather to do something more than work alongside her brothers at the store. She loved the work and never asked Maggie about her son.

Her new boss rarely talked to her about the Wheeler family, but when the news came that Christopher would be living at the inn, Becca's heart raced. Maggie explained that he had been injured in Iraq and would be coming to Captiva to rest. She didn't share more details than that, but it was enough to pique Becca's interest.

She stood on top of a large boulder and peered in the window. The lights were dimmed, and she couldn't see anyone now. She decided to throw caution to the wind and go inside—her innocent lie at the ready if anyone asked.

She walked through the rooms but saw no one. A slightly open door to the first-floor bedroom and a dimly lit lamp made it possible for her to see the front wheels of a wheelchair and a blanket over a man's legs.

The man maneuvered a few feet to open the bedroom door. Once opened, the wheelchair turned, and his blanket fell to the floor. She ran to pick it up, and the man wrenched it from her hands. She stood and looked at him, coming face-to-face with the boy she knew so many years ago.

Although she tried not to appear shocked, her face must have given her away. Christopher seemed angry at her, and even though she knew it was him, he seemed a stranger to her.

"What do you want?"

Panic set in, and she responded with her prepared excuse.

"I...um...I'm looking for my sunglasses. I worked here this morning and thought maybe I'd left them in one of the rooms."

His face looked ashen, and his eyes were without life. Her heart broke for him. She wanted to look away but couldn't. Becca waited for him to recognize her, but he showed no interest in continuing their conversation.

He turned his wheelchair around and headed back to his room. He never looked at her again, instead, saying, "If my mother finds them, I'm sure she'll let you know."

Once inside his room, he shut the door behind him.

Tears began to fill her eyes, but she willed herself not to cry. Maggie had told her that Christopher was injured, but she didn't give any details about that injury. Seeing his leg, her mind raced with questions that were impossible to answer. Christopher seemed a bitter, isolated man, and although he was someone with whom she had a brief history, it gave her no privileges to insert herself into his life.

Overwhelmed with emotion, she ran out the back door and to her bike. She jumped on and raced down the driveway, and off the property. It started to rain as she rode her bike on the sidewalk path. Water dripped down her face and she let her tears finally fall, wiping them away with the sleeve of her sweatshirt. By the time she arrived home, she was soaked through her clothes.

Becca wasn't sure what made her cry—the sight of her old friend in the wheelchair or the fact that he didn't have a clue who she was. Either way, she now had a new memory of him that she could put away with all the others and pray that Christopher's return would give her the closure she didn't know she needed.

Christopher knew what he was doing when he asked his mother if he could stay with her on Captiva Island. He needed to feel the warm salt air on his skin and rest in a place that had become his oasis years earlier. He decided that the island would be his medicine—a place that would provide a quiet, slow, and uneventful recovery. One step at a time was ironic to say the least, but he had no other choice but to focus on each moment.

He had fond memories of the island, and the young girl who became his first real girlfriend ten years earlier. He'd kept her photograph with him all these years and told himself that it was nothing more than a distraction from the horrors around him.

Laying on his bed in the barracks, he'd look at the picture whenever he needed to fantasize about his life back home. He imagined Becca in her swimsuit, hair up in a ponytail, water-skiing and having fun on Captiva's shores. He smiled when he thought back to their days playing volleyball and how she impressed him with her athletic ability.

He pushed those images out of his mind and accepted his new reality. The woman standing before him now was a stranger—an intruder. She had no right to show up like this. He wanted the inn to be his hiding place for the foreseeable future. The memories of his childhood served no purpose and, if he let them, would remain a ghost to haunt him.

Did she say she worked here?

Clutching the blanket, he turned his wheelchair toward his room, dismissing her. The next sound he heard was the slam of the back door. He could hear her footsteps crunch along the seashell-covered driveway but then a steady rain fell, making it impossible to hear anything more.

Good. Maybe she'll quit.

He wheeled his chair to the desk and pulled out a notebook. He had used it to make notes and construct letters during his time in Iraq. After he was hit, they gathered his belongings and gave them to his mother when she arrived in Germany.

He opened the notebook and turned the pages to where a plastic bag held various personal items. He pulled out a high school ring and turned it in his hands. Wilson Barker High School letters shone through the dirt. His wallet carried little inside except his license and military Common Access Card for identification, along with two family photos and one of Becca Powell—pieces of a life that didn't exist any longer.

He pushed the items aside and wheeled himself to the window. Rain pounded against the house competing with his heart's rhythm. The storm unsettled his nerves, and he couldn't shake the chill in his bones. He pulled the blanket up to cover his chest, leaned his head against the windowpane, and thought about Erin Stenwick.

She'd be twenty-six now. He remembered how much she loved

singing, and all her high school musical performances. By now she'd probably be traveling the world making music.

Christopher and Erin were part of a larger group of friends that did everything together. Erin thought of Christopher as her boyfriend, even though he didn't return the feelings.

He did his best to keep things as casual as possible, but often he had to remind her that he didn't want that kind of relationship. She'd pout for a few minutes, but then would smile and say she was only teasing. She'd said that he was her best friend and confided in him about everything, including the abuse she suffered at home.

He felt helpless to do anything about it but promised her that he'd think of a way to get her the help she needed. Surely, there were adults who could find a place for her to live until she was eighteen. He even thought about asking his parents if she could stay with them. As soon as his family returned from Captiva Island, he'd see what could be done.

He never got to fulfill his promise. Erin died the summer Christopher met Becca. She'd walked into the pond near her house and took her last breath before going under. A note left by her bedside explained that she couldn't deal with the abuse any longer.

Christopher left Captiva Island that summer, in love and committed to growing his relationship with Becca, but the pain and guilt he felt over the loss of his friend proved too much for him.

He tried to answer Becca's emails and texts but couldn't bring himself to enjoy any happiness with her. He didn't believe that he deserved it. Eventually, he stopped answering her altogether and assumed she'd get over whatever feelings she had for him in time.

Now, after all these years, he was forced to look into her green eyes once again. He vowed to stay clear of her and hoped it would be enough to allow him to focus on what needed to be done.

CHAPTER TWO

*B*eth Wheeler stared at the papers on her desk and sighed. She looked at the clock and chewed the end of her pencil. She'd promised herself that no amount of ambition served her well if she got sick from lack of sleep. The brass ring was only available to her if she put in the hours, but she also wanted a life outside the office just as much as a promotion.

After law school, she never thought she'd be lucky enough to work in the District Attorney's office. She had to pinch herself at her good fortune. Growing up, she watched her father work long hours into the night and their family suffered for it. Determined to do things differently, she'd booked activities like yoga classes, gym time, and nights out with girlfriends, and even left time to date, but her efforts were thwarted time and again.

Beth didn't anticipate the long hours in the office. She'd canceled get-togethers with her friends, her gym membership, and if not for the perseverance of her closest friends and their constant setting her up, she'd never go out at all. It seemed impossible that she'd ever meet someone to share her life with, and had given up looking until she met Gabriel Walker. Their relationship was easy from the start. He had a steady and calm personality which she'd come to depend on. Trying not to bore him with the day-to-day details of her job, she rarely talked about her work. However, when she needed to vent, he was a willing and patient listener.

With her Brooks Brothers pencil skirt and white blouse, Beth blended in with all the other female attorneys. She felt proud of her accomplishments and loved the idea that she would be fighting for those who otherwise saw their plight as hopeless. Money never factored into her decision to go to law school. Although she didn't want to work for non-profits, she never worried about her salary. She wanted to build her career on winning cases and putting bad people behind bars. She loved her work but missed the days when she had more free time to do as she pleased. Her time wasn't hers anymore, and that pained her.

Beth sat back in her chair and thought about her family. She missed her mother and sister who had moved to Florida two years earlier. Her brother Michael was busy with his family, and she rarely saw her sister Lauren, whose thriving real estate business and family obligations left little time to get together.

Her biggest concern, however, was her brother Christopher. His military career over, he returned to the US with an amputated right leg. Instead of coming home to Andover, Massachusetts, Chris chose to settle, at least for now, on Captiva Island, Florida with their mother and her new husband.

It was hard enough accepting that her brother had lost his leg, but not being able to see him in person made things so much worse. There was little chance she could take time away from work, and it angered her that her job required such sacrifice.

Thanksgiving and Christmas came and went without the family coming together like the old days. Everyone had obligations that took them in different directions. Paolo's mother died while he and her mother were away on their honeymoon in Italy. Because of that they stayed in Europe much longer than they had originally planned. Christopher's surgery in Germany made it especially difficult for anyone in the family to feel anything but sad during the holidays.

Growing up, Beth and Christopher were very close. Being the two youngest of their siblings gave them a special bond and it was for that very reason it upset Beth to not be by his side when he needed her the most. She'd called his cell phone several times and left messages that were never returned.

What's it going to take to get everyone back together again?

Her frustration mounting, she decided to talk to her boss about taking a couple of days off. A trip to Captiva to see Chris wouldn't sacrifice anything she was working on, and she'd feel better spending a few days with her brother.

Maggie Wheeler knocked on the front door of her best friend Chelsea Marsden's house. Only a few blocks from the Key Lime Garden Inn, the house sat at the end of Andy Rosse Lane.

Most mornings Chelsea would hover over Maggie's freshly baked scones, but this morning Maggie needed to talk to her best friend without Christopher hearing them.

"I thought you were going to take the curtains down. Why are they still up?"

Chelsea put her paintbrush down and pulled her apron up over her head.

"Because I'm lazy, that's why. We can't all be Martha Stewart you know."

Maggie admired Chelsea's new painting but wondered why there were two canvases side by side.

"What's the deal with the two canvases?"

Pointing to the canvas on the left, Chelsea explained. "This one's mine, and Jacqui Hutchins painted that one. What do you think?"

"What I think is that she's an amazing talent. Sarah told me that Trevor's sister would be working with you. I knew she had talent, but I had no idea she was this good."

Chelsea rolled her eyes. "That girl is a handful to be honest. She's incredibly smart, but sometimes I think she lets others influence her so much she loses confidence. I don't want to be one more person who tells her what she should be doing with her art. I'm here to guide her on her painting skills, but she needs to find her place in this industry, and the world for that matter. Let's just say that she's a work in progress."

Maggie sat and lifted her legs onto an ottoman. "Aren't we all?"

Chelsea could read her friend's mind. "What's eating you this morning?"

"The same thing that eats at me every morning—Christopher. The whole point of his coming to Captiva was to rest by the sea and do physical therapy. He's not doing either. It's been a few weeks since he returned home, and he spends most of the time in his room. He barely interacts with anyone, me included. I thought he was making some progress in Germany, but now it feels like he's regressing. I think it's been his plan from the start to come to Captiva and do nothing to get better."

Chelsea stood behind Maggie's chair, leaned down and wrapped her arms around her friend.

"You remember what the doctor told you? It's going to take time. It isn't only the physical limitations that are hurting him, it's the trauma of losing so many of his friends. You have to give him time to adjust."

"Oh, I know, but it hurts to see him like this. I feel helpless. I want all my children to be happy. Sarah and Trevor are content with their little family, Lauren and Jeff are doing great. So are Michael and Brea. Beth is settled in Boston with her job and things seem to be progressing nicely between her and her boyfriend, Gabriel. I can't stand to see Chris suffer like this. I can't imagine what his future will be. I can't picture it, and I'd hate to see him spend the rest of his life as a recluse."

Chelsea said nothing. She knew it was best to let Maggie get it all out.

"Do you know what hurts me the most? Of all my children, Christopher was always the positive, most upbeat one. Nothing stood in his way. Honestly, there were times when I thought he was crazy for being so optimistic, but he'd prove me wrong time and again. Nothing seemed to upset him. No matter how challenging a situation was, he'd push through. There was a brief time when he was sixteen when a close friend of his died. I know it hurt, but he moved on. Nothing kept him down. Now, he's in this dark place that I can't reach. I don't know what to do."

"What does Paolo say?"

"Oh, you know him. He tells me to leave Chris alone, and to give him space. I understand what he means but between you and me, I can't do that forever. At some point I'm going to have a talk with my son. He can't go on like this much longer. None of us can."

Chelsea wanted to help but other than be supportive there was little she could do.

"How about I get you an iced tea? Jacqui won't be here until two o'clock. We've got plenty of time. Why don't you tell me about Sarah and Trevor? What's the latest with them?"

Maggie was happy for the change of topic. "It looks like everything's in place for Sophia and Noah's adoption. Sarah told me the other day that she and Trevor were planning to go to the town hall to get married."

"Oh, no they didn't."

"Don't worry. I put a stop to that. No way my daughter is going to get married that way. Besides, we've got such a lovely backdrop with the beach. The inn is a perfect place to have it. We can prepare a little buffet or something. I promised her that I wouldn't go overboard, and that we'd keep it small."

"So, when is the wedding day?"

"Next weekend."

"What? How are you going to put together a wedding in a week?"

Maggie laughed, "That's just the point, Chelsea. She insists it not be anything but a small get-together. You, me, Paolo, Ciara, and Trevor's family. Noah wants to get dressed up again. Apparently, he loved wearing a suit for our wedding and wants to do it again."

"Oh, that's so sweet. How has he been doing, any seizures?"

Maggie shook her head. "None. He's doing really well. I don't know much about seizures, but I do wonder if his lack of stability before coming to live with Trevor had anything to do with his health. You should see him with Sophia. He's really taken to being a big brother."

A knock on the front door interrupted their conversation.

"Hello, where is everyone?"

Facing the door, Chelsea answered.

"We're out on the lanai."

Sarah joined them and then dropped several bags on the floor.

"I've been shopping."

Maggie got up from her chair and hugged her daughter. "I can see that. What in the world did you buy?"

"Oh, just a few things for Sophia and Noah, and maybe a little something for myself. I found a cute dress to wear for the wedding. I know I said I didn't want anyone to make a fuss, but when I saw this dress in the window at Mason's Bridal, I had to have it. And naturally had to drive over here and show it to you. Paolo said you were here."

"Oh, honey, that's wonderful. Let's see it."

Sarah opened the box and pulled out a short white dress with some lace around the hem and short sleeves.

Maggie looked confused.

"It's a dress."

"No, it isn't. It's white. See all the lace?"

Chelsea laughed and gave her opinion. "I think it's perfect. It suits you, Sarah. It's simple and classy. You're going to look beautiful in it. Ignore your mother."

"Thanks, Chelsea. You know Mom. She thinks every wedding needs to be a big flashy and extravagant affair."

Maggie shrugged. "Thanks a lot. I guess that means my wedding was overdone."

Sarah was quick to fix her faux pas. "No. Mom. Your wedding was perfect for you. You know me. I was never that girl who dreamed of her wedding day. You know that."

Maggie had to admit that it took a long time for her daughter to find the kind of love that would convince her to marry. Trevor and Sarah were perfect for each other and that made Maggie happy.

Sarah put the bags to the side and collapsed in a chair. "I'd love an iced tea if you've got one, Chelsea."

"Coming up."

"So, when you stopped over at the inn, did you go inside?"

Sarah's face turned serious. "You mean, did I see Chris? No. I talked to Paolo in the driveway. I was going to go inside but decided against it after the last time. I don't want to fight with him, Mom, but he makes it impossible. Has he left his room at all?"

"Only once since he's been home, and even then it was because I wheeled him down to the beach. The chair can't go out onto the sand, so we stopped at the end of the walk. We're going to extend the walkway area so he can see the ceremony."

Chelsea returned with Sarah's tea.

"Thanks, Chelsea."

"Mom, something has to be done. What he needs is tough love."

Chelsea interrupted her. "At the risk of butting in, I'd like to add my two cents on that. The boy needs to see a therapist.

Tough love can be dangerous if you don't know what you're doing. He's depressed and needs the kind of help only a professional can give him. Chris has seen things we can't imagine. I'd be careful to pretend any of us know how to deal with this."

Maggie nodded. "I agree. And for the record, Chelsea, you're family. You're not butting in. Besides, we'll take any advice at this point."

Chelsea's face lit up. "I have an idea. What about Sebastian?"

Maggie looked confused. "What about him?"

"Well, he's in a wheelchair too. He had a traumatic event in his later years that put him in that chair. He can walk but only with the brace and even then he has to use poles for balance. It's not ideal, but maybe it's a start. I'm sure he's been through a terrible time before accepting his situation. Perhaps he can speak to Cristopher about what it was like for him."

Maggie nodded. "Chelsea, that's a great idea. That is, if Chris is willing to talk to Sebastian. Right now, I can't get him out of his room, let alone talk to a stranger."

Sarah had an idea.

"What about at my wedding? Chelsea, you're going to bring Sebastian to the wedding, right? We'll set the walkway up so that both Chris and Sebastian can wheel out to the ceremony. There is no way Chris can refuse attending. You'll have to talk to Sebastian about our plan, but I'm sure he'd help us."

Chelsea clapped her hands together, then lifted her glass of iced tea in the air. "It's a perfect idea. Let's toast to it. There's nothing that can't be accomplished when three women put their minds to it. Come on, ladies, raise your glasses to 'Operation Get Out of that Chair.'"

For the first time in weeks, Maggie felt a glimmer of hope. Whether her son would see through their plan, she had no idea, but it didn't matter to her if he did. Someone needed to reach her son, even if it wasn't her.

CHAPTER THREE

Becca pulled the attic door down and secured the footing in place. Half-way up the stairs she reached for the light switch. Not that long ago her father went through several boxes of old items looking for things to throw away. Every time he attempted to reorganize; Becca would stop him. She hated the idea that pieces of her childhood would end up in the trash.

Her mother's death from ovarian cancer three years ago made it impossible to part with anything. Memories from the past were all she had left and fortunately her father understood her feelings. He promised Becca that he wouldn't throw anything away until she'd had a chance to go through every box.

The oldest of her siblings, Becca's mother, Julia Bradford Powell, was born and raised on Sanibel Island. Her education began in a small schoolhouse, but since there were no high schools on Sanibel, she had to go to Cypress Lake High School off island. It was there that she met her future husband, Crawford Powell, whose family owned a beach supply store in Ft. Myers.

Crawford had no interest in going to college. He wanted to

grow his family's business and with hard work, along with his father's backing, opened a small store on Captiva Island. The family kept the Ft. Myers store, but Crawford chose to stay on Captiva and run the shop there, eventually expanding the business by offering to meet the demands of tourists for jet skis, parasailing excursions, and sunset cruises.

Their children were raised on Captiva and were homeschooled for several years before attending high school off island. As soon as they were old enough, the Powell children helped out at the store.

Crawford and Julia Powell had four children, three boys and a girl. Finn, Luke, Joshua, and Becca were good kids and practically lived on the water. Expert swimmers and all-around sports fanatics, the Powell family was known for their love of the ocean. Throughout southwest Florida, their name was synonymous with adventure.

Even in her forties, Julia looked like she was still in her twenties. Vibrant and young spirited, she was as athletic as any of her children. She could keep up with all of them, until the pain and swelling in her abdomen slowed her down. She started to rapidly lose weight, and once she received a cancer diagnosis, continued to act as if nothing was wrong, keeping the illness from her children.

It was Crawford who ultimately convinced her to tell the family. Everyone said Julia was a strong person and if anyone could beat the disease, it would be her. But, since ovarian cancer is rarely found in its early stage, survival was rare.

Unlike her brothers, Becca wanted to go to college. She had dreams of attending medical school beyond her undergraduate degree and worked hard to graduate at the top of her class, even being selected as valedictorian of Stonehill College in Massachusetts.

Upon graduation, she immediately studied and took her MCAT exams, passing with a score of 517. Admitted to Tufts

University of Medicine, she excelled and had plans to focus her area of study on sports medicine.

With her mother's cancer diagnosis and subsequent death, Becca's grief was all-consuming. She couldn't understand that after so many years of research and trials, the medical industry had nothing to save her mother.

Becca was twenty-three when her mother died. Even with three brothers and a father, she felt like an orphan, untethered and without direction, and so she left school and returned home, helping out in the store and now at the Key Lime Garden Inn. Her passion for a career in medicine was lost. Her only interest now was to stay as close to her family as possible.

Becca pulled a small stool under her for support and opened the closest box. There were several smaller boxes inside with her mother's handwriting on the outside of each one. Her heartbeat increased knowing that most of the contents within belonged to her mother.

She opened the first box labeled "To Be Organized" which had several photographs stacked inside. Since photo albums made up the bulk of the items, Becca assumed the box of random photos were meant to be organized into the albums when she felt better.

She never got to finish this project.

Her mother's cancer kept her weak and in bed, and most days Becca remembered her mother sitting on the beach or sleeping in her room. When an unexpected surge of energy presented, she used that time to clean the house and cook. Becca imagined that her mother found private time early in her illness to look over these pictures.

She smiled staring at photos of her and her brothers as babies. Some of the pictures she had seen before, but there were a few that were new to her.

"What are you doing up here?"

Her father's voice startled her. He stood on the rung of the ladder and looked at her.

"I thought I'd start going through these boxes before you throw them into a dumpster."

"Aren't you being a little dramatic? I would never throw photos away, and you know it."

Becca laughed. "I know. I'm just teasing. Sit with me. I could use your brain. You can tell me who some of these people are. I can't believe how many pictures she never got to put into the photo albums."

"Maybe you could finish it for her."

Becca smiled at her father's suggestion. "I think that's a great idea."

Crawford Powell hugged his daughter and then kneeled on the floor, pulling a box closer to him.

"Let me see if I can help you with these. Give me a pile."

Becca turned a photo over and shook her head.

"Dad, who's this with Gran?"

He took the photo and then put his glasses on.

"That's Robert Lane and his wife, Rose. They were good friends. I remember mom telling me that there was some gossip back in the day that Gran and Robert were lovers. Can you imagine that?"

"Rose Johnson Lane? Isn't she the woman who sold the Key Lime Garden Inn to Mrs. Wheeler?"

"Yes. That's the one."

"Do you think the story is true? I can't picture Gran cheating on Great-grandpa."

"Oh, that's a long story. Lillian didn't share her feelings about any of this with me. Everything I know, I got from your mother. I think this is one photo that's best thrown away."

Becca didn't know why the story intrigued her so, but she put the photo in a pile with others that needed further investigation.

"Why don't we move some of these boxes downstairs? It's getting hot and the attic air is stifling. I'll put them in the dining room, and you can go through them in an air-conditioned environment."

"Thanks, Dad. I do want to finish Mom's project. I think it will make me feel close to her."

Becca's eyes began to water. "I miss her so much."

Crawford held her hand. "Me too, sweetie. I like to think that she's still with us. Just because we can't see her doesn't mean she isn't here."

"You really believe that Dad?"

"I do. I talk to her all the time. I don't think there's anything wrong with that. I feel her presence every day, and it gives me comfort. I believe that one day we'll all be together again."

He looked at Becca and smiled. "That's why we've got to live our best lives. It's what she would have wanted for all of us."

Becca nodded. "I want to make her proud of me."

"Oh, Becca. Your mother was proud of you the day you were born. You never gave her a moment of unhappiness. She's already proud of you, baby. I am too. Now, let's get these boxes downstairs. Run and get Finn to help."

Becca jumped up from her stool and quickly made it down the attic stairs. She loved nothing more than to irritate her brother Finn, and she knew that interrupting his time on the computer would do that very thing.

"Hey, Dad wants you to help bring some boxes down from the attic."

"Now?"

"No. Whenever you feel like it. Really? Yes, now."

Becca smiled as she watched her brother Finn storm out of his room. She turned on her heels and almost laughed.

"Mission accomplished."

Becca looked at the clock and sighed. Every morning she'd run five miles from Captiva through Sanibel and back but going over her mother's photos took up so much time that she had to rush to get to the inn.

She loved her job at the inn and had no intention of quitting just because Christopher made her work challenging. Three rooms needed to be cleaned and since they were on the second floor, she probably didn't have to engage with him at all.

She ran outside and got on her bike. It was a beautiful day without clouds. She loved living in a place that people came to for vacation. The streets were filled with tourists, and she waved to several island business owners on her way to the inn.

Parking her bike in the bike rack, she walked around to the back of the inn. She went upstairs to the guest rooms and pulled the linens off the beds. Once on the first floor, she'd have to pass Christopher's room to get to the laundry so she walked as quietly as she could to avoid another unpleasant confrontation.

While the linens were in the wash, she picked up the vacuum cleaner and started for the stairs but stopped when she saw him. Reaching for a book from the bookcase in the living room, he didn't notice her.

"Can I get that for you?"

"No. I've got it. Thank you."

Surprised at his polite response, she couldn't resist getting back at him for their previous encounter.

"Good to see you haven't lost all your manners. You must have gotten up on the right side of the bed this morning."

Christopher turned his chair around to face her.

"I wake up on the same side of the bed every morning. I have no choice. I need to reach my crutches."

His sarcasm didn't help, and although she believed it was stupid to pick a fight with him, she felt justified.

Just then, Maggie came into the room.

"Hi Becca. I see you've met Christopher. I'm glad you're here actually. I was wondering if you wouldn't mind taking a few minutes to change the bedding in Christopher's room. Normally, I'd do it myself, but since you're already doing laundry, and Chris isn't in there, I think this is the perfect time to get it done."

The look on Christopher's face made Becca want to laugh, but she kept a straight face.

"Mom, I don't want anyone in my room."

Maggie ignored her son and remained focused on Becca. "Would you take care of that for me, please?"

Becca didn't take her eyes off Christopher and smiled as she answered, "Of course. I'll do it right now."

She could see his anger building but since she didn't have much choice in the matter she went directly to his room.

Pulling the comforter off the bed she removed the sheets and pillowcases, taking care not to disturb any personal items. She opened the closet and found another sheet set.

Passing the desk, she saw several items. A high school ring, a notebook, and a photo. Moving closer, she could see it was a picture of a young girl joining arms with a boy. It took a minute before she realized the girl in the picture was her.

Terrified she'd be caught, Becca quickly stepped back from the desk and looked around to see if anyone saw her. Christopher was still in the living room and would probably stay there until she finished changing the bed.

No wonder he didn't want me in here.

Becca made his bed, scurried out of his room, and ran to the laundry room. She closed the door behind her and leaned against it. Her breath coming in short rapid spurts, she put her hand to her heart.

Why did he have her picture?

She knew every detail about their friendship and tried to remember exactly when the picture was taken. More importantly, she didn't understand why he was still carrying a photo of the two of them from so many years ago.

She waited a few minutes, hoping he'd gone back to his room. She opened the door just enough to peer out and see if anyone was nearby. The upstairs beds were made but she hadn't yet cleaned and restocked the bathrooms. Carrying several bars of soap and additional towels, she had no choice but to walk by the living room to get to the stairs.

Talking to herself she held her head high.

You can do this.

When she came out of the laundry room she walked as fast as she could to the stairs, but his voice stopped her.

"I suppose you'd like an explanation?"

She turned to face him.

"I thought you didn't recognize me the other night."

Christopher looked down and shook his head.

"I'm sorry about that. I…it's been difficult. I didn't mean to be so rude to you. I think I was surprised to see you standing in the middle of our kitchen. It wasn't one of my best moments."

Becca couldn't resist asking more about the photo.

"Where did you get that picture?"

He smiled and tried to make light of the situation.

"Now whose memory isn't working. Don't you remember Stacie's brother Kyle taking that picture of us?"

She did remember.

"It was right after one of our volleyball games. Your team lost that day."

"Well, that proves you don't remember, because we won, and your penalty was that you had to have your picture taken with a member of the opposing team. You picked me."

She loved that he remembered the details of that day even if she was convinced that his team lost.

"I kept your photo along with a few of my family while I was overseas. It was encouraged by the military. They figure it's good for morale."

She nodded but wondered if he was lying. The story sounded

innocent enough. After a brief awkward silence, she changed the subject.

"You must be glad to be home."

The lightness of his mood changed, and she could tell he felt ambivalence about returning to the states. The smell of the soap still in her arms was almost overwhelming.

"Yes, of course. It's good to be back."

Becca wanted to stay longer but their conversation felt forced. "I should go."

"Yes. Thank you for straightening up in there."

She nodded, and walked away, returning to what was left of her work.

Confusion swept over her, but she knew better than to focus on things she had no control over. Whatever reason he had for keeping her photograph all these years, it had nothing to do with her. At least the ice had been broken between them and she wouldn't worry about running into him again.

CHAPTER FOUR

Beth's assistant Lynn stopped her as she walked out of the conference room.

"Your sister Sarah is on the phone."

"Thank you, Lynn. I'll take it in my office."

Beth dropped her pile of papers on the corner table. Picking up her phone, she sat at her desk.

"Hey, sis. Please tell me you're not calling with bad news."

Sarah laughed. "Hey Bethy. Actually, I have good news and I hope you can make it even better. Trevor and I are getting married next Saturday, and I want you to be my maid of honor. What do you say? Can you get time off?"

"Oh, Sarah, that's great news. Congratulations. I knew you guys were engaged, but you never set a date. I take it Mom is thrilled with planning the wedding?"

"You know Mom. Always ready to entertain. This is very last minute. We only decided a couple of days ago and were planning on going to City Hall. We didn't want anything fancy. It's just now that we have Sophia and Noah's adoption in the works, it's best that we do it as a married couple."

"And Mom wouldn't hear of you getting married at City Hall. Am I right?"

"Bingo."

"Honestly, Sarah. You had to know how she'd react. But enough about that. Of course, I want to be your maid of honor. I'm thrilled to be asked, but am I wrong to wonder if you picked me instead of Lauren because you're trying to get me down to Captiva to help with Chris?"

"You're wrong, Bethy. You're my little sister and I miss you. As far as Chris goes, Mom, Chelsea, and I have a plan we're working on. However, I do think if you can get here, it might help Chris too. You guys are so close. He doesn't listen to anyone. I'd be shocked if he didn't feel better with you around."

"I don't know about that. I've called him a few times and left messages on his cell phone, but he never calls me back. It makes me want to cry."

"I know. Me too."

"Anyway, let me talk to my boss about taking some time off. I've been working around the clock, and I really need a break. I don't know if he'll agree, so say a prayer that he does. Knock on wood, cross your fingers, do whatever it takes."

"Will do. I can't wait to see my little Bethy."

Beth rolled her eyes and laughed. "Oh, I'll make sure my boss knows that he's hired 'little Bethy.' That should make all the difference. By the way, are you inviting the whole family down?"

"I'm going to call Michael and Lauren when I hang up. I hope they'll come. It's possible not everyone will attend, but it would be great if we could at least get us siblings together. Mom would be in her glory. By the way, I've decided to ask Mom to walk me down the aisle."

"Oh, that's so sweet. She'll love that, and I'm sure Michael and Lauren will come. I do know that Lauren's been working long hours. The last time I talked to her, she and Jeff were having a hard time adjusting to her absence. I don't know what's going on there but maybe at the wedding, she'll tell us. You know Lauren, it's impossible to squeeze anything out of her if she doesn't want to talk. She's so much like Mom that way."

"We all need to see each other in person, Beth. You know how strong we all are when we're together. I think part of the problem is that we're all so scattered, and now, with what Chris is going through, he's going to need our support."

"I'll talk to my boss today and will let you know. And, Sarah, thank you so much for asking me to stand up for you. It means the world to me. Love you."

"I love you, too, my Bethy."

Beth knocked on Mitchell Glassman's door.

"Got a minute?"

"Just about. I've got another meeting in about fifteen minutes. What's up?"

Glassman was an exceptional Assistant District Attorney and was quickly becoming someone that Beth looked up to.

"I wanted to ask you if I could take a little time off. I haven't had a vacation or a day off since I started. I wouldn't ask, but my sister is getting married and has asked me to be her maid of honor. Also, if you remember, I told you about my brother Chris who's come home from Iraq. He's not doing well, and the whole family wants to gather around him."

"I'm sorry about your brother. Terrible thing that's happened to him. How much time do you need?"

Beth hadn't planned on being away for more than a long weekend, but the more she thought about it, a week made sense.

"I'd like to take a week off. Including the weekends, I could be with my family for nine or ten days before I returned to Boston."

Mitchell nodded. "I think we can make that work. Why don't you have Lynn work with Kristina to bring her up to speed on your project list. Stay in touch with the office while you're down there."

"Thank you, Mitchell. I really do appreciate it."

"I hope things with your brother improve and let me know if there is anything either myself or the office can do for you."

Beth nodded. "I will."

She smiled as she closed the door behind her. She felt giddy and wanted to dance all the way back to her office but decided against it. Keeping it professional was the best way to earn the respect of her peers, not to mention her boss. For now, she'd dance up and down when she was safely behind her closed office door.

Gabriel Walker wiped his hands on the damp towel. Grabbing the broom that was leaning against the wall, he swept the floor. He'd spent the day focused on making the spindling for several rocking chairs commissioned by a New Hampshire farm. Before locking up he always cleaned his workspace, checked on the wood stove and returned calls and emails.

A cold New England wind started up a few hours earlier, but the wood stove kept the barn warm and cozy. He'd often work into the night and during the fall and winter months was glad for the small sitting area at the back of the barn. More than once he'd fallen asleep on the sofa.

Walker Brothers Woodworks in Boxford, Massachusetts thrived but even with his brother James' help, there were days when Gabriel struggled to keep up. It was a wonderful problem to have, and he never lost sight of his good fortune.

Meeting Beth Wheeler was another of Gabriel's blessings. He'd fallen hard for the woman who dropped her ice cream cone on his boot last September. It was their first date after being set-up by friends. He had no choice but to bring his niece, Willow, along on the date, since his brother and sister-in-law made last minute plans and needed him to babysit. Much to his amusement, he watched Beth spend more time talking to Willow, than him. They went to Benson's for a cone after dinner and with one sneeze, the top scoop of Beth's ice cream cone dropped on his foot. The two girls thought that was the funniest thing, and after returning Willow to his brother's house, he asked Beth to come back to his place for a cup of tea.

He remembered her making fun of his herbal teas and said that growing up, her mother insisted everyone have a cup of tea whenever they had something important to discuss.

They sat on the porch rocking chairs and talked for hours, and he looked forward to being with her as often as possible. He found it difficult to go more than a few days without seeing Beth. They talked on the phone every day and hearing her voice got him through until they saw each other again.

As he locked the barn door, Beth's car pulled up to the house.

"Hey, what are you doing here? I thought you had to work late."

"When I woke up this morning, I thought so too, but the events of the day changed all that. I wanted to run something by you. I thought I'd come out here so we could talk in person."

"Oh, that sounds like an invitation for me to make a pot of tea."

Beth laughed. "At the risk of upsetting you and my mother, how about a cup of hot chocolate instead? It's freezing out here."

"We can do that, and I promise not to tell your mother. How about I meet you inside in a bit? I've got to get more wood for the fire."

The barn sat across from a large farmhouse. Beth knew where everything was in the kitchen, so she found some hot chocolate packages and poured the contents into two mugs.

Charlie, Gabriel's dog, came running out of the bedroom and jumped up on her.

"Hey, Charlie. How's my favorite dog?"

She enjoyed getting down on the floor with Charlie. It was the best way to engage him in playtime. That, plus stealing his toys always did the trick.

Gabriel stacked wood inside near the large open fireplace while Beth mixed the hot chocolate. She carried the mugs to the sofa and watched the fire start to build.

"I love your fireplace. I've never seen one like it before."

"My brother and I built it. This house needed a lot of work when I first bought it. We did most of the work ourselves. So, tell me what's brought you out into the woods tonight?"

"My sister Sarah called. She's getting married next Saturday and asked me to be her maid of honor."

"Whoa, that's great news. She's the one living on Captiva Island with your mother, right? Can you get the time off of work to go?"

"Yes, that's her. Mitchell approved my taking a week. I'm especially happy to go because I really need to see my brother."

"Has he called you back yet?"

Beth shook her head. "No, and I'm really worried. It's not like him to not talk to me. I know he's been through a lot, but we've always been able to talk to each other about everything. He won't be able to ignore me once I'm standing in front of him."

"I'm sure he'll be happy to see you."

"Anyway, that's not why I came out here tonight. I wanted to ask you if you'd come down for the wedding. I know you have lots of work to do here, but I'm not talking about you staying down there for ten days. I'm leaving on Thursday, and the wedding is Saturday. You can fly back home right after the wedding. You'd be back at work first thing Monday morning."

Gabriel looked uneasy. "Oh, I don't know."

"What's wrong?"

"Your family, that's what. They've never met me. Won't they be unhappy that you sprung this guy on them at the last minute?

I mean, don't you think they'd like a little heads up before you bring me down there? Especially with what's going on with your brother, they're not going to want to have me hanging around."

"What? Don't be silly. My family will welcome you with open arms. You don't have to worry about a thing. It's a wedding. People bring dates to weddings all the time. It's no big deal. Trust me. It will be fine. As far as my brother goes, you're right, he's not going to want to talk to me with you in the room, but that doesn't mean you shouldn't come. I'm going to get Chris alone when I talk to him. You can hang by the pool, or the beach or take a walk. Please say you'll come?"

Gabriel couldn't say no to Beth. Her big blue eyes staring back at him with a fake lower-lip-quiver made him laugh.

"All right. You win. I'll go but promise you won't push me on your family when they want time alone with you. I'm perfectly capable of finding something to do on my own. Deal?"

Gabriel stuck out his hand and Beth took it.

"Deal."

"Good. Now, let's enjoy this delicious hot chocolate, and my masterful fire-making skills."

CHAPTER FIVE

Chelsea Marsden watched as Jacqui's paintbrush carried the ultramarine and cobalt colors onto her canvas. Facing the water, her view was perfect for creating an ocean landscape.

"Your mix of colors is spot on, Jacqui. I like how you've opened the sky, letting the light shine down on the water."

"Thanks. I never know if I'm being too heavy-handed with my strokes. Most of the time I feel like I've left too much paint on the canvas and have to rush to thin it out."

Chelsea put her hand on Jacqui's shoulder.

"It takes time to find your comfort level. With each canvas, you create a new story, but you also add to your own."

Jacqui put her paintbrush down and turned to look at Chelsea.

"If I may be so bold, what's your story? I can tell something's on your mind today. You're being too nice to me."

Chelsea laughed. "Am I really such a dour presence?"

Teasing, Jacqui said, "You're ok most of the time. I'm probably the last person you want to confide in, but I'm as good a listener as I am a talker. Does Sebastian have anything to do with your mood?"

Chelsea hated to admit that Jacqui was right about her mood. She'd been stewing over lingering comments from Sebastian's children that left her frustrated. Although she couldn't see herself sharing intimate details of her personal life with a twenty-three-year-old woman she barely knew, she found Jacqui to be wiser than most young ladies her age. That came as a shock considering how, thus far, Jacqui had made horrible decisions about her own life.

"Sebastian and I are fine. I'm not so sure about his children though."

"Uh-oh, that doesn't sound good. Are they jealous because daddy is spending too much time, not to mention most of their inheritance, on you?"

"Wait just a minute, that's quite a leap. What in the world would make you say such a thing?"

Jacqui shrugged and walked to the table, pouring herself a tall glass of iced tea.

"Well, for starters, I've got a little experience with daddy issues, and my brother, Clayton, sees everything through the lens of money. He's been known to put a monetary value on human beings. I've had a front-row seat for years watching the men in my family maneuver their way around the almighty dollar. My guess is that Sebastian's daughters are not only worried about how much money is flying out the door, but jealous that you've taken the place of their dead mother."

Chelsea hadn't considered any of this, but she had to wonder if Jacqui was right. More than once she'd suffered his daughter Samantha's icy stare. Jordan Barlowe was equally cold. At least, Peter, Sebastian's son was somewhat pleasant. Chelsea couldn't figure what she'd done to deserve such treatment.

"Of course, I could be wrong. Maybe they don't like your perfume."

Jacqui had a way with words. She could be irritatingly accurate, but without filter she often annoyed Chelsea. Chelsea had promised Trevor to look after his younger sister and help her as her confidence in her talent grew. Unfortunately, it meant Chelsea would be subjected to ongoing unsolicited commentary on everything from the current fashion trends to the latest reality television show.

Chelsea liked living alone. Except for the occasional visitor and her friend Rachel's six-week stay after the birth of her baby, most days were quiet at her home. Now, with her twice weekly painting classes with Jacqui, she longed for the peaceful sounds of the ocean waves and seagulls.

"I think it's time we get back to painting."

Maybe it was time to talk to Sebastian about her feelings. She didn't want to make a big deal out of it. After all, it's not like they planned to marry. Chelsea didn't think of her dating Sebastian as anything more than having fun. She liked her freedom, and if someone else asked her out, she'd go. She didn't feel that they were exclusive, and it bothered her that his children saw her as a threat to their way of life. However, unless she was wrong, his children had put a target on her back, and she'd need to put a stop to that immediately.

Christopher could hear his mother talking to someone out on the back porch. He wheeled himself out of his room and through the kitchen, pushing the back door with his left leg. Maggie and Paolo's sister Ciara were sitting on the porch swing when they noticed him.

"Hey, care to join us?"

"I didn't mean to interrupt."

Ciara opened the door and pushed the ramp under the frame. "You're not interrupting us. I dropped off some plants from the nursery for your mother. I was just leaving. It's good to see you, Christopher."

"Nice to see you again, Ciara."

Ciara helped Christopher down the ramp and then hugged Maggie.

"I'll catch up with you later. Say hi to my brother."

"Will do. Thank you for the plants."

"I was about to go inside and pour myself a glass of lemonade. Would you like one?"

"Yes. Thanks, that would be nice."

Maggie went inside and then quickly returned with their lemonade and sat next to him.

"I'm glad you came out. It's a beautiful day."

Christopher nodded. "You've done an amazing job with the inn, Mom, especially the garden. You must feel like you've died and gone to heaven tending this land. I know how much you loved your garden back home. This one is three times the size of the one in Andover."

"I couldn't do it without Paolo's help. It's a lot of work, but it brings me so much joy that I feel it's worth it."

They sat in silence for a few minutes before he spoke again.

"I know I've been difficult, and I also know that you don't think I've disrupted your life here, but I have."

"Oh, Chris, please don't say that. You know I wouldn't want you to be anywhere else but here. I just wish…"

"I know, Mom. You don't have to say anything. I know how much you want to help. This is something I have to get through on my own. I'm not sure how to do it, honestly, but I do know that you can't give me the help I need."

"What is it, Chris? What is it that you need?"

He wanted to cry, but he couldn't, or more to the point, wouldn't. He'd shed too many tears since his time in Germany. He needed to stay strong not just for his mother, but until he talked to Nick's parents. After that, he could allow himself to fall apart.

Nick Aiello was his closest friend and an excellent soldier. He and Christopher were stationed in Iraq at the same time. They'd been close friends since boot camp. Nick died the day Christopher was injured. They promised each other that if either of them was killed the other would visit his family and tell them what life was like for their son, and how he died an honorable death. It was the only thing keeping Christopher alive.

How could he tell his mother that he wished he'd died with everyone else? How could he explain his feelings of guilt?

"I just need time, Mom. I'm glad I came to Captiva. It's exactly as I remember it."

Maggie smiled and looked up at the sky.

"We made so many memories on this island, didn't we? You and your brother and sisters were like fish. You never wanted to come out of the water, not even to eat. I had to promise you all that you could go back in the water after you'd finished your lunch."

Christopher laughed. "After thirty minutes of course. You know that's a myth right?"

"What?"

"Don't you remember you telling us that we'd all get stomach cramps and drown if we went in the water too soon after we ate?"

"Oh, that. Well, we all believed that back then. There must be something to it though. Nobody drowned after lunch."

He smiled at the memory.

"You seem to have a good staff here. I'm sure that makes it easier for you."

"I do. Everyone has been great. You have to admit Riley and Grace know how to make delicious meals."

He rubbed his stomach. "I bet I've gained a few pounds since

I've been back. What about the rest of the people working here? How many employees do you have?"

He wanted information about Becca Powell but couldn't bring himself to come right out and ask.

"Not counting the work Paolo and Ciara do around here, I've hired three people—the chefs and Becca Powell. Becca only works a few hours a week. Her family runs Powell Water Sports a few blocks from here. She's a sweet girl. I'd never met the family until I took over the inn. She's an islander and knows Captiva and Sanibel like the back of her hand. Pity about her mother. Becca was in medical school when it happened. She quit and came back to Captiva to help with the store. It's a shame because I think she really wanted to be a doctor."

"What happened to her mother?"

"She had ovarian cancer and passed away a few years ago. I think she'd been sick a couple of years before she died, so they knew what was coming, but you can never be prepared for such a thing."

Christopher knew very little about Becca's family. All he remembered was that she had three brothers and that she lived on the island. It wasn't until a few summers after their time together that he made the connection between her and the water sports store. He felt awful that he never asked her more questions about her life when they talked the previous day. He wondered if he'd get another chance to show her that he could think about someone other than himself for a change.

He looked down at his lap and shook his head.

"It's never easy when you lose a parent."

He was still thinking about Becca when his mother spoke.

"Do you miss your dad?"

Christopher realized his mother mistook his words for sadness over the death of his father. He waited a minute before answering. He was never close with his father, but his passing was still hard to accept.

"Truthfully, I haven't thought about him much. I remember him going to all of Michael's football games. I know that Sarah, Lauren, and Beth worked harder to get his approval than I did."

"You always went your own way, Chris. That's nothing to feel bad about. He was proud of you, though. You need to know that."

For some reason that surprised him. He never thought his father gave him much thought. He knew there had to be more to the man than what he believed growing up. It pained him to think that he might never get to know his father now that he was dead.

"Maybe one of these days you can tell me more about him."

His mother smiled at that request and reached for his hand.

"I'd love nothing more."

CHAPTER SIX

Sebastian Barlowe was used to getting his way. He had two daughters and a son, a nurse, and now a girlfriend all fussing over him, and he was feeling suffocated. Determined to maintain his autonomy even with his obvious limitations, he pushed everyone away at the slightest encounter.

His daughters, Samantha, and Jordan joined him for breakfast and announced that they thought it best they move back home to help their father in his time of need.

Time of need? Those were their exact words and he wondered when the roles shifted between child and parent.

He was getting tired of his daughters' hovering and let them know how he felt.

"I've been managing perfectly fine with the help of the nurse. Why in the world do the two of you think I need more help than that? Besides, Chelsea has become rather important to me. If I need more assistance, she can help me."

"Dad, Chelsea isn't family."

Sebastian pounded the table with his fist.

"Enough!"

The women flinched as the table vibrated.

"You said what you came here to say, and you've heard my position on this matter. I don't want to talk about it again."

He was frustrated with their meddling and would ask them to leave as soon as breakfast was finished. He had plans with Chelsea this morning and the last thing he wanted was for them to make her feel uncomfortable, yet again.

It wasn't lost on him that his daughters were less than welcoming when they first met Chelsea. He understood their fear that she was taking the place of their deceased mother, but he thought by now they'd exhibit a bit of maturity on this subject. They were, after all, grown adults.

They ate their breakfast in awkward silence, until they were interrupted by the doorbell. His maid answered the door, and he could hear Chelsea's voice in the foyer. He wheeled himself away from the table and went to meet her.

"Chelsea, I'm so happy to see you. You look lovely as always."

Chelsea bent down to kiss him. "Hello, Sebastian."

"Samantha and Jordan are here in the dining room. We were just finishing our breakfast. Would you care for a coffee or something to eat?"

"Coffee would be great."

His daughters had gathered their handbags and stood at the entrance.

"Dad, Jordan, and I have to go. Hello, Mrs. Marsden."

"Please call me Chelsea. It's nice to see you both again."

Jordan bent down and gave Sebastian a kiss, and Samantha did the same after her.

"We'll call you later. Let us know if you need anything."

They walked out of the house without looking at Chelsea again, and Sebastian took notice of their behavior.

"Chelsea, I apologize for my daughters' rudeness. It's inexcusable."

"Please, Sebastian, you don't have to apologize. I think I understand what they're feeling."

"You do? Then maybe you can enlighten me because I don't approve of their behavior at all. They're grown women for heaven's sake."

"Don't get your blood pressure up. It's not worth it. Let's go outside and enjoy the beautiful day. Would you like more coffee?"

"No. I've had enough, but why don't you get a cup for yourself, and I'll meet you outside?"

He wheeled out to the lanai and waited for Chelsea to join him. The morning had started out horribly and he was glad that the rest of the day would be spent with someone he had come to admire. Chelsea had many qualities that he loved, high among them was her ability to make him laugh every time they were together.

"I hope I didn't run your daughters out by my being here."

He waved that idea away with his hand. "Don't worry about them. If it isn't one thing it's another. I swear they look for things to fuss about."

"Oh? What are they upset about?"

"Let's not talk about them. How about we just enjoy the day?"

Chelsea's face told him this conversation wasn't over.

"I'm sorry, Sebastian, but I think we need to talk about this. I know we planned to spend the day together, but I don't think I can do that with this thing hanging in the air between us."

"What thing? Are you talking about Samantha and Jordan? You don't have anything to worry about."

"You're wrong about that. Maybe you don't want to deal with it, and I totally understand, but it's very hard for me to be around people who obviously don't want me here."

He took Chelsea's hand in his. "You can't let them run you out of my life. I won't let that happen."

"With all due respect, you're not the only one with a say here. I'm used to living my life exactly the way I want it. I've purposely surrounded myself with people who love me and enjoy my company, anyone else can kiss my…"

"Don't say it, please. I hear you. I do. But you also have to understand that these are my daughters. I can't just order them out of my life so easily. You don't have children, so you might not understand what I'm saying."

Chelsea got up from her chair and abruptly interrupted him.

"I'm sick of people saying that to me. What does having children have to do with recognizing disrespect? I don't need to have children to know when someone is being rude. Your daughters have made it perfectly clear that they don't want me coming around here, and I don't see how we'll get beyond that."

Her sudden anger made him recognize the seriousness of the situation. Was he wrong to feel so strongly for Chelsea? He'd been alone and without a woman in his life for so long that maybe he didn't know how to behave in such a situation as this.

"I thought you and I were…"

He didn't know how to finish his thoughts. Chelsea tried to finish it for him.

"You were going to say, serious?"

Sebastian only nodded.

Chelsea looked uncomfortable and softened her tone of voice.

"I didn't mean to sound so angry, Sebastian. Now that we're having this discussion, I think it's important for us to be on the same page about a few things. I don't think I'll ever get serious with anyone again. I had a good marriage and a happy life with my husband, Carl. After he passed I hardly got out of bed every morning. When I finally did, I decided I'd live my life for the both of us. If Carl couldn't be here, I'd enjoy everything that he and I would have done together. I like my freedom. I hope you understand."

Sebastian struggled to absorb her words. He was certain that Chelsea felt more for him than she let on, but now, it sounded as if she was breaking up with him. In his mind he forced himself to diminish the seriousness of the situation. No matter what she was saying to him right now, he believed it was nothing more than her overreaction to his daughters' dislike for her. He wasn't used to people walking away from him, and he wasn't about to give up so easily.

"Chelsea, if this is really about my girls, I can talk to them."

"No. They've just helped me see what I've been doing. Honestly, I'm glad this has happened; it's given me the opportunity to talk to you about any ideas you might have about us being exclusive. It's good that we had this talk now, before things got out of hand."

"It sounds as if you're saying you want the freedom to see other people."

"That's always been my position, Sebastian. You can see other people too. We should be free to date whomever we wish."

The conversation had gone in a direction he never anticipated. The day was turning out to be as bad as breakfast with his daughters. While he tried to find a way to fix things, the power to make any change had been taken from him with her last statement. He believed that Chelsea was the only woman for him, but if she wanted to date other men, so be it.

"If you don't mind, Chelsea, under the circumstances, I'd like to cancel our date for today."

The expression on her face made it clear that she agreed with him.

Chelsea took her handbag and lifted her chin as she walked to the door. She turned back to him and said, "I hope we can still see each other from time to time. I'd hate to lose a good friend over this. I'll leave the ball in your court. You know how to reach me."

Chelsea walked into the house and out the front door, leaving Sebastian wondering how things could go horribly wrong so quickly. He needed time to think about his next step. He knew himself well enough to know that falling in love again after his wife's death, was no small thing. Maybe Chelsea didn't know that he was the only man for her, but he did. What to do about it was another matter, altogether.

Maggie carried a garden basket filled with newly picked tomatoes, lettuce and cucumbers into the kitchen and placed the basket on the island. Leaving the produce for the chef, she took off her gloves and was ready to walk to the carriage house for a long, hot bath when her best friend Chelsea stormed into the room.

Chelsea gathered all the ingredients to make her signature Key Lime-tini, and then looked at Maggie.

"Care to join me?"

"Chelsea, it's only eleven o'clock."

"So?"

Maggie knew better than to get on Chelsea's bad side.

"Ok then. I guess I'll join you, but first maybe you tell me what's got you in this mood."

Chelsea poured a glass for Maggie and then one for herself. She raised her glass and said, "To women and their awesomeness."

Maggie raised her glass and then took a sip.

"Nice to know we're in agreement on something. Now, you want to tell me what's going on?"

Chelsea poured out her frustration with Sebastian and his family to Maggie, and then, since she couldn't stop if she wanted to, began ranting about the nerve of the man to assume they were exclusive.

Maggie knew how to handle her friend. All she had to do was wait and let her vent, then when she calmed down, Maggie would speak. It didn't take long, and she figured the Lime-tini had something to do with that.

"I didn't know you wanted to date other men."

"Did I say that?"

"Well, yes, you did, and you told Sebastian the same thing. Am I wrong?"

Chelsea took another sip of her drink and rolled her eyes.

"I have no idea what I want. I just don't like my life being planned without my permission. It's like his whole family has decided what I want and how I feel. I'm the only one who can decide those things, and I told him so."

"Nothing wrong with that. So, what's next?"

Chelsea's tone softened and Maggie could tell there was a hint of regret in it.

"I'm not sure. I told him I wanted to be friends and still get together. I said he knew how to reach me if he wanted the same."

Maggie hated to be selfish, but she had to remind Chelsea of their plan.

Whispering so that Christopher didn't hear her, Maggie said, "Did you forget that we were going to have Sebastian talk to Chris at the wedding?"

"Oh, darn. I'm so sorry, Maggie. You know my temper. I completely forgot about that. I guess I could go back with my tail between my legs and ask him."

Maggie laughed and tapped Chelsea's hand.

"No. Heaven forbid I make you do that. We'll think of something else. That is, unless you *want* to go back."

Maggie watched her friend struggle with her thoughts. It was obvious to everyone that Sebastian was someone very important to Chelsea. Not to mention, that the man was falling in love with her. How they could come to an understanding was anyone's guess, but Maggie would do her best to bring them together if there was any possible way to do it.

"No. I don't want to go back. Right now, I think the best thing to do is to let him think about what I said."

"Maybe you need to think a little as well?"

"What does that mean?"

"It means that maybe you should decide how important Sebastian is to you? I've watched you with him, Chelsea. I think you feel much more for him than you realize. There's nothing wrong with finding love again. I highly recommend it."

"Maggie, to be honest with you, I don't know that I can let myself get that involved. I know it sounds silly, but I feel like I'd be cheating on Carl."

Maggie smiled. "It doesn't sound silly at all, sweetie. But Carl has been gone for several years now, and you have every right to be happy. Do you really think that he would want you to be alone or without love in your life?"

"No. I suppose not. It doesn't matter now, anyway. I've probably ruined any chance of Sebastian calling me again. I stormed out of his house and didn't sound like a woman in love."

"Be honest. Are you in love?"

Maggie could tell that her friend didn't want to say the words out loud for fear that once said, she would have to do something about it.

Chelsea whispered, "Oh, Maggie, I think I am. What am I going to do?"

"I'll tell you what you're going to do. You're going to sit with this for a few days. If Sebastian feels the same, you can be sure he'll get in touch with you soon. In the meantime, let's celebrate this. Love is never something to fear my friend."

The women held their drinks in the air clinking them together. Maggie was grateful there was happiness and joy filling the house once more. In a few days, her daughter would marry Trevor, and there would be more to celebrate. She hoped that love's power might help Christopher. It was the only thing she knew that could heal a broken spirit.

CHAPTER SEVEN

At six o'clock the next morning, Becca slid out of bed and threw cold water on her face. She loved getting outside before most people were up, but it always took a bit of ice-cold water to get her blood flowing. Before she could change her mind, she put on her t-shirt, shorts, socks and running shoes, and then filled her water bottle.

Taking in a deep breath of the salt air, she started on her run. Heading out in the direction of Sanibel, she could see others doing the same. Running helped clear her mind of things she'd rather not think about. It was her way of getting rid of any stress she was feeling but also allowed her uninterrupted time with her thoughts.

When she was in college, Becca never missed a morning run. She'd sprint through the paths on campus but then ventured out along the tree-lined streets of Easton, Massachusetts, slowing her pace. The small, tight-knit community of the school made her feel safe, but she never ran the town's streets alone.

This morning, she waved to people she'd known her whole life as she navigated the streets of her childhood. Her legs took her past the Tween Waters cottages and magnificent mansions nearby. By the time she made her way back to Captiva, she chose a new course, passing the Key Lime Garden Inn.

It was still early, and she told herself that she didn't expect to see anyone up and about on the property. Still, she didn't fool herself. She knew exactly why she chose this route. It wasn't as if the house sat on the edge of the street. One had to walk, or in this case, run up the driveway to get anywhere close enough to see people.

She could see Christopher sitting on the porch, and privately admonished herself for being so bold. As soon as he saw her, she instantly regretted her decision to run past the inn. She was sweaty and out of breath. It was not the look Becca wanted him to see, but she also didn't want to appear like she was avoiding him.

"Good morning, Becca. You look like you've been running for a while. What time did you get up this morning?"

"I like to get the last leg of my run on the beach. It's really good for the calves."

Stupid. That's not what he asked you.

"Uh-huh. How many miles did you do?"

"I do about four miles every morning. At least that's where I'm at right now. I've run longer. I even did a few marathons, but I need a bit more training before I do one of those again."

Christopher nodded. "I've done the Boston Marathon twice."

"Really? I'm impressed. How long did it take you?"

"Two hours, fifty-eight minutes the first time and two hours, forty-five the second."

"That's incredible. I'd love to do it myself. Maybe one day I'll get there."

She thought she should start back to her house, but Christopher continued talking.

"I ran the Marathon on behalf of my friend Erin Stenwick who passed away. She'd be our age now."

"Oh, I'm sorry. What happened to her?"

"Suicide. She drowned in the pond near her house."

"That's horrible. When did this happen?"

She could tell that he was hesitating, and suddenly felt ashamed she had pressed him for more information.

"You don't have to tell me if you don't want to. I shouldn't have…"

Christopher stopped her. "No. It's fine. She died ten years ago. I found out about it when I got home from Captiva actually."

Ten years ago, after his vacation. That had to be the summer when they were together.

Becca understood everything now. His friend had died while he was vacationing on Captiva with his family. He'd been having fun and been a carefree sixteen-year-old boy enjoying his summer with friends…with her. His world must have stopped the minute he returned home.

She couldn't look at him, but instead stared at the ground. Her voice barely a whisper, she said, "So that's why you stopped answering my emails and texts."

Christopher's words were equally soft, "I couldn't. Erin and I weren't dating, but I knew she felt more for me than I did her. We were very close, and I considered her one of my dearest friends. She had a rough home life. Her father was abusive and used to beat her and her brother. She'd come to school with bruises on her body all the time, but she'd make excuses for them. In the beginning I believed her, but then over time I guess she finally felt safe enough to tell me the truth."

"You must have wanted to kill her father. Did you tell anyone?"

He shook his head.

"No. I felt helpless. She begged me not to tell anyone, and I promised her that I wouldn't. I told her that when I got back from Captiva, we'd find her a place to stay until she was eighteen. I even considered telling my parents. I knew they'd do whatever they could to help. At least my mom would. I even thought that maybe we'd take her in. I never got the chance to do anything. By the time we returned home from Florida, she was gone."

Becca instinctively knew how Christopher felt, and how he still felt about what happened to his friend. She had to say something, anything that might help him.

"It's not your fault, Chris. There was nothing you could do. You have to remember that you were a child too."

"Of course, I know that, but I should have told an adult much sooner than I did. That's on me."

Becca climbed the stairs to the porch and knelt in front of him.

"No. It's not. Erin suffered at the hands of an adult, and you were a child. Children have little power and minimal understanding of such trauma. You can't hold on to so much guilt and regret. Erin wouldn't want that for you."

In her need to comfort and advise Christopher, Becca felt a desire to put her arms around him. They both seemed to acknowledge the intimacy of the moment and for a minute she thought he was going to bend down to kiss her. Instead, he took her face in his hands, and smiled.

"Thank you, Becca. You're a good friend."

Whatever she thought was about to happen, the mood quickly shifted and so she tapped his hand, and said, "Anytime."

Becca got up from the hardwood floor beneath her and grabbed her right foot, pulling it up behind her to stretch. She then did the same thing to the other leg.

Trying to lighten the mood, she said, "I've got to get going. I'm going to run the rest of the way home. I don't want to stiffen up."

Christopher nodded and smiled. "Run by the inn anytime, I'm on the porch early most mornings."

Becca walked down the stairs and waved as she began her journey home.

Friend. Well, at least that was progress.

Sarah carried Sophia to the car just as Trevor's truck pulled up. He opened the back door, unhooked Noah's seatbelt, and helped him out of the vehicle.

"Hey, where are you pretty ladies going?"

"I'm headed over to Mom's. I want to see Chris. After our first unpleasant exchange, I've been avoiding him, but things can't continue this way. I thought Sophia might cheer him up. What are you guys doing?"

"No plans really. We were missing you two and thought we'd come over."

Sarah teased Trevor. "Right, and I suppose the noise and dust from the construction had nothing to do with it?"

Months ago, Trevor had decided to put an addition on his house. With Sarah and Sophia moving in, it seemed the logical plan. Construction was almost complete, and shortly after the wedding, they'd be a family living under one roof.

"Why don't you come along with us? I'm sure Chris would love to see you."

Noah kissed Sophia's cheek, and asked, "Can I come too?"

"Absolutely. Why don't you get your swimsuit? You can go in the pool or maybe you and Dad can go down to the beach."

Noah's aversion to the water had finally abated and swimming had become one of his favorite things to do. Trevor took him inside and they found Noah's swimsuit and a beach towel.

When they came out, Sarah was already behind the wheel, and Sophia was in her car seat.

"You don't mind if I drive us there, do you?"

"Nope. I'll leave my truck here."

Trevor buckled Noah in the backseat and Sarah smiled and watched him through the rearview mirror rub Sophia's head. Noah had become a devoted big brother and loved to care for his soon-to-be little sister. Soon, the adoption would be official, and Sarah couldn't wait.

As usual, traffic was heavy getting over the bridge to Sanibel and Captiva, but they finally arrived right after guests of the inn had finished eating their lunch.

Maggie met them outside in the driveway.

"Hey, you guys. This is a surprise."

Sarah looked at Trevor. "I'm sorry, Mom. Is this a bad time? We should have called ahead."

"Don't be silly. I'm always glad to see you. My goodness, Noah is getting so big."

"I'm six."

"I know you are. Six is an important age. You're almost grown up."

Noah nodded, and said, "Can I go in the pool?"

"Of course, you can. Why don't you go upstairs in the carriage house and put your swimsuit on?"

"Thanks, Maggie. I'll take him over." Trevor got the swimsuit and beach towel out of the back of the car and the two of them walked to the carriage house.

Sarah pulled Sophia out of her car seat. She had been sleeping, but now, her eyes were wide open. Keeping her voice low, Sarah asked her mother about Christopher.

"I thought maybe meeting Sophia might put a smile on Chris' face. What do you think?"

"I think that's a great idea. I don't see how anyone could stay grumpy with this little girl around."

Maggie asked Sarah, "You got my message about Chelsea and Sebastian?"

"I did. I'm sorry things didn't work out between them. I really like Sebastian, and I think he's good for Chelsea."

"I wouldn't count him out just yet, but I agree with you. I think they make a good couple. You know Chelsea. She's got to be in control of everything and it looks like Sebastian is the same way. Regardless of the fact that they're both so stubborn, I think they'll work it out. At least I hope so for Chelsea's sake."

"Mom, before we visit with Chris, I wanted to ask you something."

"What is it?"

"I'd like it if you would walk me down the aisle on Saturday."

She could see that her mother was not only happy, but surprised.

"Oh, Sarah. Of course, honey. I just assumed that with your father gone, you'd walk alone."

"Even when Dad was alive, it was you who raised us kids. You never missed a soccer game or a recital. You've been by my side my whole life; I couldn't think of walking down the aisle without you by my side once again."

Her mother started to cry, and Sarah rubbed her back.

"No crying. Chris will think we're upset about something."

Maggie nodded. "Ok. Not crying. Let's go inside."

They went inside and settled inside her mother's favorite room. It was the room where the previous owner used to sit and read. It was also home to several books by Anne Morrow Lindbergh as well as other famous authors who had visited Captiva over the years.

Sarah handed Sophia to her mother.

"I'm going to knock on his door. I'll be right back."

Sarah walked through the kitchen to get to Christopher's room. She knocked and waited for him to open the door. When he didn't, she knocked again.

"Chris, it's Sarah. I thought I'd stop by for a visit. Care to join Mom and me for a bit?"

She could hear movement and realized it must take him several minutes to where he felt presentable.

"We're in Rose's room. I've brought Sophia with me. Noah and Trevor are down at the pool. How about you come out and meet your niece?"

The door opened, and Christopher wheeled himself out of his room and into the kitchen. Sarah was shocked to see the dark circles under his eyes. She wanted to cry. For weeks now she'd felt helpless to reach her brother. With any luck this visit with Sophia would help.

He followed her to the other side of the house. When they reached Rose's room, Sophia was on Maggie's lap. He wheeled himself closer to the baby, and Maggie turned Sophia around to see him.

"How old is she?"

"She just turned one a few weeks ago. I can't believe it really. I feel like it was yesterday when I found her on my doorstep. It's been an incredible year."

Christopher nodded. "For all of us."

"I'm sorry, Chris. I didn't mean anything"

He shook his head and held his index finger out to Sophia. "It's fine."

Maggie looked at Christopher and asked, "Would you like to hold her?"

Sarah worried that he might feel awkward holding the baby on his lap, but instead decided not to wait for an answer. She lifted Sophia from Maggie's arms and placed the baby onto his lap.

"Sophia, this is your uncle Christopher."

She watched him cradle Sophia in his arms and saw tears in his eyes. At that moment, she knew she had done a good thing bringing her daughter to meet her uncle. As Sophia grew, Sarah would remember this day, and all the days that followed, watching her brother play with his niece. She'd pray for his healing and felt certain that Sophia's visit might be the start of that process.

Sarah's cell phone rang. She answered it as soon as she saw that it was their sister, Beth. She put the phone on speaker.

"Hey, Beth. I'm sitting here with Mom and Chris. I brought Sophia over for a visit. Say hello."

"I'm glad you've got me on speaker so our brother can hear how mad I am at him."

Christopher looked surprised. "What did I do?"

"It's what you didn't do. Why haven't you returned my calls? I've called you three times in the last few weeks, and I get silence."

Christopher smiled. "I figured if I ignored you enough times, maybe you'd come down here and we'd get to see you in person."

"Well, it just so happens that's exactly what I'm going to do. Be careful what you wish for little brother. When I'm done with you, you're going to be glad you're in that wheelchair."

The room went silent. Shocked at Beth's words, Sarah and her mother looked at Christopher, waiting for his reaction. His response surprised them all.

"Oh yeah? Come down here and let's see what you got. I hear now that you're a suit you've lost your nerve."

Everyone laughed at the exchange and Sarah felt relief that no matter what Christopher had gone through, her little brother was still in there, and that gave her hope.

Maggie clapped her hands together.

"Oh, Beth. I'm so glad you're going to be here for the wedding. When are you flying down?"

"I'm taking the six o'clock flight out of Boston on Thursday morning. I should be at the house by noon. I get a week off. I'm so excited to see everyone. Michael called me. He and Lauren are going to fly down on Friday. Jeff and Brea are staying home with the kids. They send their love and congratulations."

Sarah was thrilled to hear that they all would be together again in just a few days.

"Hey, Sarah. I hope you don't mind, but I've asked Gabriel to come to Captiva with me. Are you all ok with that?"

Maggie spoke first. "Of course, tell him that we're all looking forward to meeting him."

Sarah agreed. "Absolutely, he's welcome."

Christopher had to get the last word in.

"Don't think because you're bringing your boyfriend that I'm going to go easy on you. It's going to take more than that to beat me."

Sarah loved listening to her siblings bicker.

"Sounds just like the old days. I can't wait to see the two of you go at it this weekend."

Beth laughed and was interrupted by her assistant.

"Listen, guys. I've got to go. I'm tying up loose ends here but I'll see you soon. Oh Sarah, by the way, thanks for letting me wear whatever I want on the wedding day. I'll be forever grateful that you're not stuffing me into a bridesmaid dress. Love you, guys."

They ended the call, and it was perfect timing because Sophia had given her final approval of her uncle Christopher by spitting up on his shirt.

CHAPTER EIGHT

The minute Becca looked at the photo of her great-grandparents with Robert and Rose Lane, she knew she'd have to visit her great-grandmother to get more details about the picture.

Her father had piqued her interest and so she set out the next morning to drive to the assisted living facility where her great-grandmother lived. Lillian Bradford got tired of Becca calling her great-grandma and long ago insisted she instead call her Gran. She said it was easier and made her feel younger than her eighty-nine years.

Becca signed her name on the visitor's log and walked toward Gran's apartment but stopped along the way when she saw her in a room with several other residents throwing a beach ball. Becca didn't want to interrupt Gran's physical therapy, so she waited, sitting on a chair outside the game room.

After ten minutes, Gran noticed her in the hall and threw the ball at another resident before turning to leave the room.

"Gran, it looks like they're not finished."

Waving her hand in the air, she said, "Who cares? I'm finished with them. Let's go hang out on the patio outside my room. Are you hungry? Today's hot fudge sundae day. You can have as many or as much as you want. At this age, they don't even care if your doctor tells you to cut out dairy. They figure we should enjoy ourselves for the years we've got left. I say, good idea."

Becca laughed at Gran. Tremendous spunk had been a notable quality of the Bradford women, and one that Becca hoped she had inherited.

"I think I'll pass. I just want to spend some time visiting my favorite person."

"Uh-oh. Something must be wrong back home. What is it? Your brother Finn giving you troubles? You send that boy over here and I'll give him a talking to."

Shaking her head, Becca smiled. "No, Finn isn't bothering me, at least not today. I was up in the attic the other day and found a photograph I thought you might like to see."

Becca pulled the picture out of her backpack and handed it to her.

Lillian brought the photo close to her face. "Oh, dear. That was a long time ago. Look how handsome your great-grandpa was."

Becca had hoped her first words would be about the other man in the photo.

"Who are the other people in the picture?"

"That's Rose and Robert Lane. They were friends of ours."

Becca felt brave and decided to go through with her plan to find out more about the rumors and gossip.

"Is that the man everyone gossiped about?"

Lillian put the photo down on the table and looked at Becca.

"Did your mother tell you about that?"

"Mom? No, it wasn't Mom. Dad said something the other night when I found the photo. I asked him about it, and he made a brief comment, but wouldn't say more. He told me that I should throw the picture away."

"But you didn't, and instead decided to play detective, huh?"

Becca suddenly felt embarrassed about the whole thing and regretted starting the conversation. They walked out onto her patio, Gran still holding the photo. They sat around a small table and Gran looked up at the sky and shrugged.

"Well, I guess there's no point in ignoring this. Besides, I think it's important that you understand just how fearless your mother was."

"Fearless?"

"You betcha. Your mother never shied away from controversy, especially if she felt that someone was being treated unfairly. She hated that I was the focus of such treatment, and she wouldn't stand for it."

"What did she do?"

"I guess the gossip got to her, so she went to Mrs. Lane and told her what was happening and how it hurt me. Mind you, your mother also dealt with kids her own age thinking her grandmother an adulterer, but she never cared about those bullies. Her singular worry was about me and was determined to put a stop to such treatment."

"Wow. That was brave. What did Mrs. Lane say?"

"There have been many heroes in my life, Becca, but none as brave as that woman. She publicly made a fuss about it, never concerning herself with the fact that her husband had been unfaithful, more than once, I might add. She wasn't trying to protect and defend him; she was clearing my reputation."

"What exactly did she do?"

"Rose told Abigail Warren, who was the biggest mouth on the island, that if she and the others didn't publicly retract their statements, and admit they were wrong, that she wouldn't give one more dime to the ladies' auxiliary. In addition, she told them that she'd never again lend her name to another of their charities."

"That's awesome."

Lillian nodded. "It was. The Lanes had a lot of power and

money on the island. Rose had Abigail by the throat and refused to let go. Not to mention that she also told Abigail that if she didn't back off she'd see to it that everyone knew of Abigail's weekly private get-togethers with Gerard Gromely off island. I'm pretty sure that was the final nail in that coffin."

Becca laughed at that last statement. "Rose Lane sounds like an amazing woman."

Lillian agreed. "She was, and I'm sorry she's gone now. I made a point to see her when I found out what Julia had done. Rose and I had tea one day so that I could thank her, but it was your mother who continued to have a friendship with Rose. They got together for tea now and then. I used to be a little jealous of their friendship. If your mother needed to talk to someone, I wanted that someone to be me, or even her own mother, your grandma. But that's not the important thing to focus on here. What happened back then would never have happened if your mother didn't step in to protect me."

"Mom was a special lady."

"So are you, Becca. You have that same fearlessness in you. I can see it in your eyes dear girl."

Becca looked down and shook her head.

"Oh, Gran, I don't know about that. I don't feel very fearless. Most days I don't feel anything at all, and if I do feel something, it's usually fear."

Becca didn't mean to say that out loud, but now that she had she couldn't take it back. She wondered if Gran had any magic to change her perspective.

"Do it afraid."

Becca didn't understand. "Huh?"

"Fear is a funny thing. We need it to keep us safe. If there is something real that is threatening our life, we need to be afraid so that we can adjust accordingly to protect ourselves. The problem isn't being afraid. It's letting fear get out of hand and control our lives when there is only something we perceive as frightening. Sometimes that means we end up being afraid of nothing more than a paper tiger. When that happens, the only way to break through is to do it afraid. Acknowledge the fear, but don't let it stop you from doing anything you truly want to do. Do it afraid, Becca. Before you know it, you won't be afraid of that paper tiger anymore."

By visiting Gran, Becca learned how strong her mother was, but she also understood for the first time, that the strength came from her grandmother and great-grandmother as well. If she could harness that resilience and courage, then maybe she'd be able to move forward.

Whatever the course of her life, she felt proud to know such incredible women. Rose Johnson Lane would forever be another to draw wisdom from, and her excitement grew stronger the more she thought about the powerful and influential women she had yet to meet.

Beth and Gabriel picked up their luggage and walked to the car rental counter. Fortunately, the line wasn't long, and they got their car and made their way out of the airport in record time. She felt his eyes on her as they drove to Captiva.

"What?"

"I'm admiring how beautiful you are."

She'd never received compliments about her looks before, and no matter how many times Gabriel told her that she was pretty, she still felt uncomfortable.

"Why can't you take a compliment?"

"I don't know. It just sounds…"

"Insincere?"

"I didn't say that."

"But, you were thinking it, right?"

Beth laughed at his candor. She couldn't argue with him because that was exactly how she felt.

"How about this, what if we both agree that because you are so happy to see your family again, you have a glow, and that healthy look makes you beautiful? Would you be satisfied with that?"

"That's perfect. I'll accept that and thank you."

Along the way to Captiva, Beth pointed out the various shops, restaurants and places that meant so much to her and her family over the years.

"You'll have to come back to Captiva when you can stay longer than a few days."

Gabriel agreed. "It certainly is beautiful."

"You'd be surprised how nice Sanibel is too. Once in a while Sanibel's water isn't as clear as it is on Captiva. It has to do with the US Army Corp of Engineers releasing water from Lake Okeechobee. When the lake water gets too high, they open the floodgates and send the water out into the ocean. The only problem is that it turns the water brown. I've noticed that the water surrounding Captiva doesn't seem to suffer the change in color. I think it's too far out and away from the lake."

"People must be furious when that happens."

Beth nodded. "They are, indeed. Imagine if you've planned your vacation and you come to Sanibel just when they decide to release the water? I wouldn't be too happy either."

As they approached the inn, Beth's heart began to beat faster.

"Is it weird that I can't wait to see everyone but I'm nervous too?"

Gabriel shook his head. "Not weird. What do you think is making you feel nervous? Is it Christopher?"

Beth was happy that they talked on speaker phone a couple of days ago. It broke the ice, but she didn't know how she would react seeing him in the wheelchair.

"I worry that I might cry when I see him."

"That's understandable. From what you've told me about your brother, the two of you are very alike. Maybe you should think of him the way you always have, instead of a changed man."

"That's just it, Gabriel. Chris has changed, and there's no point in pretending that he hasn't. I think what upsets me the most is that we've got to find a new normal, and I hate it. I'm angry, and scared and…"

Gabriel put his hand on Beth's arm.

"Focus on loving him, Beth. You can't go wrong if you do that."

The lump in her throat prevented her from saying anything more. All she could do was nod and look straight ahead toward the Key Lime Garden Inn driveway.

Maggie watched as Paolo and his landscape workers from Sanibellia put the final stones around her new koi pond. A small waterfall fell into the pond sending the fish scurrying. Paolo had wanted to add the pond to the garden area and had spent the week working to complete it in time for Sarah's wedding.

The sound of crunching seashells announced the arrival of Beth and Gabriel's car. Beth parked the car, got out and then ran to her mother. She threw her arms around Maggie, and then pulled her toward Gabriel.

"Mom. This is Gabriel."

Gabriel didn't wait for an invitation. He hugged Maggie tight and could see the pleased look on Beth's face.

"Beth has told me so much about you that I feel like I've known you forever."

"Well, unfortunately my daughter has been too busy to call her mother, so I can't say I know a lot about you, but I hope to rectify that this weekend."

Paolo came out from the garden and met the three of them in the driveway.

"Gabriel, this is my husband, Paolo Moretti. Paolo, this is Beth's friend, Gabriel Walker."

Gabriel shook Paolo's hand.

"Nice to meet you, Mr. Moretti."

"Please, call me Paolo."

Beth looked at Maggie and whispered,

"Where is he?"

Maggie rolled her eyes and shrugged.

"Where he always is—in his room. He's come out onto the porch here and there, but most of the time, he stays in his room."

Beth looked at Gabriel and said, "Do you mind if I first see Chris alone?"

"Of course not. I can wait out here."

Maggie shook her head. "No need to stay out here. Paolo and I will show him around the garden before going in. You go see your brother and have a talk. Come find us when you're done."

Beth smiled and hugged her mother.

"Wish me luck."

Maggie watched Beth go inside and crossed her fingers that a talk between her two youngest children might help her son out of his funk. No one but Beth could ever get Chris riled up. In the old days, Maggie would have to pull the two of them apart and scold them for fighting. Now, she'd give anything to see the two of them go at it once again.

CHAPTER NINE

Beth went inside and stood in the middle of the kitchen. She forgot to ask which room was his, but it made sense that he'd need something on the first floor. Walking toward the bedroom off the kitchen, she knocked and called out his name in case she had the wrong room.

"Chris? It's me, Beth. Open the door."

She could hear noise coming from inside but couldn't make out if it was her brother or not. She turned the doorknob and slowly opened the door.

"Chris?"

He was laying on his back on top of the bed, his arm covering his eyes. She couldn't bring herself to look at the rest of his body just yet and so she gingerly sat on the edge of the bed and removed his arm from his face. His eyes were red from crying, his pain impossible to ignore. She threw her body down onto his and hugged him.

"Oh, Chris. It's all right. Get it all out. I'm here now. Your Bethy is here."

They stayed like that for a long time before she sat up and

reached for the tissues. She handed them to him, and he wiped his eyes, pushing himself up against the headboard.

"I'm sorry, sis. I promised myself I wasn't going to be a mess when you got here. These moments come and go and it's impossible to predict when I might have an episode. As usual, my timing stinks."

"Since when do you apologize to me? Now I know you really need help."

He laughed at that and reached for her. They embraced again and he whispered in her ear, "I'm so glad you're here."

She squeezed him tight and answered, "Where else would I be when my little brother needs me?"

She pulled away from him and looked around the room.

"So, this is your new hideout?"

"I wouldn't call it that"

"No? What would you call it? Looks to me like you've decided to climb into the coffin while you're still breathing."

She walked to the window and opened the blinds, letting light into the room.

They both knew that Beth was picking a fight with him.

"Oh, I get it. This is where tough love comes in, right? When the psychiatrist doesn't work, send in the family, and shame him into getting back to normal. Well, I've got a news flash for you. This is the new normal. You see that wheelchair, and these crutches? Take a good look at my leg, Beth. Can you see? This right here is my new normal."

She looked down at his leg and wanted to cry, but she didn't. She refused to let him think she saw his situation as abysmal.

"I see you, Chris. I see all of you, but you only see an amputated leg. What exactly is your plan? You realize you can only stay in this room for so long. Eventually, you're going to have to get out into the world and deal with life just like everyone else."

He didn't answer her, but instead looked down at his mangled leg. She waited for him to say something—anything that made her feel that she was getting through to him.

If only he'd get angry. At least that would be a sign that he's feeling something other than hopelessness.

Her voice barely a whisper, she said, "You are so much more than this, Chris. I'd hate to think that all those men and women who died, did so in vain."

His eyes wide, she'd struck a nerve.

"Don't talk about them like that. You don't know what you're saying."

"Oh, I think I do."

She looked out the window and studied the landscape, giving him a minute to think about her words before she continued. When she did, even sitting on the bed, something in his posture changed.

"Every single brave soldier who dies fighting to preserve our way of life, doesn't die in vain if we go on living and serving others. You don't have to be in the military to make a difference in this world, Chris, but I promise you this. You'll never honor them by hiding out in this room."

Beth had come to Captiva to reach into her brother's heart and give him hope. If no one else could reach him, perhaps she could. For now, she'd leave him to think about what she'd said. Maybe he'd see her words as a challenge and return to the competitive person she'd known all her life. She opened his door and looked at him once more before joining the others outside.

"I'd really like it if you'd come out to meet my boyfriend. I want the two most important men in my life to be friends. Take your time and come look for us when you're ready."

She left his room and closed the door behind her. Searching for her mother and Gabriel, Beth tried to stay distracted enough to avoid thinking about her brother's slow descent into darkness. She did what she could. The rest was up to Christopher.

After a tour of the garden and the new koi pond, they walked down to the beach before going upstairs to the carriage house to see Maggie and Paolo's place. The newlyweds had brought back many items from Paolo's childhood home in Italy to decorate the place. The look was a mix of Italy and summer beach cottage, and it suited their personalities perfectly.

Beth looked out the window and saw Riley help Christopher out onto the porch. Her joy at seeing her brother outside of his room was palpable.

"Mom. Look."

Maggie smiled, and hugged Beth.

"Looks like your talk did the trick. Let's get downstairs."

Beth led the way as everyone joined Christopher on the porch.

Christopher's eyes had cleared, and he smiled as they approached.

"So, this is Gabriel?"

They shook hands and then Christopher pointing to Beth said, "Is she as much trouble as a girlfriend as she is a sister?"

Gabriel looked uncomfortable, but smiled and answered, "Well, I wouldn't know anything about what she's like as a sister, but she's pretty great as a girlfriend."

Riley carried a platter with a large pitcher of lemonade and glasses followed by Grace who had made sandwiches for the group. It was a wonderfully informal gathering and Beth loved that Gabriel started to relax.

Paolo was particularly interested in Gabriel's woodworking and furniture making business and asked what seemed like a million questions before Maggie stopped him.

"Paolo, he's on vacation. Give him a break. I'm sure the last thing he wants to do is talk about work."

"Oh, I don't mind, really. I love what I do."

Just then, Chelsea came around to the back of the house and screamed when she saw Beth.

"Bethy! Come here and give me a hug. You have no idea how much we all miss you."

Beth loved Chelsea. She felt the woman to be kind as well as colorful and was pleased that she lived so close to her mother.

"Chelsea, this is…"

She didn't get to finish her introduction because Chelsea finished it for her.

"Gabriel. Wow, Beth. He's a handsome one. Come here and give me a hug. I'm a big hugger."

Gabriel complied and Beth stifled a laugh watching Chelsea refuse to let go of him. Her mother had to intervene.

"Ok, Chelsea. That's enough, leave something for Beth."

They all enjoyed their lunch and spent the rest of the day coming and going to and from the beach. Beth and Christopher spent more quiet time together before heading off to bed. Michael and Lauren would be here tomorrow, and Beth looked forward to seeing Sarah, Trevor, Noah, and Sophia too. Her heart was full of joy and anticipation for the next few days. She would be with her family again, and that meant everything to her.

Maggie got up early and tried to be as quiet as possible in the kitchen. She wanted her family to enjoy a beautiful breakfast buffet and promised Riley and Grace that she would work with them first thing in the morning. Up at five o'clock, she walked across the driveway and entered the inn on her tiptoes.

She started on the scone batter before anything else and made sure all the vases were filled with flowers from her garden. Her blue hydrangeas were perfectly bloomed and ready to be picked, so Paolo went outside to gather them. When the bushes were planted two years earlier, Paolo worked the soil to produce the most beautiful and varied colors possible. Now, with Sarah's wedding only hours away, the flowers covered every available table to be enjoyed by everyone in attendance.

Satisfied that the table was set just right, Maggie heard activity on the second floor and before long, Beth and Gabriel came down for brunch. Christopher took considerably longer.

Every time he showered, Maggie listened for sounds that he'd fallen. Even with the chair placed inside the shower, she still feared he'd hurt himself. She reminded herself to have a talk with him about his starting physical therapy again. But decided that was a discussion for another day. This weekend would be dedicated to happy family time.

Lauren and Michael arrived, and Christopher joined them in the dining room. Just as he wheeled himself into the room, everyone stopped talking. He managed to lighten the mood with a joke.

"Was it something I said?"

Everyone laughed and Michael shook his brother's hand, pulling him into a hug.

"Hey, big brother. Glad you could make it down."

Lauren bent down and hugged Christopher.

"Hey, Chris. Jeff and the kids send their love."

Michael and Lauren hugged Beth and said hello to Gabriel.

"Gabriel, nice to see you again."

Sarah and her family arrived and joined everyone.

"Hey, hey, the gang's all here."

Maggie laughed, fully aware that the loud noises in the dining room were about to go sky-high.

Michael called out to Sarah.

"Hey, here's the bride and groom, and the two small humans."

Noah went immediately to Christopher.

"Why does your chair have wheels?"

Maggie watched her son deftly handle the situation.

Without missing a beat, Christopher answered him.

"Because I got hurt and they had to take part of my leg away, so it helps me get around."

Noah was confused by that, so he squatted down and tried to look under Christopher's blanket.

Maggie panicked and reached for Noah, but it was too late. Christopher pulled the blanket off of his lap and exposed his limbs to everyone. Although dressed in jeans, one pant leg was folded under the right stump making the injury obvious to Noah.

The room was quiet except for Noah, who wasn't done asking questions.

"Does it hurt?"

Christopher shook his head. "Not so much anymore."

"Will the leg grow back?"

"No."

Maggie almost cried at her son's bravery. So that his nephew wouldn't think him any different than anyone else, Christopher picked up Noah and put him on his lap.

"You can still sit on my lap anytime you want, ok?"

Noah nodded and smiled, putting his arms around his uncle's neck.

Lauren's message from Maggie's mother lightened the mood in the room.

"Oh, Mom. Grandma wanted me to tell everyone that she's sorry to miss the wedding, but she's going to have a blast on her senior cruise. She also said that I should remind Trevor about something she told him at your wedding."

Sarah looked at Lauren and then back at Trevor.

"What did Grandma say to you?"

Trevor shrugged and tried to look innocent.

"Something about the Garrison women being strong-minded."

Maggie laughed. "That's my mother for you. She forgets that you all are Wheelers too."

Paolo added his opinion to the discussion, "She's right about the strong-minded part though."

Maggie gave a soft slap to her husband and laughed.

Sarah agreed with her grandmother's assessment.

"I'm proud to be strong-minded, but just in case, you still have a few hours to get out of marrying me, Mr. Hutchins."

Trevor took a sip of his mimosa. "Not on your life, Sarah Wheeler."

CHAPTER TEN

*S*arah looked into the mirror and placed her hand on her cheek. Her foundation barely covering her freckles, she laughed at her attempt to look glamorous. She'd been an outdoor girl all her life, and hardly ever wore more than a bit of mascara on her lashes. Her sister Beth insisted she add more color and presented Sarah with a palette of pink and blush shades for her lips.

"Pick something on the darker side. You want the color to last a long time."

"Beth, it doesn't matter how much lipstick you put on me. The minute we have our first kiss as husband and wife, it will be gone or at least smeared."

"No. Not these. Trust me. I know how to put makeup on. These are lip tints. They stain your lips for twenty-four hours at least."

Sarah pushed the lipsticks away. "Are you kidding me? I don't want something that's going to need turpentine to get off."

Beth didn't budge. "No. Today is special, and you need to look your best. Don't worry, you won't need turpentine or anything else, it comes off with this cream."

Sarah took the jar from Beth and stared at the ingredients. She felt certain that somewhere on the list would be a toxic mix of chemicals typically used by mechanics.

Aloe juice and coconut oil were first among a plethora of natural ingredients that Sarah felt comfortable putting on her face. She gave in and let Beth take over.

"Just sit back and enjoy the pampering. That's the best thing about weddings, people wait on you all day long. I should have been born a princess."

Sarah looked at her sister in disbelief. "Excuse me? I thought you were."

"Very funny."

"Seriously, Beth, you and Chris have had more attention being the babies of the family. The two of you got away with murder."

"A lot of good that did us. Look at us now. I'm struggling to find my place in the world and Chris wants to leave it."

Sarah sat up and admonished her sister.

"Don't say that. Chris is going to be fine. He just needs time."

The two women didn't know what to say after that, so they were quiet for a few minutes. Sarah suspected Beth shared her worry, and if she was honest with herself, had to admit she didn't believe her own words. Staying positive kept her from feeling scared for her little brother, even though the truth was that she had little control over his suffering.

Beth smiled and changed the topic.

"Let's not feel sad today. It's your wedding day. Pick out whatever makeup you want. You're going to look beautiful, no matter what you wear. You always do. I'm going to get changed. Mom should be up here any minute."

Sarah looked down at her engagement ring and thought about the last two years of her life. So much had changed and much of it without her planning. She laughed when she thought about how hard she tried to stay single and without children. With every relationship she had one foot out the door, ready to run away from love.

Without any effort at all, Trevor Hutchins and her two children, who she would soon adopt, turned her world upside down. Now, she believed with everything in her heart that she couldn't live without them.

She stepped into her wedding dress just as Maggie came into the room.

"You look beautiful, honey."

"Thanks, Mom. Is everyone ready outside?"

"Yup, even Christopher. Lauren wheeled him down to the beach. Noah is right up front with his father. He looks adorable. Once she got Chris in place, she took Sophia from me, so I could come up here and be with you."

Beth joined them and looked beautiful in a long hibiscus print maxi dress. In her hair, a single plumeria flower behind her left ear finished the look.

Sarah was impressed. "Wow, Bethy. You look gorgeous."

Beth opened a small box and presented a white hibiscus flower for her sister.

"I know you didn't want to make a big traditional fuss today, so I thought since you didn't have a veil, why not a pretty flower for your hair?"

Sarah's eyes started to fill with tears. "You see, Mom. This is why I chose Beth. She knows exactly what I like."

She hugged Beth and asked her to put the flower in her hair.

"I'm not any good at this. Will you do it?"

"I will if you promise not to cry. I've spent the better half of the morning on your makeup. It won't do to have it dripping down your face before the ceremony even begins."

Beth weaved the hibiscus into Sarah's hair, turned her sister around so that she could face the mirror, and stepped back.

"What do you think?"

"It's perfect. Just the right touch. Thank you, Bethy."

She looked at Maggie and sighed.

"I guess we're ready."

Beth handed Sarah her flower bouquet and grabbed her own.

"I'll go ahead of you. See you down there. Good luck."

Maggie waited until Beth was gone to say a few words to Sarah.

"Before we go down, I just want to tell you how very proud I am of you. You could have chosen any career or path for your life, and I'd support you, so I don't want you to misunderstand what I'm trying to say. It's not that I'm proud of you for choosing marriage and children. It's not that at all. It's that you looked deep into your heart and decided to be happy. It's as simple as that. You chose you. It's the only thing I ever wanted for you. How you found your way there was up to you."

Sarah put her hand to her mother's face.

"Thank you, Mom. I had a good teacher."

Chelsea thought she was seeing things. Everyone had walked down to the beach to find a chair for the ceremony. She'd gathered her wrap around her shoulders and had turned to join the guests when she saw him. Sebastian Barlowe had come to the wedding, and his daughter Samantha pushed his wheelchair toward her, her sister, Jordan followed alongside them.

Sebastian looked stunning in his tuxedo, and as much as Chelsea wanted to run to him, she held back, waiting to see what his daughters had to say.

"Hello, Chelsea. I hope I've not been too presumptuous showing up like this, but you did invite me."

Before Chelsea could speak, Jordan interrupted her.

"Mrs. Marsden, we want to apologize for the way we've treated you. It must seem like you've been dealing with a couple of children instead of two adult women."

Samantha agreed. "After you left the other day, our father called us back to the house. To be honest, we were surprised when he shared his feelings for you. Our mother's been gone for several years now, but I think you never truly get over the death of someone you love."

Jordan continued. "We know that's something you would understand given the loss of your husband. We're truly sorry for the way we've behaved. Our brother, Peter couldn't be with us today, but he wanted to offer his apologies for anything he might have said that was disrespectful."

They didn't wait for Chelsea's response, but instead, they began to walk away, leaving their father with Chelsea.

Chelsea stopped them. "Wait. Thank you for coming here today. I'm sure it wasn't easy for you. I do accept your apology. I'd ask you to stay, but it isn't my event. I hope you understand."

Samantha shook her head. "We only wanted to stay long enough to talk to you. Jordan brought her car and followed behind the van. We thought we'd leave Dad here with you and he can text us when he's ready to leave. The van's technology is equipped to handle the wheelchair, but one of us needs to drive him back."

Sebastian put his hand up and asked his daughters to wait. He wheeled closer to Chelsea and took her hand in his.

"Do you accept my apology, too? I don't want to assume anything. I won't stay unless you want me to."

Chelsea smiled, and bent down, kissing him softly on the lips. She stood and looked at the women.

"We'll call you when he's ready to go home."

Walking toward the beach holding Sebastian's hand, Chelsea didn't need to think about the future. He'd taken a leap of faith by coming to the wedding. The least she could do, was to follow his lead.

As a local guitarist strummed some of Sarah's favorite songs, the guests took their seats. Paolo sat in the left front row with his sister, Ciara. Sophia fussed briefly in Lauren's arms, but soon settled down. Michael and Gabriel sat next to Lauren.

Maggie took Sarah's arm in hers, and watched as Beth walked in front of them, barefoot on the sand. Sarah and Beth had decided to walk down the aisle without sandals, but Maggie couldn't bring herself to go that far. She figured the mother of the bride had to stay somewhat formal even if her daughter's wedding was anything but conventional.

Devon and Eliza Hutchins sat in the front row on the right. The rest of his siblings were there, and Maggie wondered how the two families would mingle during the reception.

Noah stood at the front with his father. Trevor looked as relaxed as ever, and it surprised Maggie that even though Noah wore a little tuxedo, Trevor chose a long cream-colored tunic and pants. He wore a Hawaiian lei around his neck and half of his long hair was pulled back and tied with a blue ribbon.

Neither Sarah nor Maggie's soon-to-be son-in-law were very religious. To hear Sarah tell it, they were both still searching and spiritual. Maggie wasn't certain what that meant exactly, but she was happy to know that at least her daughter believed in something greater than herself. So, it surprised her to hear Trevor's vows.

He took Sarah's hand in his.

"Sarah, you, and I have chosen to take this journey through life together, and along with Noah and Sophia will build a family. Our lives have been forever changed by things we had little control over. I know some call it destiny, but I'm not sure that's how I see it. I tried to find something already written that could express my feelings as precisely as

possible. And although I'm not a religious person, I found something that touched my heart and my spirit. I believe with all my heart, that in this life, you and I have a mission to fulfill. So let me tell you what I feel our time on this earth will look like. This prayer speaks to me, and I hope it will you as well:

Lord, make me an instrument of your peace:
    Where there is hatred, let me sow love.
    Where there is injury, pardon.
    Where there is doubt, faith.
    Where there is despair, hope.
    Where there is darkness, light.
    Where there is sadness, joy.

O divine Master, grant that I may not so much seek
    to be consoled as to console,
    to be understood as to understand,
    to be loved as to love.
    For it is in giving that we receive,
    It is in pardoning that we are pardoned,
    And it is in dying that we are born to eternal life.

Sarah Wheeler, I love you with all my heart. I want to make this world a better place with your help. I think that our love has a greater purpose, and I can't wait to see where it takes us."

Grateful her dress had one small pocket to hold a few tissues, Maggie wiped her eyes.

    Sarah spoke next.

. . .

"Trevor, as you know, when we first met, it was far from love at first sight for me. The reason for that is clear to me now. I simply didn't know who you were. I didn't know that you were the type of man who'd get out of his car and chase down a stray dog, or that you'd carry a spider outside to save its life. I didn't know that you'd give up your seat if someone older needed a chair. I had no idea what kind of father you'd be, or why you needed to keep your tea bag in your cup long after the tea had been steeped in hot water."

Everyone laughed and Eliza Hutchins nodded in agreement.

"Growing up, I was never that girl who wondered about her future husband or longed for her wedding day. I didn't dream of the perfect man for me, mostly because I had no idea what I needed in a partner. But that didn't matter. Somehow, without any effort on my part, the universe brought you to me. The most perfect person to share my life with. On top of that, you brought with you a wonderful little boy to love. Noah and you have made my life complete, and as if I wasn't blessed enough, one morning, not that long ago, a little baby girl was left at my door.

I'm sure there are going to be moments of difficulty and stress, but I know with everything I am, that I never have to worry whether I'll be strong enough to get through it, because I'll have you to carry those burdens with me. I love who we are, and I can't wait to begin the most incredible journey with you, Noah, and Sophia. I love you more than any words can say, but you have my promise to be yours and only yours for the rest of my life."

When the officiant pronounced the couple husband and wife, everyone clapped, screamed, and whistled. Beth handed Sarah her bouquet and the newlyweds walked back down the aisle.

Maggie had planned the ceremony and reception exactly as Sarah requested—no fuss, very informal and it was to look like nothing more than a family get-together. No matter how hard she tried, she couldn't ignore the traditions that had been passed down from generations. And so, she pulled Sarah aside and placed a small box in her hand.

"I got a little something for you."

"Mom, you didn't have to."

"Don't be silly. It's your wedding day. If I can't give you a gift on this day, then when? Come on, open it."

Sarah opened the box and took out a necklace that looked similar to the one her mother wore. A heart with Sarah and Trevor's name surrounded by two smaller hearts. Noah and Sophia's names were etched in the center.

"Oh, Mom. It's just like yours. I love it."

"Well, it's not exactly like mine. I've changed the center heart on mine and of course I have five smaller hearts, but I figure you can always add to yours."

Sarah laughed. "Oh, my goodness. Don't say that just yet. I'm still learning how to be a mother to the two I've already got. Will you put it on for me?"

Sarah turned and lifted her hair. Maggie hooked the clasp and then put her arms around her daughter.

"You never know what life has in store for you Sarah Wheeler Hutchins. Today is the beginning of an amazing journey. Some days it will feel like you're riding a wave and have no idea where the wind will take you. Other times it will feel more like a roller coaster. My advice is just ride the wave. You'll be surprised how much you love where you end up."

CHAPTER ELEVEN

As the sun set, two fire pits were lit and music continued to blare from the speakers. Dancing had slowed down and so did the songs. A soft breeze caressed Maggie's face as she and Paolo danced. He held her close and started to hum along with the music.

"I'm learning new things about you every day. I didn't know you had such a good voice."

"As long as you like it, that makes me happy. I'll sing to you every day if you want."

Maggie laughed. Paolo was incredibly sweet to her, and their marriage had been a wonderful blessing to them both.

"Paolo, do you see what I see?"

They looked over at Christopher and saw him wheel his chair over to Sebastian Barlowe.

"Oh, I hope Sebastian might have some advice for Chris. If anyone knows what Christopher is going through, it's him."

"I hope Chris will listen to him. It's a good sign that he's the one approaching Sebastian and not the other way around."

Maggie looked over at Chelsea who was sitting alone at the table.

"Paolo, I want to talk to Chelsea for a minute. Do you mind?"

"Of course not. That is, if you promise to come back and dance with me again."

As the song ended, Paolo dipped Maggie and then kissed her on the lips.

Chelsea clapped at them. "You two make such an elegant-looking couple. That was quite the dance."

Maggie sat next to Chelsea and fanned her face. "We might look good, but I think my hot flashes are wilting me."

Chelsea laughed. "You and me both. Do you see where your son is right now?"

Maggie smiled and leaned closer to Chelsea.

"What triggered that? Did Sebastian have anything to do with it?"

The twinkle in Chelsea's eye gave her away.

"I promise you, Maggie, I had nothing to do with this. It was subtle, but Christopher came over and asked Sebastian about his van. It's nothing fancy, just a Chrysler Voyager, but it's equipped to handle a wheelchair. Someone has to drive it of course, but it's very roomy. I've driven it myself. The next thing I know the two of them are wheeling themselves over to the van."

Maggie felt relief. "I don't care what the reason, I'm just glad the two of them are talking. Does Sebastian know how Chris has been dealing with his situation?"

Chelsea nodded. "He does. He told me that Christopher's attitude didn't surprise him, because he went through something similar after his accident. It's not unlike the stages of grief one goes through when there is a death. Losing a limb is a death of sorts. In Christopher's case, he not only lost his leg, but many of his friends too. None of us can imagine his pain. Sebastian might be the closest thing to someone who does."

Maggie looked over at Sarah who was dancing with Noah.

"Can you believe Sarah is married with children? Talk about miracles."

Chelsea put her hand on Maggie's arm and leaned in closer.

"Speaking of married with children, did you hear about Rachel?"

"No, what?"

"Well, you missed the last lunch-bunch get-together, so you didn't get the latest."

"Honestly, Chelsea. I've been so busy with the wedding planning and dealing with Christopher, I haven't had a minute to myself."

"Oh, I know that. I told everyone you'd be with us at the next one in two weeks. Anyway, apparently that jerk of a husband of hers finally signed the divorce papers and agreed to a nice settlement for her. Even though he didn't want Everly, he's agreed to pay child support."

Maggie rolled her eyes. "Isn't that big of him."

"Anyway, Rachel's decided to sell her house and move down to Cape Cod to be with her sisters Hannah and Lucy. They each have their own homes, and Rachel said there's no way she wants to live with either of them. A new start for her and the baby sounds like the right thing, if you ask me."

Maggie smiled. "That's wonderful news. This way, she'll have family close by. It's too bad the sisters don't have children. It would be nice for Everly to have cousins. Will she go back to teaching at some point, do you think?"

"Good question. I asked her, but she said she wasn't ready to think about that right now. Her main focus was selling her house in Andover and then getting her, and the baby moved. Her sisters will help and of course Jane, Kelly and Diana offered too. I think she'll be just fine. I told her to buy something big enough so all of us could have girl vacations on Cape Cod."

When the music stopped, Beth and Gabriel walked over to their table and Beth dropped onto the chair next to her mother. She took a sip of her lemonade and sighed.

"I'm pooped."

Maggie laughed. "Really, at your age? I've been watching the two of you dance. You could be on that dancing show on tv."

Beth's eyes went wide.

"Are you kidding? I used to be able to dance for hours non-stop. Not so much now. Must be all those hours sitting at my desk. I'm not getting enough exercise. I have a health club membership, but I never seem to get there. Where's Christopher?"

Maggie pointed to Sebastian's van. "Over there with Sebastian. He was asking him about his wheelchair accessible van, but I'm hoping they talk about more than that."

Beth shrugged. "Do you think it'll do any good? How many of us have already tried? I'm thrilled Sebastian is here though. Heaven knows we can use all the help we can get."

Christopher watched Sebastian with intense scrutiny. Nothing in the man's persona would suggest that he was unhappy with his life in any way. Cheerful and confident, Sebastian wheeled in front of his van and turned facing Christopher.

"So, are you thinking about buying one of these for yourself?"

Christopher shrugged. "I'm not sure. What kind of gas does this thing use?"

"It runs on regular gas."

"Are they expensive?"

"This one cost me forty-three, but they can go higher than that. This one is side entry, but they sell rear entry ones too. I can't tell you how convenient these things are. I hate feeling trapped. I like to get around. The only thing that was a challenge was having someone available at all times to drive me anytime I want. I have a full-time nurse so that helps."

The thought of depending on anyone bothered Christopher. The money it took to have a full-time nurse didn't help. He'd never have that kind of money, nor would he want the same life that Sebastian Barlowe lived. They were completely different people, with one exception.

"How long have you been, I mean when did...?"

"You mean how long have I needed a wheelchair? It's been almost eleven years now."

Christopher immediately regretted his question.

"I'm sorry about your wife."

Sebastian looked down at the ground and sighed.

"She was a wonderful woman. An incredible mother and amazing wife. She didn't deserve to die so young."

Christopher wondered how Sebastian managed to come out of such a horrible and traumatic experience to be such an upbeat and happy person.

"It wasn't easy in the beginning. I didn't want to live and was angry that she died, and I didn't. I felt guilty about that and angry at God. Everyone around me suffered. It was an ugly time. Even now I struggle. Do you know why I have someone drive this van for me? It's because I won't get behind the wheel of a car ever again. I can't do it."

"I can imagine, but is it just that time heals or was there something else that helped you move on?"

Sebastian smiled and nodded. "My children. I have three, two girls and a boy. They're grown people now, but eleven years ago they still needed their father."

Christopher could better understand Sebastian's outlook. He pulled himself out of a terrible situation, and for the sake of his children, did everything he could to keep living. Christopher didn't have children, nor did he have anyone that depended on him. Even if he did, he didn't believe he was strong enough to see a future. In his eyes, everyone would be far better off without him around.

Sebastian wheeled his chair up alongside Christopher and looked him in the eyes.

"No matter what you think about the world and the people in it, I can tell you now, that you haven't got a clue. I thought I had all the answers, but I was a stupid man. It wasn't until this accident that I came to believe what I do now. That is, that everyone struggles every single day in one way or another. You don't need to be in a wheelchair, or lose a wife, or anyone else to learn this lesson. Some understand the value of being alive and what it means to give to others without such a hit on the head. Some like me, and maybe you, need tremendous loss before they wake up. However, you get there, Christopher, I promise you there is beauty on the other side."

Christopher turned his chair and watched as Sebastian wheeled himself back to Chelsea. He couldn't go back to the party right away and decided to sit with his thoughts a bit longer.

He let his mind go quiet and listened to the sound of the ocean waves. He breathed in the salty cool air and looked up at the stars. He knew in the larger scheme of things, that he was no more than a speck on the earth, and that gave him some comfort.

His troubles seemed insurmountable from his wheelchair, but from a different perspective, they barely registered among the vast amount of suffering in the world. He had no idea what Sebastian was trying to tell him, but he believed he'd be lying to himself if he said he didn't care.

Whatever it was that gave Sebastian peace and contentment, Christopher wanted to know more. It was the first moment since the bombing that his curiosity led him to a place of hope. What he planned to do about it, he still didn't know.

Lost in his thoughts, he didn't hear his sister Lauren walk up beside him.

"Penny for your thoughts?"

Christopher smiled and shook his head.

"Oh, you don't want to waste your hard-earned money like that."

Lauren leaned against the van's bumper and rubbed her arms.

"It's getting cooler."

Christopher pulled his blanket off his legs and offered it to her.

"Thanks."

Lauren wrapped herself in the blanket and looked down at his legs.

"Are you angry?"

Christopher didn't understand.

"What? Do I look angry?"

"No. Maybe that's the point. I mean, come on Chris, I know you. You've got to be really angry at your situation. Doesn't it make you want to scream?"

Christopher laughed and shrugged his shoulders.

"Are we talking about me or you?"

Lauren sighed.

"I don't know. Maybe you're right and it's me who feels like screaming."

As his oldest sister, Lauren had lived her life much removed from Christopher's world. They didn't have much in common, and hardly ever had a face-to-face about anything except what she didn't approve of him doing. She had been an extension of their mother, and that's how he always saw her. Not this. Not two grown adults having a deeply personal discussion.

"Do you want to talk about it? I realize I'm your little unmarried brother and probably have zero wisdom to help you, but I can listen."

"What makes you think this has anything to do with marriage?"

"Oh, I don't know. Maybe because Jeff and the girls aren't here. Or maybe because Sarah and Trevor seem so in love and it's hard to watch. Maybe you've become a cynic about marriage and the whole happily-ever-after fantasy?"

Lauren smiled at him. "You know, you're a lot smarter than you look. How about we get back to the party?"

They started back toward the tables. Lauren stopped before they reached the others.

"No matter what you think, Chris, I still believe in all this—love, I mean. I'm thrilled for Sarah, and anyone else who can find happiness in this crazy world."

She looked at Chris and put her hand on his shoulder.

"Even you."

They laughed at her teasing, but Christopher didn't miss the subtle message. He'd now heard from two people tonight who still believed the world a good place. He had much to do before he could agree with them.

CHAPTER TWELVE

Becca finished her run and headed back to her house to get a final cup of coffee before riding her bike to the Key Lime Garden Inn. She had a full day ahead of her. Cleaning up after Sarah Wheeler's wedding would take her several hours, and she was curious to see the rest of Christopher's family.

As soon as she parked her bike, she walked around to the back of the inn and saw Riley and Grace already pulling the linens off the outdoor tables. Becca was jealous that the chefs worked the wedding. They had a front row seat to the event, and as much as she wanted details about the day, she didn't dare ask.

"Good morning. Looks like we've got a lot of work to do."

"You've got that right. Grace and I tried to do some of the clean-up last night, but it was so late. Maggie told us to go home and save it for the morning."

Laughing, Becca added, "And me."

Smiling, Riley agreed.

"Well, yes, that too. Listen, we've got outside, why don't you go inside and start cleaning the downstairs rooms before anyone wakes. The two guests checked out yesterday before the wedding, so Maggie cleaned them herself. But I think the other rooms will need new towels when people come downstairs. Also, the living room has several half-full glasses that need to be put into the dishwasher."

Becca nodded. "Got it."

She went inside and to her surprise, everyone had already convened in the kitchen.

"Oh, I'm sorry. I didn't know you all were in here."

Maggie put her coffee down and walked over to Becca.

"Everyone, this is Becca Powell. She joined our Key Lime family a couple of months ago to help out with the housekeeping. When she's not working here, she works at her family's store a few blocks from here. Becca, this is Michael, and my daughter, Lauren. Over next to Chris is my youngest daughter, Beth and her boyfriend, Gabriel and of course, you already know Christopher."

"Nice to meet you all. If everyone is out of their rooms, I'll replenish your towels. Does anyone need anything before I go up?"

Michael answered, "Becca, I think I need another bar of soap for the sink. Thanks."

She nodded. "No problem, I'll check everyone's supply. Enjoy your stay."

Becca couldn't wait to leave the room. She could feel Christopher's eyes on her the whole time. She went to the linen closet and gathered enough towels to replace the used ones in each room. Dropping the towels into the washing machine, she then placed new bottles of shampoo and additional bars of soap where needed. She made every bed, and hoped that by the time she'd finished, everyone would have left the kitchen.

At the foot of the stairs, Christopher, Beth, Gabriel, and Maggie were talking so Becca tried to squeeze past them, but Christopher's wheelchair was in the way. She placed her hand on his armrest to balance herself and for a moment their hands touched. When she realized her mistake she pulled her hand back quickly. They looked into each other's eyes briefly, but it was long enough for Beth and Maggie to notice.

Mortified, she excused herself and ran to the living room to gather the wine glasses. She was breathing heavy now, and her mind raced with how best to finish her work and get out of there. She felt awkward and in the way. The Wheeler family needed privacy and time together, what made her think she could do her job today and not be noticed by anyone?

Stupid. Just Stupid.

She carried the glasses to the kitchen and sensed Beth following her.

"Becca, why don't you come with us today?"

Confused, Becca wasn't sure she'd heard right.

"I'm sorry, what?"

By now, the others had followed Beth into the kitchen.

Maggie spoke up. "That's a great idea."

Christopher seemed as confused as Becca.

"What are you talking about? She can't come."

Everyone turned to look at Christopher. His resistance drawing suspicion.

Becca could tell he was just as uncomfortable as she was. Looking at Maggie she asked,

"I'm sorry, what are we talking about?"

Maggie answered, "Well, Lauren and Michael plan to spend the day at the beach and Paolo and I thought we'd join them. Beth wanted to show Gabriel around, so I suggested they take in the Greek Festival in Ft. Myers. You've been to that before haven't you Becca?"

Becca's heart sank. The last thing she wanted to do was spend the day with Christopher and his sister, Beth. Barely audible, she responded, "Yes. I know the one."

Maggie continued. "Riley, Grace, and I can finish up here. You go on with them and have a good time."

She couldn't be sure, but something in Beth's smile seemed to suggest Christopher's sister had more on her mind than eating Greek food. Whatever it was, Becca would have to be on her toes to stay one step ahead of Beth Wheeler.

Sitting in the back seat, Becca watched as Gabriel helped Christopher into the car. Gabriel took the crutches and placed them into the trunk along with the wheelchair. He then got into the back seat and sat next to her, leaving Beth to drive them to the festival.

Beth handed a printed flyer on all the festival events to Becca and Christopher just before they got on the road. "There are lots of things to do there, but since you've been before Becca, which events do you think we should see?"

Becca looked over the list and picked things that would require sitting. "Other than the food, it's always fun to watch the tradition folk dancers."

Beth didn't seem interested in that. "Are there any carnival rides?"

Christopher piped up, "Knock it off, Beth."

"What did I say? Just because you won't ride doesn't mean the rest of us have to sit it out."

Becca thought Beth cruel for suggesting such a thing but wondered if his sister had a particular motivation for what her family called "poking the bear."

Gabriel took the flyer and looked over the events. "To be honest, Greek food is a favorite of mine. All I care about is getting a gyro sandwich and maybe later some spanakopita. I love their logo, 'Gone Greek'. I can relate."

He pulled the paper close to his face and chuckled. "Uh-oh."

Becca didn't like the sound of that. "Uh-oh, what?"

"It looks like they have a bungee jump."

Beth pounded the steering wheel. "Yes!"

Christopher looked at his sister. "Are you nuts? Tell me you're not going to do a bungee jump."

Beth said nothing but looked at him and beamed.

He pleaded with Gabriel. "Can't you stop her?"

Gabriel shook his head. "I haven't been able to yet."

Until now, Christopher hadn't addressed Becca directly, but this latest topic made him frantic. "I suppose you plan on jumping too?"

Something about his tone irritated her. She couldn't stand another minute of condescension. "Yes. I think I will."

He turned to face forward and shook his head, and that pleased Becca beyond words.

Christopher wouldn't admit his fear, but he felt scared for both his sister and Becca. What if the darn thing broke? Either one of them could be killed. Although he hadn't heard of anyone getting hurt, he quickly searched his phone for bungee-jumping horror stories.

His sister admonished him for being such a baby.

"Really, Chris. You're such a worrywart."

"A worrywart? What are you eighty years old? Who says that anymore? I'm just being practical, that's all. These things are dangerous."

They pulled into the parking lot and paid the attendant.

"Put that phone away. I'm doing it, and you can't stop me."

They got out of the car and Gabriel lifted the wheelchair out of the trunk and parked it alongside the passenger door. Christopher waved the crutches away. "I don't need those. Just let me turn my body around and keep the wheelchair locked in place."

They made their way to the entrance and Gabriel paid for everyone even though Christopher objected.

"Hey, man, I can pay for myself."

Gabriel pushed Christopher's money away.

"It's my treat. It's the least I can do to thank your family for your hospitality."

Beth got behind Christopher's wheelchair and pushed it forward.

"It's a lot of walking so I hope you don't mind having someone push you."

Christopher shook his head, and said, "No. I don't mind."

Beth responded, "Good."

As soon as she said that she pushed Becca behind the wheelchair instructing her to push Christopher the rest of the way.

Christopher couldn't believe what Beth had done. It was a deliberate move intended to make him feel uncomfortable.

With their hands stamped, the four of them made their way into the festival. Music and dancing off in the distance drew them into the crowd. To the right, long lines of people stood waiting for their food. There were tables of Moussaka, roasted leg of lamb, Greek salads, and lasagna-looking Pistachio.

Beth laughed, watching her boyfriend drool over the food.

"I guess we better feed Gabriel before we do anything else. What about you and Becca, Chris, are you guys hungry?"

Synchronized, Christopher and Becca shook their heads. They stood to the side waiting for Beth and Gabriel to get their food.

Several minutes went by before anyone spoke. Christopher looked up at Becca.

"I hope you realize that this wasn't my idea."

She frowned and looked away from him.

"Clearly."

"What does that mean?"

"It means that you couldn't be any more insulting, that's what it means."

"Insulting? How was I insulting?"

"You didn't have to be so rude about my coming here. I mean

it sounds like you wouldn't be caught dead spending one minute with me."

Christopher didn't know what to say. He never wanted to hurt Becca. The truth was that she'd been on his mind for days and he didn't know what to make of it. He had plans that didn't include her and yet, he was troubled by how much her opinion of him mattered, and how often he wanted to hear her voice.

"I'm sorry. I didn't mean to imply any such thing. It's just…"

Beth and Gabriel joined them making it impossible for Christopher to finish his thoughts.

Gabriel had so much food in his arms, that Beth suggested they find a table somewhere. Once they were seated, Becca decided to get something to drink. "Chris, do you want something?"

"A bottle of water if you don't mind. Thanks."

When Becca left the table, Beth stared at her brother.

"What's with you? You have a permanent scowl on your face. It seems particularly directed toward Becca. Don't you think you might be protesting too much?"

"Meaning?"

"Meaning, I think you like the woman and you're doing your darnedest to fight it."

"You don't know what you're talking about."

"Maybe. I could be wrong I guess, but when was the last time that happened?"

There was a brief pause before the three of them laughed so hard that Christopher had tears spilling from his eyes.

Becca returned with their drinks, and they relaxed under the canopy enjoying the music and Greek folk dancers. After a few songs, Beth got up from the table and looked at the bungee jump.

"I'm ready if you guys are."

Christopher shook his head. "Oh, man."

The four of them made their way to the jump and Beth and Becca got in line.

Beth taunted her brother. "Too bad you're such a chicken, Chris."

She looked at Becca and smiled. "Don't you think it's interesting that it's the women who are the bravest?"

Christopher's anger building, he no longer felt fear, but rather, a challenge. He wheeled up to the person running the ride and asked if they'd ever had an amputee jump before.

"Yeah, of course. Since I've been running this thing over the years, I've had a few. Although some have done it elsewhere, we're not really equipped to let you jump in the wheelchair."

"I don't need the chair. I'll jump without it."

Becca looked shocked. "I don't need to jump, Chris. We were just having fun. Seriously, you don't need to do this."

"Yes I do. You can sit it out, but my sister and I have to do this."

Becca walked back down the ramp and stood next to Gabriel.

"Your girlfriend and her brother are crazy, you realize that, right?"

Gabriel nodded. "This isn't news to me."

Beth went first.

They watched as she entered the metal cage, and two harnesses were wrapped around her body with a third near her ankle. Once in place, the cage traveled high up over the park.

Minutes later they heard Beth's scream and saw her drop from the platform. Christopher felt sick to his stomach and no amount of his sister's laughter could calm him. Determined to be as fearless as Beth, he took deep breaths and waited his turn.

Beth bounced several times, and then she finally slowed down enough for the rope to place her onto a padded square. Two men ran to unhook her harnesses. Her face red, she fist-pumped the air and laughed.

"That was awesome. Chris, you're going to love it. I promise you."

He wasn't so sure, but there was no way he would let his

stomach dictate. Gabriel ran up and helped him into the cage. The man inside secured the harnesses in place and Christopher gave a thumbs up as the door closed. Considering the last few months, and his desire to not be alive, Christopher suddenly wanted to live, at least through the day.

He held onto the cage for dear life and said a quiet prayer.

Lord, I've done some crazy things in my life, and I know you're busy, but could you please not let me die today?

He looked at the rope attached to his left ankle. He had the urge to bend down and make sure it was secure, but instead he stared off into the horizon, wondering how he'd let himself get talked into this.

When he reached the top, he looked down and could see the others. He looked at Becca and thought for a moment how comforting it was that if he were to die today, the last thing he would see was her face.

The attendant counted down as he raised his arms to his sides. Like a bird he decided to let go of everything. He let his body drop, the air rushing past him as he flew.

In that moment he felt free. Surprised at how light he felt, he wanted to hold onto the moment forever. He rose in the air several times, but he wouldn't close his eyes. He needed to take in everything around him. The sensation was hard to describe, and although he would later laugh and talk about the experience with his sister, Gabriel, and Becca, he kept the feeling of freedom close to his heart.

CHAPTER THIRTEEN

By the time the four of them made it back to Captiva, it was dinnertime. Becca never expected to be invited to join them, but Maggie made her feel welcome.

"I'm glad you all had fun today, but it doesn't have to end now. Becca, you're welcome to join us for dinner."

If Christopher had resisted she would have politely declined the invitation, but instead he surprised her.

"Yes, please stay."

"Of course. Thank you. Let me give my father a call just so he knows not to hold dinner for me."

She went outside and called her father.

"I'm sorry it's last minute. I should have called earlier. I hope you don't mind."

"Don't be silly. We were so busy at the store today; all we could manage was hotdogs on the grill— not your favorite."

Becca laughed. Her mother was an excellent cook and most of the time her father and brothers depended on Becca's cooking if they wanted healthy food. Pizza, hotdogs and the occasional spaghetti and meatballs had been a typical dinner when it was just the boys.

"Thanks, Dad. I won't be home too late. Love you."

"Love you more."

She ended the call and went inside.

Maggie filled her glass with the white sangria Riley had prepared. "Becca would you care for a sangria?"

"Yes, thank you. It looks delicious."

They all gathered around the dining room table and Riley carried out the family's favorite summer meal.

Maggie raised her glass and gave a toast. "First, I'd like to say that we're thrilled that Beth insisted you come down for the wedding, Gabriel. We've loved getting to know you and we hope you'll return soon. Make sure you bring my workaholic daughter with you though. Second, I want to say how happy you all make me. It's been wonderful having all my kids with me, even if it's only been for a few days. Here's to family."

While everyone's glass was raised, Michael lifted the fried chicken platter and grabbed a breast.

Beth rolled her eyes. "As usual, Michael gets the first piece."

"What? I can't help it if you've lost your touch. You snooze, you lose."

Corn on the cob, mashed potatoes and tossed salad added to the meal and everyone immediately dug in, leaving little space to talk.

Michael yelled out to Riley and Grace. "You guys have to leave here and come up to Massachusetts with us tomorrow morning. I love to eat so you'll be very appreciated."

His mother wouldn't hear of it.

"Not on your life, buster. They belong here with me. I'd have to shut my doors if my guests had to depend on my cooking."

Lauren disagreed. "Not so, Mom. I learned everything I know from your cooking."

"Yeah, which is why Jeff is the cook in your house."

That got everyone laughing.

Becca loved watching the Wheeler family enjoy each other's

company. She imagined a lively home with lots of love and laughter in their house over the years. Even Christopher seemed happier for the first time in weeks. It was obvious that, like her, he gained strength from the love and support of a close family.

Maggie passed the potatoes to Becca.

"Who cooks at your house, Becca?"

"That would be me. A perfect example is tonight. Since I'm eating here with you all, my brothers and father are eating hotdogs."

Gabriel gave his opinion on that. "I love hotdogs."

Beth hit him in the arm. "Is there anything you won't eat?"

Gabriel thought about it for a moment and then nodded, "Yes. SPAM. I don't like SPAM."

Beth smirked. "I'll keep that in mind if ever we travel to Hawaii. They love it there. It's practically on every menu."

Maggie looked surprised. "Really? I didn't know that."

"Next time I'll make a big Italian dinner for all of us. We'll have several courses. You'll need to prepare to sit here for about three hours," Paolo said.

Gabriel's eyes widened. "Beth, make sure I'm here for that."

When dinner was over they all went out onto the porch. Maggie and Paolo sat on the swing and the others found a comfortable spot in one of several chairs and rocking chairs.

Becca sat on the steps instead and knew that soon she would have to return home. She was lucky to have a close family herself, but it didn't stop her from appreciating the Wheeler clan.

Maggie interrupted the silence. "You know what this reminds me of? Andy Griffith's house. Remember how Aunt Bee, Andy and Opie would sit out on the porch and Andy would play the guitar and sing?"

Michael looked at his mother and teased her. "None of us can play an instrument, Mom. If you want, I can sing to you."

"Very funny."

Beth shared her thoughts on the matter.

"Please don't, Michael. I've heard you sing. It's not pretty."

Christopher looked over at Becca and wondered what she must be thinking. He wanted to get her alone to talk, but it seemed impossible with everyone here. He didn't care what his family thought and chose to address her directly.

"Becca, would you like to go down to the beach? We might as well take advantage of the walkway since it's still out there."

She was glad but surprised at his boldness to ask her in front of his family. Everyone's eyes on her, she worried they'd grill him later.

"Sure."

She got up from the stairs and wheeled him down the ramp and through the garden toward the walkway. Christopher thought it would lighten the mood if he made a joke of it.

"So, is it just me or do you feel a burning in your back from everyone staring at us?"

Becca laughed. "It's not just you."

They both smiled and for the first time Becca felt she'd finally gained his friendship.

They reached the beach, just as the sun was setting over the water. Throngs of people were there to witness an event that happened every night at this time.

"You know, I've lived here all my life, but I still get goosebumps at the sunsets. Isn't that silly?"

Christopher shook his head. "No, not silly."

Becca dragged a chair next to him. "Looks like it was left here from the wedding."

Christopher laughed. "I guess someone knew you'd be needing it tonight."

They sat in silence for a while before Christopher spoke.

"Do you like your job?"

"Which one?"

"I meant working at the store with your father and brothers."

"I love taking people out on the sunset cruise. Usually, my brother Joshua or Finn drives the boat, but sometimes I do."

"Yeah, I can see how that would be fun, but do you see yourself doing this for the rest of your life?"

Becca knew where this conversation was headed. She'd had the same talk with her father, and she'd always pushed the discussion off for another time.

"I don't know what I'm going to do. I keep telling myself that I've got time, but that's not really true. I'm almost twenty-six, and I know I've got to make some decisions."

"You didn't like medical school?"

Shocked at his question, Becca asked, "How did you know that I went to medical school?"

"My mother mentioned something about it once."

"Anyway, it's not true that I didn't like medical school. I loved it actually."

"So, why quit?"

Becca sighed. "It's complicated." She didn't want to be rude, but if she knew he was going to ask her questions about medical school, she would have gone home an hour ago.

"I'm sorry. It's really none of my business."

"What about you?"

"Me? Oh, well, I've got a million offers from high-paying corporate jobs in Boston and I've been offered a position as president of the biggest investment firm in the city."

"Not at all funny."

"What did you expect me to say? It's not like I've got people lining up to hire me. Listen, I'm not feeling sorry for myself, at least not today. I just know the reality of my situation. Right now, I have to take things a day at a time. I guess, like you said, it's complicated."

Becca didn't want their conversation to turn depressing, so she decided instead, to look up at the stars.

"Have you ever thought how tiny we really are?"

Christopher looked up. "It's funny you say that. I was thinking that very thing last night."

She turned to look at him and the sudden darkness had made it difficult to see the features of his face. But that didn't stop her from feeling the warmth of his kiss. It was light and he didn't linger on her lips.

"I wondered what that would feel like."

"You've thought about my kissing you?"

Becca looked out at the water.

"I wondered if I'd remember it. It was a long time ago."

"Did you?"

"I remember you pulled my hair back from my face and kissed me. I remember everything about that day."

What she didn't tell him was that she was certain she'd never forget it. He was the first boy to ever kiss her. That kind of thing stays with a person forever.

The next morning, Chelsea opened her front door and looked at a half-asleep Jacqui Hutchins on the porch.

"You're late."

"I know. I'm sorry. I was up really late last night."

"Did you at least have fun?"

"Don't I always?"

Chelsea had lost patience with the woman before she entered the house.

"I'm curious, Jacqui. Are you planning on partying your way through life, or do you have a more stable future planned?"

"I thought I was here to paint, not get a lecture from you."

Chelsea looked at her watch and thought about all the things she could be doing today that didn't involve her spending time with this spoiled child. She walked to the front door and opened it.

"Time for you to go."

Jacqui looked surprised. "What?"

"You need to take some time to figure out what you want out of life. No one said you can't party all day and night. If that's what you want, go for it. But I'm a busy woman and I never signed up to babysit you. Come back when you're ready to get serious about your life. I don't care if you never paint again. That's completely your choice. As for me, I've chosen a life as an artist, and I take that very seriously. So, get out of my house so I can paint."

Chelsea expected Jacqui to pout, but instead she apologized.

"I'm sorry, Chelsea. You're right, of course. I'm a mess."

Against her better judgment, Chelsea closed the door and pulled Jacqui by the arm out onto the lanai and dropped her onto a chair.

"Do you have any idea how old I am, Jacqui?"

Jacqui shook her head. "I don't know, sixty?"

Chelsea had planned to pour herself an iced tea, but instead reached for the vodka and dropped two cubes of ice into the glass. She sat down next to Jacqui, took a sip of her drink, and looked her in the eye.

"I'm fifty-one."

Jacqui made a face. "Oh, sorry."

"That's not the point. The point is that it took me years before I'd allow myself to finally fulfill my dreams of becoming a real artist. Oh, I dabbled now and then but mostly, I treated my artwork as a hobby. Do you know why I did that?"

Jacqui shook her head again.

"Because I didn't believe in myself. I thought no one would ever buy one of my paintings. But even without making a dime, I didn't believe I had any real talent. I felt like a fraud. Do you know what turned that around for me?"

This time Chelsea didn't wait for her to respond.

"The first time I ever showed my work at a gallery on Sanibel.

I was fifty years old. Imagine that. I'd been painting for thirty years before I let myself feel vulnerable before hundreds of people. Sure, it was great that so many bought my paintings, but that wasn't where the real success was. For the first time in my life, I put myself out there on something that really mattered to me. What really matters to you? Do you have any idea?"

Jacqui looked like she was going to cry. It wasn't Chelsea's intent to make the woman fall apart, she only wanted to shake her up and help her to see that she was wasting time—not just Chelsea's, but her own.

"If you're not careful, your life will pass you by and if you're lucky you'll be middle-aged like me when you wake up. That's if you're lucky. The more likely scenario is that you'll never wake up, and won't that be a pity?"

Jacqui quickly got up from her chair and put her apron on. She walked to her canvas and looked at the landscape she had created.

Chelsea tried not to look at Jacqui's face but could see out of the corner of her eye, the young woman wiping tears away with the sleeve of her shirt.

"Do you think I should change the color of the sky?"

Chelsea smiled. "Nope. I think you've made some very good choices. You're on the right path. Keep going."

CHAPTER FOURTEEN

For whatever reason Maggie couldn't get Lauren out of her mind. Although her daughter hadn't confided in her, she felt something terribly off and couldn't let Lauren go back to Massachusetts without talking to her.

The first pot of coffee gone, Maggie started a second. As soon as it was brewed she poured herself a cup and took a deep breath before going out onto the back porch.

Lauren leaned against the railing and jumped when her mother moved behind her.

"Oh, honey, I'm sorry. I didn't mean to startle you. Would you like a cup of coffee?"

Lauren shook her head. "No, thanks. I've already had two. If I have another, I'll never sleep on the plane, and I really need to sleep on the plane."

"Didn't you sleep well last night?"

Lauren turned to face her mother and crossed her arms in front of her chest. "I haven't slept well in months."

"Do you want to talk about it?"

Maggie sat on the porch swing and gestured for her daughter to join her.

Lauren sat next to her mother and shrugged. "I don't know if talking about it will do any good. Jeff and I have been seeing a marriage counselor for months. So far, all the talking hasn't helped. All we seem to do these days is argue."

"Argue? What about?"

Lauren sat back against the cushion and pushed against the floor with her foot making the chair swing. They enjoyed a minute of rocking before she answered.

"Ever since I went back to work, Jeff has turned into someone I don't recognize. At first, everything seemed fine. He loved being a stay-at-home dad and I loved being back at work. I grant you it's a bit unconventional, but so what? We were happy. But slowly, over time, things changed. He's gained weight, stopped shaving, and generally has given up on any intimacy between us. If he'd get off the sofa long enough to kiss me, that would be a huge improvement."

"He's not neglecting the girls is he?"

"No. Not at all. He's been really great with them. Gets them to school and back, helps them with their homework, and is there at every soccer game. It's just me he doesn't have any interest in. He doesn't seem to appreciate all the hours I put in at the office. I'm constantly working to provide for the family, and all he wants to do is watch soap operas."

Maggie tried not to laugh but it occurred to her that Lauren and Jeff's role reversal might have gone too far.

"It's funny to hear you say this, Lauren. I remember several conversations with your father about his long hours. I used to think that his work mattered more to him than I did. I'd spent all day, every day, taking care of the house and you kids, and I felt your dad didn't understand what I was going through at home. I couldn't relate to anything he did at the office, most especially his need to work around the clock to, as he put it, 'provide for the family.' Is there more to this that I'm not seeing?"

Lauren squirmed in her chair and wouldn't look her mother in the eye.

Maggie grabbed Lauren's chin and pulled her face toward her.

Panic reached her stomach remembering Daniel's solution to their marital troubles.

"Lauren, be honest with me. Is there someone else?"

"It's complicated, Mom."

Maggie felt herself getting angry and tried to keep the conversation focused on helping her daughter. Projecting her past situation wouldn't help anyone.

"No. It's not. You're either having an affair or you're not. Which is it?"

Lauren shook her head.

"Nothing's happened."

"I need more than that, Lauren. What exactly are we talking about?"

"There is someone at work, but the truth is I find him to be annoying. He keeps flirting with me, and I have to admit when I'm not frustrated by him, I like the attention, but that's as far as it's gone."

"But?"

"But what? Do you really think after what Dad put us through, that I'd ever cheat on Jeff? It's not that, Mom. It's the feeling that in my head I've let someone sweet talk me to the point of feeling better about myself. Then, I immediately feel guilty about it. Please don't misunderstand me. I'm not a cheat. I love my husband, and I miss him."

"Why do you think your couples therapy isn't working?"

Lauren shrugged. "I'm not sure. If I had to guess I'd say that there's too much talking and not enough listening."

Maggie smiled and rubbed her daughter's back.

"That sounds like a real possibility. Maybe you're on to something. As long as the two of you want to fix things I'm sure you will. The best advice I can give you is to never give up. Keep talking and keep listening."

Lauren nodded and then smiled at Maggie. "Thanks, Mom. I will. I promise."

Michael joined them on the porch wheeling his luggage behind him. "Lauren, are you packed? We've got to get going. Where's your suitcase? I'll get it for you if it's ready to go."

"No need. I'll run upstairs and get it."

She opened the screened back door and then stopped long enough to turn to her mother.

"I honestly don't know what any of us would do without you, Mom."

Maggie laughed and got up from the swing. "Oh, I don't know. Somehow, I think you'd manage just fine."

Christopher came out onto the porch using his crutches for support. Although he had a way to go, Maggie felt her son had made positive progress this weekend.

Gabriel and Beth joined them on the porch. Gabriel hugged Maggie. "Thank you for having me. I've enjoyed every minute of it."

Maggie liked Gabriel and hoped he'd be back with Beth soon. "You're very welcome. I hope you visit Captiva again."

Just then, Sarah and Trevor drove up, blocking Lauren's rental.

Sarah jumped out of the car and ran to Michael. She squeezed her brother tight. "Oh, I don't want to let you guys go. It was so good to have you here."

Lauren came back down and watched Sarah and Michael hugging in the driveway.

"The two of you better not cry or I'll lose it. I swear."

Maggie beamed with pride at Christopher for trying his best to stand while saying goodbye to his siblings.

Everyone hugged and Beth turned to her mother before leaving. "Gabriel and I are going to drive down to Ft. Myers beach. I want to show him around and then we're going to have a bite of lunch before his flight. Do you need anything while I'm off island?"

Maggie shook her head. "No, nothing. Chris and I will be here when you get back. Drive safe."

Maggie and Christopher waved their last goodbyes as the two cars turned out onto the road. When they were out of sight, Christopher turned and eased onto a chair. Maggie looked at her watch.

"I've got a couple of guests checking in this afternoon. I best get inside and get the place ready. Do you need anything?"

"Nope. I'm fine. I think I'll sit out here for a bit. It's another beautiful day on Captiva Island. I don't know why anyone would live anywhere else. I know there's a world out there, but the truth is, I'm happy staying right where I am for the rest of my life."

Maggie looked at her son with a mixture of worry and anger.

"That's my life, Chris, not yours. I know you've got some thinking to do. There'll be plenty of time to sit on the porch and rest, but don't rest too long. Take the time you need, but then get on with it."

She didn't wait for his response, but instead, went inside the house. For weeks, she'd kept her concerns to herself and didn't push her opinions on her son. Those days were over. The time had come for her to be straight with Christopher.

If she could, she'd undo all the pain and hurt that haunted him every day, but that wasn't within her power. Instead, she'd do what she'd always done. She was his mother, and her love and support would have to be enough. Anything more would have to come from him.

The weekend had been a wonderful celebration of love, and by all accounts a great success for her family's desire to be together once again. Grateful for her blessings, she tried not to ask for more than that.

After lunch at The Whale on Ft. Myers Beach, Beth and Gabriel headed to the airport. She was glad that they had a few hours alone together. When she pulled up alongside the JetBlue entrance, she got out of the car and ran into his arms.

"Have a wonderful flight. I'll be home before you know it."

She wrapped her arms around Gabriel's neck, and they kissed.

A security guard looked impatient and didn't let their kiss keep him from doing his job.

"Miss, you've got to move along now."

Beth watched Gabriel walk away. She rolled her eyes and waved at the security officer.

"I'm going. I'm going."

Pulling away from the curb, she glanced in the rearview mirror for one last look at Gabriel, but he had already gone inside.

It would take an hour to get back to Captiva, so she decided to play her Spotify playlist. She had already connected her cell phone to the car's Bluetooth pairing so by the time she left the airport; she could sing along to one of her favorite songs.

Startled when her cell phone rang, Beth answered the call with the hands-free feature.

"Hello?"

"Hello Beth, it's Mitchell Glassman."

"Hello. How are things back in Boston?"

"That's why I'm calling. You remember how we left things with the Andresen case? There's been a change. My schedule is crazy, and I've told the judge that you'll be taking over as lead prosecutor on the case."

Beth's jaw dropped and she wondered if she'd heard right.

"Mitchell, is this a joke?"

"No joke. I want you to handle this. I'll be available for advice or anything else that you need, but this is yours."

Beth had always dreamed of one day getting her day in court, but she had no idea it would be so soon. It couldn't have come at a better time. She didn't know what to say, until it suddenly dawned on her that the timing might actually be horrible.

"Mitchell, are you saying that you need me back in Boston right away?"

"No. I'm sorry, I should have explained. Stay with your family as originally planned but understand that you've got some catching up to do when you get back. I'll schedule a meeting for first thing next Monday so that I can bring you up to speed. It looks like we've got about ten days before jury selection. Oh, by the way. You're going to need help with the research. I'm assigning Heather O'Conner and Alice Bellows to assist. Sound good?"

Beth didn't hesitate. "Yes. Of course. This is incredible. Thank you, Mitchell. You won't regret giving me this opportunity."

His voice was loud and clear. "Let's hope not."

Becca pulled the plastic tote from under her bed. She sat on the floor and opened it, looking for her admissions paperwork from years ago. She sifted through folders and notebooks, finally finding what she was looking for. She read the acceptance letter and thought back to the day the letter carrier delivered it. She'd opened the letter, read it, and ran screaming through the house waving it in the air.

Her family celebrated her accomplishment with a party and evening bonfire on the beach. Friends and family attended the event, and Becca felt on top of the world. She'd felt powerful and filled with promise for her future. Her mother had been sick, but everyone believed she would get better and would beat the cancer once her chemotherapy was completed. But that proved to be nothing more than wishful thinking.

Becca opened Netter's *Atlas of Human Anatomy*. Flipping through the pages, she barely remembered a thing about her studies. She'd been consumed with fear about her mother, and it affected her work. Surrounded by brilliant minds and educated doctors, her frustration grew, knowing that she had little power to help her mother.

When her mother died, Becca lost interest in a medical career. Time and again she'd ask herself, what was the point of studying if in the end she was powerless to save her mother?

Becca put the book back inside the tote and covered it. She pushed the box back under her bed, kicking it with her foot.

Angry, she pulled her knees up toward her chest and wrapped her arms around her legs. Rocking back and forth, she started to cry. It wasn't the first time she'd tortured herself this way. Keeping the books under her bed seemed an unnecessary punishment. Maybe it was time to have another bonfire.

CHAPTER FIFTEEN

Christopher grimaced as he looked at the photos online. He had several windows open so he could jump between them. Stories of the bombing filled the screen, and although there were countless opinions on the event, there wasn't one single report from anyone who was actually there. If there were survivors like him, they weren't talking. To think that anyone could speak for the dead was ludicrous.

He closed the laptop and pushed it away. Anger once again began to consume him, and nothing would satisfy his need for revenge. He didn't know what to do with those feelings. He was stuck on this island, in this house and this chair, and would be indefinitely. His fingers searched inside his shirt pocket for the ring.

Holding it in his hand his thoughts turned to Nick Aiello and Christopher's desire to fulfill his mission.

Since he couldn't drive, he'd need someone to go with him. His sister Beth was the only one he could trust with this. As much as he wanted Becca with him, he'd already decided to protect her from the ugliness of that day.

His mother was in the kitchen with Riley and Grace.

"Mom, would you please put the ramp down for me? I'd like to go outside."

"Of course."

He looked down at his cell phone and sent Beth a text.

Not sure where you are, but when you have a minute, come look for me in the garden.

He wheeled the chair down the ramp and onto the garden walkway. Paolo was picking tomatoes and waved when he saw Christopher.

"Hey, Paolo. Do you need any help?"

"Sure. You can help me pick these tomatoes. Here, take a basket."

Christopher picked several tomatoes and placed them inside the basket. He admired the life Paolo and his mother had made here on the island. Everything seemed peaceful and with little drama.

His thoughts were interrupted by his sister calling out to him from the porch. She walked toward Paolo and her brother and laughed.

"Do my eyes deceive me or is my brother actually working in the garden?"

Beth took one of the tomatoes from the basket and bit into it.

"There is nothing as wonderful as a freshly picked tomato off the vine. You guys are so lucky to eat food directly from the garden every day. I'm jealous. My plants back home don't thrive the way these do."

Christopher smirked. "I guess you just don't have Mom's green thumb after all. Or maybe you're not getting outside enough."

Beth laughed at her brother's attempt to start a squabble with her, but she resisted.

"It's true. I could definitely use more vitamin D. So, are you actually helping Paolo or are you being a nuisance?"

Paolo didn't hear their conversation as he had moved further down to the back of the garden.

"Unlike you, I decided to take in a bit of sun today."

This seemed as good a time as any to make his request.

"How about you keep me company near the gazebo? I'd like to ask you something."

"OK. Yeah, sure. I'm game, but don't be surprised if I fall asleep. For some reason I'm wiped out today. Must be all the weekend fun."

Beth helped Christopher to the gazebo.

"I'm going to get a glass of iced tea. Do you want one?"

"Yeah. Thanks."

Beth returned carrying two tall glasses.

Now that she sat across from him, he didn't know how to begin. He enjoyed the iced tea and waited a few minutes before speaking.

"Beth, I want to ask a favor of you. I want you to come with me somewhere."

She put her tea down and leaned closer to him.

"Where?"

"I want to go see a friend's wife. I have something to give her."

Beth didn't mince words.

"Is this friend of yours dead?"

Christopher nodded. "It's something I've got to do. I promised him that I'd go see his wife if anything ever happened to him. There are things he'd want me to tell her."

He waited for a response but was surprised when she answered him right away.

"If this is something you have to do, then you've got to do it. It doesn't matter what I think or anyone else. Of course, I'll go with you."

Christopher smiled. "When you say it like that, you make me wonder if you think it's a bad idea. Do you?"

"Chris, I only worry about you. I'm sure your friend was a

wonderful man and I'm truly sorry that he died, but will going to his family make things better for you? It won't change a thing."

Looking beyond her at the inn, he whispered, "I know. But we've always known that wasn't the point of the visit. If I died that day instead of Nick, he'd be right here, right now, talking to you about me. He'd be telling you how much I loved my family and how I talked about you guys all the time. He'd probably even tell you a few indelicate things that we did over there. And he'd give you this."

He placed Nick's ring on the table in front of Beth. She picked it up and looked at it, confused.

"Wilson Barker High School—what's this?"

"It's Nick's ring. He had mine, and I'm guessing his family has it now. We swapped rings and promised to exchange them when the time came."

Beth could see in her brother's face how important this trip was. She wanted to help him do whatever he needed to do to feel whole again. If visiting his friend's wife would help him, she was all in.

"Where does his family live?"

"Vero Beach—a little over three hours from here. I'm going to call her before we leave, just to make sure she doesn't mind us coming."

Beth still looked worried, and Christopher hoped she wouldn't change her mind at the last minute.

"Chris, can I ask you something?"

"Of course."

"What happens after you meet with her?"

"Huh?"

"What I mean is, will this bring you the kind of closure you need to move on with your life?"

He didn't have an answer for that. The purpose of seeing Nick's family had nothing to do with him and everything to do with Nick. Suddenly he felt his eyes tear up.

"I honestly don't know, Bethy. I wish I could tell you that it would heal whatever is broken inside of me, but I can't. All I can do is go see her. I need to talk about that day and she's the only person I can do that with."

His sister reached for his hand.

"In that case, I'm honored that you've asked me to come."

He wanted to make fun of her to lighten the mood. She'd laugh if he said he asked her just to have someone to drive the car. He didn't realize until this moment, that he truly needed his sister to be there. He couldn't stand the thought of the both of them crying, so he made fun of her anyway.

"Don't go getting all mushy on me. If I'd lost part of my left leg, you'd be staying here."

They both laughed, but also knew their bond hadn't been lost after all these years. If the trauma of this year hadn't changed their relationship, he was convinced that nothing could.

Christopher watched as they passed the houses along Dahlia Lane.

"Number eight, there it is."

A small one-story ranch style home with a stucco roof came into view and Beth pulled her car into their driveway. She turned to look at him.

"Nervous?"

"A little."

"Come on, let's do this before you change your mind."

She brought the wheelchair out of the trunk, and they slowly went to the front door, aware there was someone looking out at them through the window. A tall older man opened the door before they could ring the doorbell.

"Hello. I'm Nick's father, Frank, let me help you inside."

Beth and Frank lifted Christopher's wheelchair over the door threshold. Two women and a teenage boy stood up the minute they entered the large living room.

"This is my wife, Mary, and our son, David, and this is Nick's wife, Kayla."

"I'm Beth and this is my brother, Christopher. It's nice to meet you all."

Mary had made a platter of cheese and crackers and put out some grapes. A pitcher of iced tea and one with lemonade sat next to the tray. His mouth dry, Christopher could barely swallow, and his stomach wouldn't allow him to eat a thing. Beth, on the other hand, accepted a glass of iced tea.

Framed family photos were placed around the living room and a single photo of Nick in uniform stared back at him. The air of awkwardness hovered over them, and Frank did what he could to break the tension.

"So, you were stationed with our Nick in Iraq?"

Christopher nodded. "Yes. But we'd been friends from day one at boot camp."

Mary spoke up, "Nick's letters to us said he found base camp much like a small town. That made me feel better. On Frank's side of the family, we have several members in the service, so it's been a way of life for us, but for me, I didn't grow up in that world, so I was more nervous about Nick enlisting than everyone else."

David had been sitting on the arm of the sofa, but his face changed when he spoke. Excited, he moved closer to Christopher.

"I'm going to be a Marine too. As soon as I'm old enough, I'm going."

Mary looked horrified. Her hands shaking, she spoke harshly to her son.

"David, sit over in that chair and leave Mr. Wheeler alone."

Kayla seemed equally nervous. He couldn't wait any longer, he had to say what he'd come to tell them.

"Nick and I were very close. In the beginning, when you don't know anyone it can be hard. Even if it's what you wanted to do from the start, you still feel unsure of things. If you're competitive like me, you start to compare yourself to the other guys. Every time you stand in front of the drill sergeant, you start to think about how you're going to be this perfect soldier. Nick and I had our fair share of complaints, but mostly, when we weren't competing against ourselves, we were with each other. It got to be a game."

Frank nodded. "Nick was a good Marine."

"He was. He beat me most of the time, but somehow I didn't mind."

Kayla interrupted Christopher.

"Can you tell us about that day? They told us that everyone died. We were surprised when you called. We didn't know anyone survived the blast."

Beth put her hand on Christopher's shoulder for support.

He took a deep breath and shared everything he remembered about that day.

"We were in the mess tent getting lunch. There were tons of service members, but also some American civilians, and contractors. I believe there were several others from different countries. Nick had just gotten his food and was walking by me. I was standing in line ready to get my lunch. He got a seat at a table near the line. After he sat down he turned to me and made a joke. He said I shouldn't fill up my plate too much because he'd noticed I'd gained weight. He thought about it for a minute and then said never mind. He said he wanted me to get as fat as possible so he could keep on beating me."

David laughed at that. "Sounds like something Nick would say."

Christopher paused before continuing. "That was the last thing he said to me. They said when the bomb went off, shrapnel went everywhere. Some of it hit my leg. I don't remember anything except laying on the ground. The dirt and dust were everywhere. I couldn't see two inches in front of me. I must have passed out from the shock. When I woke up, I was in the hospital. Your son and I were like brothers. We shared everything. We agreed that if anything ever happened to either one of us, that we'd visit the family of the one who died. I told Nick all the things I would want him to tell my family, and he did the same."

Christopher looked directly into Mary's eyes. "He wanted me to tell you that he understood how scared you were for him, but that even if he knew for certain that he was going to die, he'd make the same choice. He'd still enlist. He wanted you to know that he didn't die in vain. He died doing exactly what he wanted to do, and he's asking you to accept that."

Mary wiped her eyes with a tissue and nodded. Frank put his arms around his wife and pulled her close.

He then looked at Frank.

"Nick told me that he looked up to you his whole life. He knew how much you wanted to become a Marine yourself and how much it hurt when your brothers got in, but you were rejected because of your asthma. He said that serving in the military as your son made him proud, that he thought of you often and that he hoped you were proud of him as well."

When Christopher looked at Kayla, he could see that she'd been crying.

"Kayla, I hope you don't mind that your husband told me every detail of your life together. He shared what it was like the first time he kissed you, and how much you didn't like him when you first met. He told me how much he loved you and couldn't wait to have children with you one day. He made sure that I tell you that he lied to you only once, and that was the day he told you that he'd had tons of girlfriends before you. He said he didn't want you to think he was a loser and that he couldn't get a date. The truth was that as soon as he met you, he was glad he hadn't been with anyone before you. You were his soulmate and his reason for everything."

Kayla composed herself and sat up tall against the back of her chair. Christopher looked at Beth who reached inside her handbag and pulled out Nick's ring.

"One of the things Nick and I did early on was to swap high school rings and, if the day ever came, we promised to return the ring to our family."

He handed Nick's ring to Kayla, and she wiped her eyes finally understanding.

"Wait." She ran upstairs to her room and quickly returned. "I thought they'd made a mistake when they gave me Nick's things. I didn't know."

Christopher gave Nick's ring to Kayla and then held his own high school ring for the first time since boot camp. His fingers wrapped around the ring, and he squeezed it in the palm of his hand. Dropping his head in his other hand, he broke down and cried.

Beth pulled Christopher close and rubbed his back. Whispering to him, "It's all right, Chris."

He'd done everything Nick had asked of him, except one.

He remembered one night, the heat making sleep impossible, he and Nick lay in the dark on their bunk beds.

Nick looked over at Christopher and whispered, "Hey, I forgot something."

"What?"

"I forgot there's one more thing you got to do if anything ever happens to me."

"What's that?"

"Live. Live for me."

CHAPTER SIXTEEN

Beth kept her eyes straight for most of the trip home. She had lots to say to her brother, but the truth was that she needed more time to think about how to phrase it all.

"There's no way I could have eaten their cheese and crackers, but now I'm starving. You want to get something to eat?"

"Yeah, sounds good."

"Let's go to Bahama Breeze. I love that place. We can eat outside."

They had made it to Rte. 41 in Fort Myers just before dinner. She parked the car and opened the door, but Christopher stopped her.

"Hey, I should have said this three hours ago, but thanks for coming with me today. Notwithstanding the driving logistics, I'm not sure I could have gone there without you."

"No problem. Don't be surprised when I come to you to reciprocate."

Christopher smiled. "Anytime."

They were seated at an outdoor table in the corner, giving them plenty of room as well as the privacy Beth needed. She waited until they'd ordered their food and drinks had been served.

"So, listen, I've been thinking. I think you should run the Boston Marathon next year."

Christopher looked like he was going to spit out his drink.

"Pun intended, run that by me again?"

"I'm serious, Chris. You've run that thing a few times already, right?"

"Twice."

"Twice, fine. So, what does that tell you?"

"That I can run a marathon with two legs. That's what it tells me."

"Oh, come on. You and I know that's hardly an excuse. There are tons of people who run with prosthetic devices. You wouldn't be the first."

"Beth, can we please take one thing at a time? Wasn't today a big enough step forward? I'm having a hard time keeping up with you."

"I don't know. Maybe it's the lawyer in me, but when I see a situation that needs to be addressed, I deal with it."

"What situation are we speaking about?"

"Chris, you don't have any direction or plans for the future. You've been recuperating, I get that, and I think you needed time, but that time has passed."

"Oh, because you say so? I'd like to be the one to decide that."

"You are so stubborn. You're fighting me just because that's what we do, or at least that's what we've always done. But we're not kids anymore. If you seriously take a look at your life, you'll agree it's time to move on and decide how you want to spend the rest of your life. I'm talking about you finding passion for something again. I think training for the Boston Marathon is a good motivator."

Their food came and Christopher started eating right away. Beth feared it was his way of avoiding their discussion, but she hoped he might be thinking about what she said. She figured while she had a captive audience, she'd throw fuel on the fire.

"You could train with Becca."

The look on Christopher's face made it clear she had hit a nerve.

He put his fork down and took a sip of his drink before he answered her.

"Why would I want to train with someone who works for Mom?"

"Oh, don't you dare go there. You and I both know that Becca is more than that to you. I have eyes you know."

"Can we please change the subject?"

She had to back off, even if it meant she'd save the conversation for another time. Beth held her hands up in the air and gave in.

"Fine. I'll change the subject. I've got news."

"Does this news have anything to do with me?"

"No, actually. It's all about me."

"Good to hear."

"I'm going to court on my very first case. Well, not my first case, just the first one that I'm going to lead."

"Fantastic. That is news. What's the case?"

"Guy stabs his son during an argument. His son was fourteen. He says the kid came at him with a knife and it was self-defense. "

"But you don't believe that?"

"I believe that the boy did come at him, probably with the intention of killing him."

"But?"

"But I also believe the kid was out of his mind from years of abuse that he took from his father. He snapped, and probably couldn't take it anymore."

"Is that enough to put the guy behind bars if he really did kill his son in self-defense?"

"Probably not, but I'm going to try."

"What makes you so certain that the guy had been abusing his son?"

Beth looked at Christopher and was reluctant to tell him the rest. She remembered how hard it was for him after his friend Erin died when they were kids. She had no choice but to be honest with him.

"The boy's teacher noticed several bruises on his body. She reported them to the authorities, and I guess several visits to the home were made, but no arrest. I'm going to get his sister to testify. She witnessed the fight. I'm convinced the son wasn't the only one he was abusing. I think she's terrified to speak out against her father."

Beth looked at her brother for a reaction. Christopher's jaw clenched and she could see the pain of that awful time return to his face.

"I know you don't like to talk about it, and I also know how much it still hurts, but maybe we both can help Erin."

"Meaning?"

"We can't do anything to bring Erin back, but we can do our part to make the world a better place, and we can do it in her name."

"Are we back on the marathon thing?"

"Come on, Chris. You know I'm right. You ran the Boston Marathon twice to honor Erin. Why not start a foundation or do something going forward that honors her life? She's not the first child who's been abused, and she won't be the last. I refuse to sit by while another child's voice is silenced."

She hated to force the issue, but there were too many lives that needed saving. Her brother's, not the least of them.

Her voice shaking, she looked him in the eye.

"It's the least I can do, and it just might be the most important work either of us will ever do."

～

Beth hoped that the rest of the drive home gave Christopher much to think about. Even though he wouldn't admit it, Beth knew she was right about Erin. From the moment of her death, her brother became a different person. He had as much drive for helping people as she did, and she assumed it was his motivation for enlisting in the Marines.

He had a big heart and she wanted to see him use it. She was right about his interest in Becca too. She could see it whenever they were in the same room together. With only a few more days before she returned to Boston, she'd have to move fast.

Beth liked Becca and thought that once she left the island, someone needed to be there for her brother. She decided to visit Becca at her home as soon as she and Christopher made it back to Captiva. Unannounced, of course.

Beth's car turned the corner, and she watched her brother look out the window at Powell's as they passed. It took all her restraint not to tease him about it. The Key Lime Garden Inn came into view, and they waved at their mother as they turned into the driveway.

"How'd it go?"

Once in his wheelchair, Christopher gave his mother a thumbs up. Beth got his crutches from the back seat and carried them into the house. Paolo put the ramp down and once inside, they gathered in the kitchen, whispering so they didn't disturb the guests.

Beth opened the refrigerator to get a soda. "I'll let Chris tell you more, but I think it went really well."

Christopher agreed. "It did. It was emotional as you would have expected, but all in all I think it went well. Do you and Paolo mind if we talk more about this tomorrow? I'm really tired and want to rest in my room for the night."

"Of course. It was a big day. How about you, Beth? We were thinking of going up to our place and maybe call Chelsea to come over for wine, snacks, and a game of cards."

Beth pretended to be too tired. "I think I'd like to chill in my room too. Maybe watch some tv or read a book. If I get a second wind, I'll walk over later."

"Sounds good. Well, goodnight you two. We'll probably be up late. Come over later if you haven't fallen asleep."

Beth nodded and walked upstairs to her room. After a few minutes waiting for her mother and Paolo to go next door, only one guest sitting in the living room paid any attention as she sneaked out the front door.

The full moon lit up the sky and the music coming from the outdoor restaurants rang through the streets as tourists walked toward the water. Beth loved this time of night. Not quite dark and the sun had already set. The steady breeze off the water cooling the night air.

She knew Powell Water Sports would be closed, so she had no choice but to go directly to the Powell home next door, hoping that Becca would be there. If she wasn't, Beth would have to get to her before Christopher talked to her at the inn tomorrow.

Becca answered the doorbell.

"Beth. Hi."

"Hey, Becca. I know it's kind of late, but I wondered if you had a few minutes to talk?"

"Sure. Let me get my sneakers." Becca was gone for only a minute before yelling to her father that she'd be back soon.

"Is everything all right over at the inn?"

"Oh, yeah, everything's fine. I wanted to talk to you about my brother, Christopher."

Beth watched Becca's face for reaction.

"Is Chris ok?"

"Yes. He's good. Becca, you're going to find out that I'm not good at minding my own business. I couldn't help but notice how the two of you are around each other."

"What do you mean?"

"Well, when we were at the Greek Festival for instance, the

two of you looked very uncomfortable around each other. Is there a reason for that?"

"Chris has been nothing but polite around me, Beth. I'm sure it's more my fault than his. I've got three brothers and we harass each other all the time. I think Chris and I just fall into that place of sister/brother snarky remarks. He doesn't mean anything by it and neither do I. Since we've got history, it makes it even easier to tease each other."

"What do you mean, that you've got history?"

Becca looked confused and Beth was suddenly glad she had pursued talking with her.

"Oh, I guess that's right. I never said anything to your mother or anyone in your family about that. If Chris never said anything either, it explains things."

They came upon the ice cream shack, and Beth decided to keep the conversation as casual as possible. She wanted to jump up and down with this news but played it cool.

"Do you want a cone? I'm paying."

"Sure, thanks. I'll have a small chocolate chip."

"One small chocolate chip and one small strawberry please."

While waiting for the cones, Becca brought Beth up to speed on her brother's summer romance with her ten years ago. She explained how he stopped answering her emails and texts and how, only recently, she came to learn about his friend Erin's suicide.

They picked up their order and continued walking along the various shops and restaurants.

"I remember Erin. It was a shock to everyone in town. He took it really hard, and it certainly explains why he stopped emailing and texting. It must have come as quite a shock when he returned home from Iraq injured as he is. How has that been for you?"

"It's made me so sad to see him give up on life the way he has. I haven't said a lot to him about that though. It's not my place."

Beth took a chance that her hunch was right.

"You still have feelings for him though, don't you?"

Becca nodded but didn't make eye contact. "I do care."

"Are you in love with him?"

Becca stopped walking and turned to look at Beth.

"Why are you asking me all these questions? Has Chris said anything to you about me?"

"Not really. At least he seems to be resisting the very same thing you are. I wonder why that is?"

Becca scratched at her scalp, just under her ponytail tie.

"I don't want to be rude, but I'm not in the habit of talking about my feelings with someone I barely know."

Beth knew she didn't have the luxury of time, so she got right to the point.

"Becca, I'm going back to Boston in a few days, so I don't have time for you and me to become best buddies. I'm going to give this to you straight. I think my brother is in love with you, and I think that you're in love with him. He's got a huge uphill road ahead of him, and I'm not sure how successful he's going to be without the support of someone who cares deeply about him. His mother and his family will always be there for him, but we're talking about a person who will stand beside him for the rest of his life. Now, if you're not going to be that person, that's fine. If you are, then I suggest you get on with it because I think he needs you. I might be crazy, but I think you need him too. Just think about it."

Their walk around the block returned them back to Becca's home. Beth waved as she walked back to the inn, leaving Becca standing in the middle of the street with her ice cream cone melting.

Beth had a history of injecting herself in her brother's business and she felt certain that nothing in the past could hold a candle to this night. Maybe one day, he'd yell at her for talking to Becca the way she did, but it didn't matter to her right now.

She'd saved her brother's life twice in one day, and she smiled at her success. Whether Christopher would be as impressed with her, only time would tell. For now, she'd enjoy the last few days on Captiva Island, starting with a card game back at the carriage house.

CHAPTER SEVENTEEN

Although sad to leave Captiva, Beth felt excited for what awaited her in Boston. She wanted to tell Gabriel about it but decided to wait until she could explain everything in person. She closed her suitcase and zippered it shut. She walked downstairs and wheeled her luggage to the front door.

Carrying a pile of linens for the laundry, Becca met her in the hallway.

"So, you're off then?"

Beth nodded. "Yup. I'm returning to the land of overcoats and snow."

Becca laughed. "I'm sorry to see you go."

Beth didn't know whether to stand her ground or apologize.

"I hope I didn't upset you the other night. I just couldn't go back to Boston without talking to you. I hope I get to see you again, Becca."

"Thanks, Beth. I understand that you only want the best for your brother. He's lucky to have you in his life."

"I could say the same to you."

Beth could sense she'd made Becca uncomfortable once again.

"I've got to get back to work. Safe travels."

Beth sighed and watched her walk down the hall. She'd made herself clear and hoped it was enough to bring Becca and her brother closer. Only time would tell.

Beth walked into the kitchen and found her mother at the table breaking off the ends of newly picked green beans.

"Hey, Mom. I'm ready to go. I've got just enough time for a cup of coffee before I've got to head to the airport. Is Chris up yet?"

"He hasn't come out of his room this morning, but I did hear some movement in there. I'm sure he'll be out to say goodbye to you. Let me get your coffee. I was thinking of having another cup myself."

"What time did you get up this morning? The kitchen smells amazing."

"Paolo and I went for our usual early morning walk, and then I came in to make my scones. I think we were on the beach at five-thirty."

Beth shook her head. "You two are incredible. I'm so glad you found someone, Mom. I mean it. You and Paolo make a great couple and I can see how happy you are. After everything you've been through, it's so wonderful to see you in such a good place."

Maggie handed Beth her cup and kissed her head.

"Thank you, honey. You and Gabriel make a lovely couple as well. Do you think the two of you might get married?"

"I'm not sure how Gabriel feels about that, but I do know that he's the one for me. If he asked me, I'd say yes even though I'd rather wait a few more years before getting married. I really want to give my career as much as I can and that makes marriage and children difficult. As Grandma says, I've got time."

"Yes, your grandmother definitely has opinions about everyone else's life. You do what you think is best, and I agree it's a good idea to first focus on your career. Just don't work so hard that you forget to have fun."

Christopher came into the kitchen and joined them at the table.

"What's this about having fun? I didn't know Beth had issues with having a good time. Seems to me she's been having fun all her life. Time to get to work, sis."

"Very funny, and I might say the same to you."

Maggie interjected. "Don't start you two. Your sister is going back home and you're going to miss her when she's gone. I know I am."

Christopher smiled and leaned in closer to Beth.

"I'm just teasing you. You know I'm going to miss having you here to talk to. I mean it when I say, I'm glad you came to Captiva."

He looked down and seemed to struggle with his words.

"I never could have ..."

Beth didn't want to make him revisit the events of their time at the Aiello's, so she put her hand on his and stopped him.

"I know, Chris. You don't have to say anything. I'm happy I went with you. You know I always have your back, right?"

Christopher nodded.

"And I've got yours."

Maggie cleared her throat to interrupt them.

"Beth, honey. You've got to go, or you'll miss your plane."

Maggie handed Beth a bag. "I packed a couple of scones for you to eat before you fly. You didn't have a bit of breakfast."

"Thanks, Mom."

She hugged her mother and then the three of them went out the back door and onto the porch. Beth waved before getting in her car. Her moist eyes made it difficult to see, so she wiped her eyes and fought to keep her tears from falling.

So much had happened during her time on the island, it felt strange leaving in the middle of such events. Christopher would find his way; she was sure of it. With any luck, Becca would help him along the next step in his journey. It might take time, but something told her that Becca needed Christopher as much as he needed her.

～

The soft warm breeze caressing his face, Christopher felt so relaxed on the porch that he almost fell asleep. With more guests checking in today, he knew that Becca would be working this morning. Hoping for a few minutes with her, he stayed on the porch, waiting for her to come outside. Her bike was parked in its usual spot, and he could hear her voice inside talking to his mother. It was almost one o'clock before she stepped outside onto the porch.

"Hey, Becca. Nice to see you."

She waved and continued to walk down the steps heading to her bike. He panicked that she hadn't lingered to talk with him. Nervous, he blurted out anything he could think of to keep her here.

"How long are you planning on working here?"

Becca stopped and turned to look at him.

"I'm sorry?"

"I asked you how long you plan on working here?"

Becca walked back to the house and stood at the bottom of the steps.

"Do you mean today? I'm done here but I've got to work at the store the rest of the afternoon, and I might have a sunset cruise to run tonight. Why do you ask?"

Christopher felt stupid, but the thought had crossed his mind more than once, that there must be more to her ambitions than just working on Captiva Island. He didn't want to offend her, but still, he persisted.

"You mistake my meaning. What I'm trying to understand is why someone as intelligent and strong as you obviously are, doesn't want to do more with her life than change bed linens and do laundry."

Becca joined him on the porch.

"I didn't know you were such a snob. You think it's below me to change sheets?"

"That's not what I meant."

"Oh, I know what you mean. Do you have any idea how many people it takes to run an inn, or a hotel or any other establishment so that rich people can take vacations and throw their money away like it was nothing? I like my job and I'm grateful to have it. Maybe if you spent your days thinking about how you might find something to focus on other than yourself, you too could feel useful."

He never expected the conversation to go so horribly wrong.

"Becca, I'm pretty sure people thought my time in the military was pretty darn useful."

She put her hand up to stop him.

"Don't do that."

"Do what?"

"Don't use your time serving our country like that. Everyone appreciates and respects what you've accomplished as a soldier. And I completely understand the idea that once a Marine, always a Marine. But what are your plans going forward? Are you planning on sitting on this porch for the rest of your life thinking about how you once had two legs?"

Christopher's anger building, he couldn't control his words.

"Funny coming from someone who gave up medical school to spend her days playing with tourists. I'd call that being a hypocrite. What makes you think you can judge me? From where I sit you seem content with hiding out on Captiva instead of doing something you've always wanted to do, probably something you were born to do."

He regretted the words the minute he said them. He'd struck a nerve and could see the pain on her face. He didn't know how to fix what he had broken, but he felt certain any progress they'd made had just evaporated before his eyes.

Becca quickly walked to her bike. Christopher didn't know how to undo what he'd done. He felt physical pain knowing that he'd hurt her. He was surprised how deeply he cared about Becca and decided that whatever it took he'd find a way to apologize.

∽

Beth pulled her car into her driveway. She was finally home, and decided a long, hot bath would relax the tension in her back. The flight wasn't a long one, but it was the Andresen case that she blamed for her stress.

Before she did anything, she called Lauren to tell her she was home and to bring over the mail when she had a moment.

"Hey Beth. How was your flight?"

"It was fine. I can't believe how cold it is though. Makes me think seriously of moving permanently down with Mom."

"You'd never make it there. You love New England too much."

Beth agreed. She loved the snow and skiing just as much as the beach.

"How are things with you guys? I didn't get to talk to you too much at the wedding."

"Yeah, everything's fine. I'll stop over later and drop off your mail. I can't stay and talk though. I've got a showing tonight if you can believe it. I never show a house after dinner, but it's unavoidable. I'll leave it all in a bin at the front door. I've got to run, but maybe we can get together sometime next week?"

"Sure. I've got some catching up with work to do, and I've got a case I'm leading so I'm going to be super busy myself for a while. I'll call you when I can stop by for a visit. Right now, all I want to do is get into the tub with a glass of wine."

"Sounds perfect. I remember the days when I used to have time to do that."

Beth laughed. "In that case, I'm going to sound like Mom here for a minute. Don't work so hard that you can't have a little fun now and then."

Beth still could hear tension in her sister's voice.

"I'll see what I can do. I'll talk to you later. Love you."

"Love you too."

Beth knew that something was off with Lauren. She guessed that it had something to do with Jeff, but she wasn't sure. Hopefully, when they got together next time, Lauren would feel comfortable enough to share what's been going on with her. Until then, all she could do was pray it was nothing serious.

After she unpacked, Beth spent the next hour relaxing in the bathtub. When she was finished with that she made herself a salad and enjoyed a nice Pinot Grigio. She thought about her time on Captiva. Grateful she had the weekend with all her siblings, she still missed the old days when they were young and with little responsibility.

She looked at the markings on the wall near the kitchen doorway. Her mother had made them as each child grew, making a big fuss over their progress. She pulled a few photo albums off the bookshelf and sat back on the sofa. She smiled remembering how she used to debate the major news with her father. Their heated exchanges making her mother insist they stop fighting which they always responded with "Who's fighting?"

From an early age, she'd always been a champion for those who couldn't defend themselves. Stray animals always found their way into the house, and she'd give away her allowance to strangers begging for money whenever she saw them.

She made the decision to become a prosecuting attorney so that she'd be able to put bad people behind bars. She had to be careful and stay objective to do her job properly, but when it came to children, she was fiercely determined to wipe the planet clean of abusers.

Looking through the photo albums she searched for images of

their yearly family vacation to Captiva looking for familiar spots that were unchanged.

She put the photos down on top of the coffee table and ran upstairs to her room. She stood on her toes to reach a box on the top closet shelf. When she got it, she placed it on her bed. Opening it, she saw several photographs of the friends she had met on Captiva. There was a keychain and postcards from the island, and in a small plastic bag were several seashells that she had collected.

Beth carried the seashells back downstairs and placed them on the glass hutch in the living room. She went to her suitcase and unzipped the front pouch, pulling out another small plastic bag filled with seashells she had picked up on this trip. She placed them among the old shells, mingling the past with the present.

The photo albums, the markings on the wall, and now the seashells all represented pieces of her life. She didn't feel sad but rather gathered her bathrobe, took a sip of her wine, and sat back on the sofa. She pulled her feet up and smiled, pleased with herself that she'd come to embrace all of the moments of her life thus far.

Updating Gabriel on the latest news was first on her to-do list. She didn't want to tell him about her job on the phone, so she'd call him before bed and plan to get together tomorrow after work.

Beth was ready for this new challenge at work and decided that as scared as she was about failing, she felt equally excited about succeeding. Focusing on doing her job, and making a difference mattered more than anything else. There was no telling what she could accomplish with that attitude.

CHAPTER EIGHTEEN

Christopher watched as Chelsea helped Sebastian into his chair. They'd come to visit his mother and Paolo. The four of them sat under the gazebo for tea and cake. There was no sign of Sebastian's wheelchair, but the laborious movements to adjust his brace and cane were difficult for Christopher to watch. It wasn't Sebastian he focused on, but rather Chelsea and her ever-present, and loving attention to the man.

He imagined Becca years ahead, helping him into his chair. In his mind they were older and lived on Captiva. He couldn't stand the thought that Becca would remain on the island never doing more than taking care of him. She needed to get on with her life, and the best way to do that was to convince her to return to medical school.

Along with helping her to move forward in her career, he realized he also needed to distance himself from her life. The last thing he wanted for her was to be his caretaker, and knew that if they gave in to their attraction for one another, she'd never walk away from him. He couldn't let that happen. He struggled to find a way to help her accept what was best for her.

His first move was to get real about his feelings for her. He was falling in love with Becca, probably for the second time. She had once again touched his heart and excited him every time they talked. She was smart, fun, challenging, and a pain in the neck, but he had to admit, at least to himself, that he loved her more than he had a right to.

He had no idea how she felt about him, except to think that right now she couldn't stand the sight of him. He had insulted her in the worst possible way and couldn't imagine her feeling anything but disgust and contempt for him. He hated that, but at the same time, maybe it was exactly what was needed to help her leave Captiva.

He had another, more practical idea. What he needed was someone else in his corner—someone with whom Becca had complete respect and love. Someone like her father, Crawford Powell. But how? He didn't want to show up at Powell Water Sports. The island gossips would be talking about him as he wheeled himself through town. Perhaps Becca's father might come to him if he asked.

Sebastian and Chelsea had invited his mother and Paolo to an event off island the next day and would be a perfect time to talk to Becca's father.

With guests out for the day, and everyone else out on the lawn, it was an ideal opportunity to not be overheard. He went into his room and shut the door. He Googled the store information and called the number.

A man answered, "Powell Water Sports."

"Hello, may I please speak with Crawford Powell?"

"Speaking."

"Mr. Powell, this is Maggie Wheeler's son, Christopher. My mother owns the Key Lime Garden Inn."

"Yes. I know Maggie. What can I do for you, Christopher?"

"I'm sorry to be so vague, but I'd rather not talk to you on the phone. It's about your daughter, Becca."

"Is anything wrong? I know she works at the inn a few times a week. Is there a problem?"

"Oh, no sir, I'm sorry, I didn't mean to imply there was anything wrong with her work. This is a more personal situation. Becca and I were friends when we were kids. I've been away in the military for a few years and…"

"Christopher, I do know about your situation. You know how things are on the island. The people here know everyone else's business. I'm sorry about what you went through over there. Thank you for your service. What you've done with your life is commendable. I'm sorry I haven't had a chance to come by and meet you in person."

For once, the gossips were useful, saving him from having to get into the details of his life over the phone.

"Well, about that sir, I was hoping that you and I could get together in person and talk tomorrow. I have to be honest with you though, I'd rather Becca not know that we're going to meet. She's already sort of mad at me."

Christopher could hear Crawford chuckle on the other end of the line. He hoped that was a good thing.

"My daughter has very strong opinions which you no doubt have already figured out. I tell you what, why don't I come by and pick you up tomorrow around noon? We'll drive over to Sanibel, and I'll buy you lunch. That way we'll have privacy and be away from the busybodies. Becca is going to see her Great-grandmother tomorrow, so she won't wonder where I've gone. Sound good?"

"That's perfect. I'll see you at twelve. I'll be outside in the driveway."

"Great. See you then."

The phone call turned out better than he'd hoped. Now, all he had to do was figure out how he was going to convince Becca's father that he wasn't in love with his daughter?

The next day as he sat on the porch drinking his morning coffee, Christopher marveled at his luck. He realized that he'd unknowingly created a problem for himself. Staying immobile and always at home made it impossible to go anywhere without having to explain himself.

Since his mother would be off island for the day, and Becca would be visiting her great grandmother, he'd picked the perfect day to escape.

Maggie and Paolo came out of the carriage house and walked across the driveway. His mother wore a casual summer dress and sandals, and Paolo had on jeans and a pink, untucked linen shirt and loafers.

"You guys are looking sharp. I don't know what you've got planned for today, but you're going to be the best-looking couple there. So, where are you headed and how long do you think you'll be gone?"

"Oh, you know Chelsea, she's always got more than one adventure crammed into her days. I expect we won't be home until after dinner. You don't have to worry about food. Riley and Grace are here if you need anything. Ciara is coming over this morning to work on the computer and do some paperwork."

Christopher panicked. Ciara would most definitely give him away. If it came to it, he'd have to ask her to keep quiet about his leaving the inn.

Maggie bent down and hugged him.

"What are you going to do today?"

Christopher held up a book he'd removed from the bookshelf.

"It's nice and peaceful around here. I figured with everyone gone, I'd spend some time reading. I'll be fine. You better get going, you don't want to keep the Activities Director waiting."

Maggie laughed and waved at him as she walked to their car. As soon as they were gone, he went inside and got showered and shaved. He had plenty of time to get ready, but he didn't want to make Ciara suspicious by fussing over his looks. He finished in record time and made his way back out onto the porch.

Two guests came downstairs and walked by him with their beach towels and suntan lotion. Playing host, he smiled at them. "Have a great day."

"Thank you, you too."

Ciara's car pulled up to the back of the inn. She got out of the car carrying her briefcase.

"Hey, Ciara. Mom said you'd be by. How are you?"

"Hi, Chris. I'm well, thanks. It's a beautiful day and definitely not one to be sitting inside doing paperwork, but it's got to be done. I've got to pick up Noah from school today to help Sarah out. She's got to bring Sophia to the doctor, so I said I'd get Noah."

"Is Sophia ill?"

"No, nothing like that. It's just the usual check-up by the pediatrician."

Trying to sound nonchalant, he asked, "Oh, good. What time does Noah get out of school?"

"Noon. It'll take me about thirty minutes from here, so I best get to work so I can leave."

Relieved he didn't have to lie to Ciara, he nodded. "I'll leave you to it then. I've got a good book I'm about to get into."

He had two hours before Crawford was due to pick him up. He took that time to think about what he would say to him. He'd already gone over the words in his mind at least twenty times, but nothing felt right. Every time he found the right words, he'd think of her green eyes, and would lose his train of thought. In the end, he decided to forget everything and let his heart speak.

Ciara's voice made him jump. "Well, I'm off. You have a good day."

"Will do, you too. Say hello to Sarah and everyone."

At exactly twelve o'clock, Crawford Powell's 1985 Chrysler LeBaron Woody station wagon drove over the inn's seashell-paved driveway. Christopher left his wheelchair behind, preferring to use his crutches. It took a while to make it down the ramp on his own, but it was worth it to meet the man standing.

"That's quite the car you've got there."

Crawford beamed at Christopher. "Ah, she's my baby. Nice to meet you, Christopher. Is it Chris or Christopher?"

"I answer to either one."

Crawford opened the passenger door and helped him into the car. Once inside, he ran his hand over the dashboard.

"This is a pretty sweet ride. I don't blame you for loving it the way you do. The cars they make today don't have the character of the old ones."

"Exactly my thinking. Of course, not everyone feels the same way we do about that. Nothing new under the sun as far as I'm concerned. Every new car looks the same to me."

"What are you in the mood to eat?"

"I like everything so I'm easy to please."

"That's what I like to hear. I love the cheeseburgers at the Lighthouse Café. Let's stop there if you don't mind. They've got a great outdoor eating area."

"Sounds great."

They talked about music, old cars, and the Red Sox. Three subjects Christopher could ramble on about for hours. He smiled when Crawford talked about The Rolling Stones.

"People say that Mick Jagger is too old and that the Stones should disband, but I don't agree. Have you seen them in person? That guy has more energy than anyone I've ever seen at his age. Even younger kids can't keep up."

"I agree. I hope they continue for many more years."

The small talk continued until they reached their destination.

Crawford found a parking space as close to the front door as he could get. Christopher accepted the man's help in getting out of the car, but soon after, waved him off.

"I can take it from here."

The hostess sat them in the corner garden area which kept them shielded from the hot sun. After they placed their orders and got their beers, Crawford seemed anxious to hear what Christopher had to say.

"So, I'm glad to finally get to meet you, but I'm more than curious why you wanted to talk to me."

Christopher cleared his throat and took a sip of his beer before saying a word. When he was ready, he leaned in to speak.

"As I mentioned on the phone, Becca and I knew each other years ago. My family and I often vacationed on Captiva, and one year, when I was sixteen, we hung around together on the beach with our friends. It was a long time ago, but I guess I hurt her when I stopped answering her emails. It's a long story as to why, and it really doesn't have anything to do with what I wanted to talk to you about."

Suddenly, his plan to quickly say what he'd come to tell her father didn't matter. Unprepared to speak from the heart, he took a deep breath to calm down. He regrouped and started again.

"Here's the thing. I think Becca feels something for me still, and I'm concerned that she'll continue to throw her life away feeling sorry for me. She should go back to medical school and get on with her life, but it seems to me that she's stuck somehow."

Crawford didn't say a word but looked directly at Christopher and smiled, letting him continue.

"I know about her mother. I've no doubt that Becca suffers because of her mother's death. I'm no psychiatrist, but I think anyone would have a hard time with that."

Crawford wasn't smiling anymore, which worried Christopher. He stopped talking and even though he had more to say, he feared that by talking about his dead wife, he'd overstepped. He didn't know what to say next, so he waited for Crawford to speak. When he did, his words shook Christopher.

"You're in love with my daughter."

"I...I'm."

He couldn't finish but stopped and then let his heart do the talking.

He nodded.

"I care very much for her."

"And you believe that Becca is in love with you?"

"I do."

"Well then, why did you need to talk to me?"

Crawford asked a simple question that Christopher suddenly realized he couldn't answer.

The waiter placed their plates in front of them and asked if they needed anything else. Both men shook their heads no. When the waiter left, Crawford continued.

"Listen, Chris. I completely agree with you that Becca should return to medical school, but I can't force her to go back. She'd be an incredible doctor. Her interests have always been in sports medicine, and I know that she'd be perfect in that role, but again, I can't insist she do something she doesn't want to do. My question for you is why not have this conversation with her instead of me?"

"Well, I'd like to, Mr. Powell, but she's stubborn, and right now I don't think she'd let me read her the weather report."

"What exactly did you do?"

"I told her that she was hiding out on the island afraid to go back to school. I asked her if she wanted to spend the rest of her life doing laundry and playing with tourists."

Crawford whistled. "Whoa, you're a much braver man than I. What made you take that approach?"

Christopher hated to admit Becca was right, but it was time to come clean with her father.

"Because your daughter told me the same thing. She said that

I was hiding out at the inn and that I was afraid to move forward. She asked me if I planned on spending the rest of my life sitting in a wheelchair."

Crawford took a bite of his cheeseburger and Christopher could see a crinkle in the corner of his eyes—evidence of a humorous reaction.

"She was right, wasn't she?"

Crawford's mouth was full and so all he could do was nod his head. He swallowed and sat against the back of his chair wiping his mouth with his napkin. He looked across the table and said, "Can I ask you a question?"

"Of course."

"Have you ever seen Becca cry?"

"No, why?"

"Because I've only ever seen her really fall apart twice in her life. The first time was when a boy she cared deeply for stopped answering her emails and texts. The second was the day we buried her mother. Both of those events, I watched my daughter feel like her world had ended, and there was nothing I could do about either one."

Christopher's heart raced and he started to sweat.

"I would have done anything to keep my little girl from the pain of losing faith in the world and in herself. My job has been and will continue to be her father. You, on the other hand, have an opportunity to give my daughter a reason to feel hopeful about her future. If you love her, then tell her. If you can't do that, then give her a reason to leave this island and go back to medical school. Make her see that to be as far away from you as possible is the only way she'll ever be truly happy and willing to open her heart to someone else."

Crawford took a sip of his beer and then continued.

"I know you've been through a lot yourself, and I won't judge you for whichever road you choose. All I ask is that if you truly love her, then do what's best for her."

Christopher flinched at Crawford's words. Realization that he'd always had the power to influence Becca's choices scared him. It was the first time he truly felt a coward. He had tried to relinquish any responsibility by giving the control over to her father. Now, he saw himself through Crawford's eyes and felt foolish.

Whether Crawford respected him or not, he couldn't tell. All he knew in that moment was he'd lost respect for himself, and what he intended to do about it he had no idea.

CHAPTER NINETEEN

Beth hadn't been back at her office for more than five minutes when her assistant tracked her down.

"Mitchell wants to see you in the conference room."

"Now?"

"Right now."

Beth got up from her chair and straightened her skirt. Hoping for new information on her case, she hurried down the hall to the meeting. Heather O'Conner and Alice Bellows were seated at the table and Mitchell was standing. She pulled open the glass door and went inside.

"Beth, welcome back. I hope your brother is doing better."

"Thank you, Mitchell. He's well, and my sister's wedding was perfect."

She sat at the table opposite Heather and Alice and waited for an update.

"So, here's where we are at this point. Gunner Andresen has been denied bail and it looks like we've got several people to look at for this jury. Defense is concerned about the fact that one of the jurors has a child who died recently. It wasn't murder, it was cancer, but nevertheless, she'll be disqualified for sure. I want the three of you to get back there tomorrow and take a close look at the remaining potential jurors to see what we've got."

Beth already felt uncomfortable with the way Mitchell was delegating. It was her job to tell Heather and Alice what their assignments were. If she was to head up this team, she'd have to talk to him about it when the meeting was over.

"Heather, I want you to get a meeting with the social worker who's been assigned to the sister. She's been living with her aunt for the foreseeable future. They've been keeping an eye on her. Tell them that we need to talk to that girl and coordinate a time when we can meet. I assume she'll need to be supervised the whole time we talk to her."

Alice looked down at her file.

"The sister's name is Katlin. She's twelve. Which one of us is interviewing her?"

"I am."

Beth didn't realize she had said the words out loud, but looking at Mitchell's face, she could tell he didn't want to argue about it.

"Fine. Alice let Beth know when you schedule the meeting. Let's see what the kid has to say."

Beth was horrified.

"Mitchell, with all due respect, we can't just march into the room and interrogate the girl. She's a child."

"She's a witness." His voice was loud, a tactic he often used to silence others.

"Be that as it may, I'll need to talk with whomever has already spoken with her. I need to gain her trust. If she hasn't told anyone what she and her brother went through, then there's a reason."

"I'm sure she's terrified of him, even if he is behind bars," Heather said.

Mitchell interrupted, "We've only got days before this trial begins. We're running out of time. Without the sister we don't have enough to convict. If it was self-defense, and the sister corroborates that, it doesn't look good. She saw her brother go after the father with the knife."

Mitchell paced around the room and then stopped, looking at Beth he said, "Get the sister and more if you can. See if there are any other witnesses to his constant abuse. Without that, I'm not sure we'll win this thing. That's it for now."

We? I thought he was removing himself from the case.

Heather and Alice got up from the table and left the conference room.

Beth didn't move.

"Mitchell, can we talk?"

"What's up?"

"Maybe I'm crazy, but didn't you tell me on the phone that you wanted me to be lead council on this case?"

"Yes I did."

"Well, it doesn't look like it. You took control of this meeting and basically dictated orders to the rest of us. Maybe I misunderstood, but I thought this was going to be my big break. Does everyone in the office know this is mine?"

"Look, the DA expressed his concern with you being lead council. If it were up to me I'd have no problem with it. I mean, it was my idea in the first place. With my schedule, I thought it made sense. We've shifted a few things around so I can better handle it."

Beth felt defeated and angry. She'd told her family about her big chance and now, she'd have to go to them and say she remained a newbie lawyer with the same responsibilities as always.

Mitchell must have sensed her disappointment.

"Hey, listen kiddo. This isn't a big deal. You still have all my support and it's a good opportunity to show what you can do. I plan to rely heavily on you. If you think you've got something that will help us win this case, go for it. I've got your back on this."

He has my back.

She suddenly felt like she had a target on it. She'd planned a romantic dinner with Gabriel tonight and was excited to share her good news. Now, all she wanted to do was go home and crawl under her comforter and never come out.

She took her notebook and walked out of the conference room. She felt everyone's eyes on her, and true to her nature, instead of looking at the floor, she stared back at anyone who dared say one word to her.

Maybe Mitchell was lead council, but that didn't stop her from keeping her focus on what really mattered. A child was dead, and another was one of the walking wounded. Lead council or not, she'd do everything in her power to make sure Gunner Andresen paid for what he'd done.

Becca tiptoed into Gran's room. She held a tall strawberry ice cream soda, Gran's favorite, and sat next to her bed, waiting for her to wake up.

Ten minutes passed before the woman moved and looked over at Becca.

"How long was I asleep?"

"I'm not sure. You were sleeping when I got here ten minutes ago."

Gran struggled to sit up in the bed, so Becca jumped up to help her.

"I hate having old creaky bones. Makes moving difficult."

She looked beyond Becca and smiled.

"Is that what I think it is?"

Becca brought the treat to her. "Strawberry ice cream soda, your favorite."

"Oh girl. You certainly know the way to my heart."

She sipped the delicious drink through a straw.

"Careful or you'll get a brain freeze."

"I best take it slow then; I can't afford to lose any more brain cells. Pull the chair close and stay a while."

Becca did as she was told and noticed how weak Gran was. Something had changed since their last visit. Gran seemed more frail than she remembered.

"How are you feeling?"

"I'm all right. You don't have to worry about me."

Becca reached for the monthly schedule of events at the assisted living facility.

"Looks like they've got a piano player coming at one o'clock. It's a sing-along. Do you feel like going? I can take you down."

Gran moved her hand in a dismissive gesture. "Nah, I'm sick of hanging around with all those old people. I'd rather stay here with you. So, tell me about your life these days. What have you been up to?"

Becca wanted the focus to stay on Gran, but knew resistance was useless.

"Well, I've been working a lot. It's tourist season you know."

"Uh-huh. That sounds exciting, and when I say that I'm being sarcastic. What else you got?"

Becca started to tell her about Christopher and their fight but didn't know how to approach the subject. Gran decided to press her for more information.

"Why don't you start by telling me about the young man you're in love with?"

Shocked, Becca quickly denied that she was in love with Christopher. "Gran, I never said…"

"Stop right there."

Gran took another sip of her ice cream soda. "You've never lied to me before, Becca Powell. I don't think you should start now, do you?"

Becca looked down at her hands, twirling the bracelet on her wrist. Gran was right, she'd never lied to her before, and she didn't keep much from her either. The problem was that Becca had been lying to herself these last few days, but she couldn't ignore the truth any longer.

"His name is Christopher Wheeler. I met him ten years ago when his family came to the island. We never saw each other again until recently when he came home from being in the service in Iraq. He was injured and has one leg amputated just above the knee. He's living on the island now."

Gran nodded. "So, what's the problem?"

Becca explained everything that had happened since Christopher came home. When she was finished, she waited for Gran to say something.

"I like his sister. That girl's got hutzpah even if she was wrong. What is her name again, Beth?"

Becca nodded. "What do you mean she was wrong?"

"She had no right to ask you to look after her brother. You don't say such a thing unless…"

Gran paused and scratched her chin.

"Unless what?"

"Unless you're in love with this boy. That's a horse of a different color."

Gran was famous for quoting *The Wizard of Oz*.

"When you love someone, you don't give a lick if they're sick or injured. You want to be with them no matter what. If you're not in love with him, then don't give it another thought. You just think about yourself and what you want your future to look like."

Becca stayed silent, letting Gran's words hang in the air.

"What do you think about what Christopher said to you? Something about wasting your time doing laundry and hiding out? I know what you told him, but my question is, is there any truth to what he says?"

"I can't answer that."

"You mean you won't answer it. Becca, I can't tell you what to do, but I'd hate to think that you're giving up something you truly love. Since you were a little girl you were always bandaging up your brothers and anyone else who would sit still long enough for you to play doctor. I think you even wrapped my ankle in gauze once when you were ten. Do you remember that?"

Becca laughed. "I remember. I think I even wrapped Izzy, our cat in that stuff."

Gran frowned. "I hated that cat."

"Gran!"

"Well, I did. Anyway, your mother used to tell everyone that you were going to be a doctor. We all had to buy you medical supplies for your Christmas presents. What kid wants medical supplies for Christmas?"

They both laughed at that. No one said anything again for a few minutes, and then Becca noticed Gran seemed sad.

"Becca, I won't be here to talk to you like this much longer. I know my time is coming."

Becca's eyes started to water.

"Don't say that. You're going to be here for a long time."

"Listen to me, girl. I've outlived my daughter and my granddaughter, but I can't stay here forever. I want to be with your Great-grandpa. I miss him. I miss them all. So, you've got to be strong and get on with your life. Stop living in the past. Stop thinking that you've got all the time in the world. You don't. None of us do. Listen to your heart and then make your choices. Listen to your heart, Becca."

How often she'd heard her mother say the very same thing to her. She couldn't see how that was possible. *How could she listen to her heart when it was broken?*

"Roll the bed down, Becca. I'd like to take a nap. Why don't you run along now? Thank you for my strawberry ice cream soda. You're a good girl."

Becca took the soda from Gran's hands and placed it on her nightstand. She rolled the bed down and stood next to it. As Gran fell asleep, Becca looked around the room, her eyes landing on a framed photograph of her mother, grandmother and Gran, their arms around each other, laughing at the camera.

Three women whose strength and wisdom had guided Becca since she was a child. In that moment she made a promise to herself that whatever choices she made going forward, she'd keep this picture in her mind. Their lives would carry on through her, and she knew in her heart that she'd never take their sacrifices and love for granted ever again.

Beth put away her laptop and checked on the roast chicken in the oven. Gabriel was on his way, and she couldn't wait to see him. So much had happened since their time together in Florida. Her brother's meeting with the Aiello family and her better understanding of his attraction for Becca was first on her list of things to talk about. The latest changes to her job, although upsetting, needed to be shared with him as well. She longed for his perspective and comforting words and hoped by the end of the night that she'd feel better about her situation.

She heard a car door shut and went to the front door to meet him. As soon as she opened the door she ran into his arms and buried her face in his neck.

"Hey, I guess you missed me."

When she stayed in his arms longer than usual, she knew he could tell something was wrong.

He held her tight and stroked her hair. When she felt ready, she pulled back and he could see the redness in her eyes.

"Hey, what's this? You've been crying. Tell me what's wrong."

Beth held his hand and they walked into the house. She tried to reassure him that everything was fine, but she couldn't be sure that was true. She poured wine into two glasses and handed Gabriel a glass as they moved to the sofa.

She told him everything that had happened since they last saw each other, and when she was done she smiled. "Honestly, I know I'm over-reacting. I'm just disappointed."

"Beth, I know how excited you were about this, but you're going to get your opportunity to shine. Every single day you approach your job with such dedication and commitment. You work hard and have a passion for what you do. Don't you think that's enough?"

Beth thought about that for a minute and agreed.

"You're right. I'm lucky to have this job and I'm going to have to get used to disappointments. I know I won't win every case, but I also know even if I lose, I'll go right back into the fire and fight just as hard for the next person. It's what I signed up for after all. If I let a little thing like my ego get in the way, I'm doomed."

Gabriel smiled and put his hand on her face. "You're going to be an amazing attorney. You're not the type to let much stand in your way. Something tells me that you've been like that your whole life."

Beth moved closer to him and loved how good it felt to snuggle up against him. His wisdom made him all the more attractive, and she had to admit that she had very little in her life to complain about.

"I hope you're hungry. I've got your favorite roast chicken and root vegetables in the oven."

"I thought I smelled something familiar, and yes, I'm starving. You certainly take good care of me."

"Right back at you. I don't know what I'd do without you."

He kissed the top of her head.

"You won't ever have to worry about being without me. I'll see to that."

CHAPTER TWENTY

Christopher had a lot to think about. From the start he'd struggled with his feelings for Becca. Helping her to live her best life was the kindest thing he could do. His affection for her would need to be put aside. His actions in the coming days carried weight, and her father knew it. Crawford's advice was jarring, but understandable. He only wanted his daughter safe and protected from more pain and confusion.

Christopher wanted the same and didn't believe that he was the one to make her truly happy. He had too much baggage, and regardless of how committed he was to his healing, he couldn't allow Becca to sacrifice the rest of her life on his account.

Four guests were sitting on the porch drinking wine and talking about the Bubble Room's desserts. They were loud enough that even in his room, he still couldn't hear himself think. He wanted to apologize to Becca and decided to call her.

She answered his call on the first ring.

"Hey. Everything ok?"

"Yeah, um, I just wanted to apologize for the other day. I didn't mean to be such a jerk."

"Well, some things can't be helped, I guess."

She was teasing him, which he took as a good sign.

"I'm sorry too. I shouldn't have said what I said. You've been through a lot, and I sometimes forget about that. Am I forgiven?"

"Of course. Yes. You're forgiven."

She didn't say anything more and the silence was palpable. He wanted to see her.

"What are you doing tonight?"

"Nothing. Just hanging around. You?"

"It's a full moon. I was going to sit outside on the porch, but the guests are out there and they're pretty loud. I think they've had more than a few drinks."

Becca laughed. "I can come over if you'd like. We could go down to the beach and enjoy the quiet…that's if you want to."

"I'd like that."

"Great. I'll see you in a few."

Christopher could hear Becca in the kitchen within minutes of their phone call.

"Hey, that was fast."

"I took my bike. Let me put the ramp down at the door."

He hated to interrupt the guests, but he had no choice but to go past them.

"Excuse us, everyone."

Becca navigated the wheelchair down the ramp and chose the path leading toward the beach. They didn't need to go out that far. The moon was large in the sky, and it shone down on them, lighting the way. She locked the chair in place and ran back toward the shed to find a tall camping chair. She placed it next to him and pulled her legs up, her arms holding them in place.

"This was a great idea. You'd be surprised how many times I've come down to watch the full moon. I'm glad to share it with you this time."

The moon singled her out and illuminated her face. He always thought Becca beautiful, but tonight she glowed.

"Me too. Mostly, I'm glad we're not fighting anymore."

She smiled and looked at him. "I am too."

He rehearsed what he would say to her all day, and felt the time was right to make his move.

"You were right. What you said before. I have been hiding. The truth is I couldn't see my life beyond the walls of my room. Nothing mattered to me except going to see my friend Nick's family. I haven't told you about Nick. He died the day I lost my leg."

He told her everything about that day, and the day he and Beth went to see Nick's family.

"How did you feel after you fulfilled your friend's wish?"

"I won't say closure, because I don't think you ever get closure on the death of a loved one, but I'm glad that I kept my promise. It didn't have any impact on how I saw my life going forward. I was still stuck, that is, until you."

"You mean what I said to you the other day?"

"No, not just that. I mean, I have to admit you did knock some sense into me, but ever since you came back into my life, you've been a good friend to me. I'm not sure I've been a very good friend to you though. I've been a jerk actually. I'm surprised you're still talking to me."

Becca laughed and punched him in the arm.

"You haven't been that bad. But thank you for admitting it. That's something at least."

He chose his words carefully.

"I hope you and I will stay good friends for a long time. I lost one friend years ago because of the loss of another. I don't want to do that again. I want us to remain friends. I hope you'll always stay in touch and let me know how you're doing. I promise to answer your emails and texts this time."

He could see the disappointment in her eyes. It killed him to lie like this, but to tell her how he really felt would keep her tethered to him and possibly Captiva for the rest of her life.

Her response caught him off guard.

"Of course, Chris. I'm glad we're friends. I'd hate to think I'd never hear from you again. No matter where we are in the world, we've got to reach out now and then, okay? I won't forget you, and I hope you won't forget me. I wish you the best...always."

He wanted to kiss her but realized it would be a mistake. Even though he'd never get the chance again, he knew it was best to keep things platonic.

Ready to take his next step, he took a deep breath and continued.

"I've made some decisions about my future too. Back in Germany, after the surgery, they wanted to fit me for a prosthetic leg. I didn't want to live, let alone spend hours in physical therapy with constant appointments required to get the leg just right. I blew them off and would barely speak to the doctors. I was in such a bad place I didn't see the point in doing anything to prolong my life. I've had time to rethink all that. I'm going to talk to the Veteran's Administration and see what I can do about getting a prosthetic device."

"Chris, that's amazing. I'm so happy for you."

He smiled, pleased to see her so excited.

"Thanks. I should have done this months ago. I have no idea what I'm up against, but I'm happy I've made this decision. I haven't told my mother or anyone else about it, so for now, keep it to yourself."

"I will and thank you for sharing your news with me. It means a lot."

He didn't know how to feel. It was a bittersweet moment. He thought back to what her father asked of him.

"All I ask is that if you truly love her, then do what's best for her."

Letting her go hurt him deeply, but he stood firm in his decision that it was indeed what was best for her. In time, she'd come to see that he was right.

Becca waved to Christopher as she rode her bike down the inn's driveway. She pedaled as fast as she could, letting the warm, salt air hit her face. Passing businesses and restaurants she pedaled across the street and onto the bayside dock. The sand-slick road under her tire made her skid. She fell onto the asphalt paved parking lot, scraping her knee.

Pulling herself away from the bike, she kicked it with her foot. Standing, she put pressure on her leg to see if she could walk. Nothing happened on the island after ten o'clock, and so the streets were quiet. Grateful no one saw her, she limped to the end of the dock, and sat on a stump.

Her dirty hand pushed her sweat-soaked hair away from her face, leaving a dirt mark on her forehead. She wanted to cry but didn't know the reason for it.

What was she so upset about? Had their fight sealed her fate? Did she overstep and make him feel that they could never be more than friends? How did this happen?

After a few minutes of rest, she picked up her bike and walked the rest of the way home, struggling to understand her talk with Chris. When she got home, she got into the shower and washed away the dirt and tears. She needed time to think about what to do. Confused and frustrated over her inability to understand how Christopher could misread her attraction for him, she wrapped her bathrobe around herself and sat on the end of the bed trying not to cry.

The house landline rang, and she could hear her father talking.

"This is he…when? I see. Yes, thank you for calling."

She could hear her father's footsteps. When he reached her door, he knocked.

"Come in."

"Hey, sweetheart. That was the assisted living nurse. Gran passed away in her sleep about thirty minutes ago."

A deep guttural wailing from somewhere inside her raged from her body.

"No! No!"

Becca bent over holding her stomach. She started to fall when her father caught her. They both fell to the floor and sat leaning against the bed, his arms around her.

"I know, baby girl. I know. It's going to be all right. She didn't suffer. She's with your mom now."

He stroked her hair and let her cry for as long as she needed. They remained like that for several minutes. Becca couldn't imagine her life without her Gran. She was the last connection to her mother and with her passing, Becca felt like she'd lost her all over again.

Later, when she tried to fall asleep, she lay in her bed thinking about her last visit with Gran. Becca smiled remembering how happy her great-grandmother was drinking her favorite strawberry ice cream soda. She could picture her in heaven, telling everyone what to do. That image made her laugh. Later, when she was almost asleep, Becca thought back to her childhood fantasy of becoming a doctor. Her Gran never forgot the Christmas of medical supply gifts.

"What kid wants medical supplies for Christmas?"

"What kid, indeed."

CHAPTER TWENTY-ONE

Beth placed her briefcase on top of the table and waited for the social worker to bring Kaitlin Andresen into the room. She'd been questioned by several people and jumped through many hoops to get to this day.

The door opened and a woman followed the young girl into the room.

"Kaitlin, this is attorney Beth Wheeler. You remember what we talked about? She wants to ask you a few questions and all you have to do is be honest about what you saw and what you know. Are you still willing to talk to this attorney?"

Kaitlin nodded.

Beth looked at the young girl. "Hi, Kaitlin, my name is Beth. It's nice to meet you. I want to ask you a few questions, and I promise you can ask me any question you like as well."

Kaitlin sat at the table across from Beth.

"Kaitlin, I'm so very sorry about your brother. I lost my father two years ago and it was very sudden. I know how sad you must be. I wanted to ask you about your father. Would that be ok with you?"

Kaitlin looked over at the social worker.

"It's all right, Kaitlin. You can tell Beth whatever you want."

Kaitlin nodded, her eyes not contacting with Beth.

Beth opened her folder and looked at the paperwork before her. She wouldn't let Kaitlin see any photos of her brother and so she turned them face down. She looked at her notes and then looked at Kaitlin.

"Your father says that it was an accident. He said he didn't mean to kill Tyler but that he was just defending himself, and that it was Tyler who attacked him with a knife. You were there. Is that what you saw? Is your father telling the truth?"

Kaitlin shook her head. "Not exactly."

"Can you tell me what you saw?"

Kaitlin hesitated briefly before speaking. Her hands trembling slightly, she answered Beth.

"Tyler came home later than he was supposed to. He worked at Santorini's Pizza. He went out with his friends after work instead of coming home. My dad was really mad when Tyler got home. I was in my room, but I could hear the yelling and the stuff they were saying."

"What did you hear?"

"I came down the stairs because I wanted to help Tyler from getting beat up again. My dad yelled at me to go back upstairs to my room, but I didn't want to leave Tyler."

Beth handed the girl a box of tissues when Kaitlin started to cry. Beth waited for her to catch her breath.

"It's ok, sweetie, what happened next?"

"My dad started yelling really loud at Tyler. There was a kitchen knife on the counter, and my dad said that Tyler should be careful because next time he was going to use the knife on him, and then I'd be next. He was acting crazy and saying scary things. He said our mother was no good and that he was glad she left us. I don't remember what Tyler said to him that got him so mad, but he turned and punched Tyler in the face. Tyler fell on the floor, and I ran to help him. He told me to go upstairs and lock the door, but I didn't. I stayed. Then Tyler got on his feet again. He ran into the kitchen and got the knife and then came back to hit dad. Tyler's face was all bloody from getting hit. He was crying when he went after him."

"So, your brother was just trying to defend himself and you. Is that right?"

Kaitlin nodded. "He was scared. We both were scared. That's how things always were though. We were always scared. I don't remember the last time I wasn't afraid."

"Did you believe your father when he said that he'd use the knife on you and your brother?"

"Yes."

"Had he ever threatened either of you like that before?"

"Yes. One time he said that one day he was going to shoot us and then turn the gun on himself. Our neighbor heard it too, so she called the police. The police had already been to our house a few times before."

"What happened when the police came?"

Kaitlin shrugged.

"They talked to my father and then left. I don't know what they talked about."

Beth needed more. She had to get to the details of the killing.

"Kaitlin, how did your father kill Tyler?"

Her tears began to fall again, but she tried to continue her story. Choking back the tears, she said, "My dad got the knife from Tyler and then he just started stabbing him. I was screaming and telling him to stop, but he wouldn't. I thought I was going to be next, so I ran out of the house and to the neighbors' and started banging on their door."

"And that's when they called the police?"

"Yes. I never went back into the house again. I saw them take

Tyler out on a stretcher and my dad was handcuffed and put in the police car. We called my aunt, and she came and got me."

"That's your mother's sister?"

"Yes."

"Kaitlin, I know how difficult this is for you, but I need you to be as clear and honest as you can please. First, you need never worry about your father gaining custody of you. You'll never have to see him again, no matter the result of his trial. You're in no danger. He'll never hurt you again. Can you please tell me how often your father beat Tyler?"

Beth knew the answer, but she needed to hear it from Kaitlin.

"Almost every day."

Beth hated that she had to ask the next question, but it was necessary.

"Did your father ever beat you?"

Kaitlin didn't hesitate.

"Yes. Not as much as my brother, but a lot."

Beth sighed. "Kaitlin, is there anything else you want me to know?"

The girl stared into Beth's eyes and answered, "If my brother didn't try to kill him, I would have."

Becca called Maggie to tell her about Gran.

"I'm so sorry to hear this news, Becca. From what I've heard, your great-grandmother was a wonderful woman. Don't worry about us here. Ciara and I will take care of the rooms. You just take whatever time you need, and please offer my family's condolences to your father and brothers as well."

"Thank you, Maggie. I will."

When Becca ended the call, she wondered if it was a mistake not to call Christopher. She decided against it assuming that

Maggie would tell him. There wasn't anything he could do anyway, and she needed to keep him at a distance for the time being. She didn't want him to feel an obligation to be by her side during the funeral. She would stay close to her family and trust that she'd see things clearer in a few days.

The next few days were filled with telephone calls, funeral planning, and quiet moments of reflection. Her father had picked up Gran's belongings at the facility, and the boxes sat in the garage, waiting for someone to go through the items. Crawford looked at Becca for guidance.

"I don't know what to do with her things. Maybe you'd like to go through her stuff and take what you want? I'm sure we can donate whatever you don't wish to keep."

"Maybe after the funeral. I'm not up to it just now."

"I understand. I'll put the boxes in the corner, and you can go through them when you're ready."

When the morning of the funeral arrived Becca's brothers along with members of the community, carried the casket into the hearse. Her mother and the rest of her family members were buried in a cemetery off island. The limos traveled to a small church in Ft. Myers and after the church service took them all to her final resting place, next to her husband.

Becca watched everyone walk to their cars but didn't move. She walked a few feet to her mother's grave. Crawford followed Becca and put his arms around her as they stood before Julia Powell's headstone. Her brothers standing awkwardly nearby, Becca leaned on her father.

"It feels like the day we buried Mom. I can't believe she's been gone this long. Seems like we were standing here just the other day."

"I know, honey."

Becca smiled. "At least Gran will spice things up in heaven. Can't you just see the three of them? Gran, Grandma, and Mom dancing on the clouds."

"I'd say you've got three angels up in heaven watching over you now. You're a very lucky young lady. Not everyone has three angels."

Becca thought about that. Her life had been on hold for so long, she was going to need all three of those angels to help her take the next step.

She hugged her father. "We should go."

She wanted to get back home and pull the tote out from under her bed. She had some thinking to do, and if she wasn't too late, a future to plan.

Sarah sent a group text to everyone in her family.

Sarah:I'm trying to get approval to video the adoption. Who's in?
  Maggie:Are you kidding me? Absolutely.
  Lauren: What time will it be?
  Sarah:Ten o'clock tomorrow.
  Lauren:I can do that.
  Beth:Can't wait. Count me in.
  Brea:Michael's working right now, so I'm speaking for the two of us. We'd love to be included.
  Chelsea:Woohoo. This is so exciting.
  Christopher:Who's getting adopted? Only kidding. :-)

Sarah:Great. Trevor is checking with the members of his family. I can't promise anything. Courtrooms are pretty fussy about recording inside the courtroom. Keep your fingers crossed. I'll let everyone know tonight and get you all the link. Noah is so excited, and of course Sophia doesn't understand any of it. Love you guys!

. . .

When she ended the group text, she sat on the sofa and put her head between her legs. Trevor came running into the room.

"Are you ok?"

"I feel a little faint."

"Take deep breaths and I'll get you some cold water to drink."

She waited a few minutes before sitting up straight. Trevor came back with the water, and she drank the whole glass in one gulp.

"Whew. That was weird."

"Did you eat anything this morning? Maybe you need something in your stomach."

"No. Actually, I felt a little nauseous, so I skipped breakfast this morning."

"Ah, well, that's your problem. How about I make you a sandwich or I can heat up the leftover pasta dinner from last night if you want?"

"I'll take a sandwich and some iced tea. Thanks."

"Sarah, you've been so busy with the kids and your work, not to mention planning for this adoption. I think you're overdoing it."

"I know. It's just that we've waited so long for this, and I don't want anything to go wrong. Did you check with your family about the Zoom call?"

"Yup. Everyone is in, even Clayton. I'll put together the list and create the Zoom link. You eat."

The butterflies in Sarah's stomach wouldn't subside. They were only hours away from her legally adopting Noah and Sophia, and Trevor adopting Sophia. Her children were her world, and no one was more surprised about it than Sarah. So, it was understandable that she worried something might go wrong.

But Trevor was right. She couldn't be a good mother if she didn't take care of herself first. She knew it was time for her annual physical, but she put it off in favor of focusing on her new husband and children.

Feeling something wasn't right she'd make an appointment with her doctor as soon as the adoption was done. For now, her children needed all her attention, and she didn't want to miss one minute of celebration worrying about nothing.

CHAPTER TWENTY-TWO

The courtroom didn't look anything like what Sarah had seen on television. Somehow she thought the judge would be sitting high up on an elevated platform while she and her family would stand below. Instead, his desk was small and accessible. Everyone engaged with the judge as if he were sitting in their living room.

"I understand that you wish to video this event for your extended family?"

Trevor did the talking for the family.

"Yes, Your Honor."

"That's fine. Happens all the time. You can set up your laptop at the end of my desk and video from there. We'll begin shortly, so I'll give you a few minutes to get everyone signed in."

Trevor sent the Zoom link to everyone on the list, and one by one, each family member's face appeared on the screen. The judge even waved to the camera which made everyone laugh and feel more relaxed.

Noah stood next to Trevor and Sarah, who held Sophia in her arms.

"Can you raise your right hand please? Do each of you

solemnly swear or affirm that the testimony you are about to give will be the truth, the whole truth, and nothing but the truth, so help you God?"

They responded in unison, "Yes."

Facing Sarah, the court assistant to the judge read from a document and asked her if she was asking the judge to grant the adoption of Noah and Sophia. Sarah responded, "Yes."

"Can you please state the name of your son and daughter?"

"Noah James Hutchins and Sophia Eloise Hutchins."

She turned to Trevor and asked him the same with regards to Sophia.

The judge then spoke. "It is my pleasure to sign and date this adoption."

He looked at Noah and Sophia and spoke, "Welcome to your forever home."

Claps from everyone in the courtroom, as well as cheers from the laptop screen, erupted. Even the bailiff and strangers in the back of the room celebrated the new family.

Happy tears fell from Sarah's eyes and Trevor pulled his new family into a group hug.

Sarah looked at the laptop screen.

"We're going over to Trevor's parents' place for cake and ice cream. Mom, do you, Paolo Chelsea and Chris want to come over?"

Christopher answered before his mother could.

"I wish I could, but I've got an important conference call I've got to take." He blew a kiss into the screen and turned the camera on their mother.

Maggie looked confused, and Sarah sensed that this call was something their mother knew nothing about.

"Paolo, Chelsea, and I will be along shortly. We can't wait to celebrate with you all."

"I've got to clean up the mess I left in the carriage house. Give me a few minutes and we can pick Chelsea up and head over to the Hutchins' place."

Paolo walked toward the back door, leaving Maggie to talk to Christopher.

"Ok. I'll be ready in a few minutes."

Maggie sat back in her chair.

"Chris, you know I've tried to stay out of your business, but do you mind telling me what this conference call is about?"

She was surprised when he didn't hesitate.

"I have a call in to Dr. Jacobs from the VA. I've decided to get a prosthetic device for my leg."

Maggie had prayed for a sign that her son's future lay beyond the walls of the inn, but she worried that day might never come. Making plans for a prosthetic leg was the first step towards his independence, and she could barely contain her excitement.

"That's fantastic, Chris. I remember in the first few weeks when the doctors talked about it. You wanted nothing to do with it, or them."

He put his hand on hers. "Mom, I'm so sorry that I've put you through so much these last months. I couldn't see anything but my own pain and anger. I never thought about how it must have been for you."

"I know, honey. I don't know that I would have done anything different if I were in your place. I'm your mother so I see you as my baby. A mother loses her mind when her child is hurt, and she can't make it better. All I could do was wait."

"No, Mom. You did more than wait. You've supported me my whole life, not just these last few months. If it weren't for you, who knows how I would have turned out. You've been my biggest cheerleader since I was born."

She'd waited for the right time to share her thoughts about his opinion of his father. This seemed the perfect opportunity to shed light on something she'd never talked about before.

"Christopher, I wasn't your only cheerleader. I know you always felt that your father didn't love you. You've not said those words exactly, but that's the impression I've had. Am I wrong?"

"Why are you asking me this now?"

"I want to know. Did you feel that your father loved you?"

"Mom. I've come to believe that I suppose he loved me in his own way. It's just that…"

Maggie finished his thought. "You never felt it because he never showed it?"

Christopher shrugged. "I guess. It's all right now. I'm a grown man. If you're worried that I think I'm angry at Dad or that I struggle with my childhood somehow, forget it. I'm fine. Honest, I'm ok."

Maggie reached for her handbag and pulled out a dark brown leather wallet.

"I've kept this wallet in my bag ever since you came home from Iraq. I was waiting for the right time to show it to you, and only you. I don't want your brothers and sisters to feel upset about it, so if you don't mind, I think this is something we keep only between us."

Maggie handed the wallet to Christopher. He carefully opened it and saw his father's driver's license on the right and several credit cards on the left.

"Dad's wallet."

"When I went to the funeral home, they gave me this. He had it on him when he died."

"Why did you want me to see this?"

"Look under the license."

Christopher wiggled his finger behind the license and pulled out a single photograph.

"It's my military photo."

"There's something else behind that."

Christopher reached inside and found a small piece of paper with crayon letters written on it.

To the best dad in the world. Love Chris

"Your father talked about how proud he was of you all the time. He only carried one photo in his wallet. Not one of his wife or his other children—only a picture of you. He loved you very much, Chris. I know you're all grown up and maybe you don't need to see this. But I think that maybe you do."

Maggie could see she was right. Christopher's eyes were filled with tears. She placed her hand on his face. "Your father wasn't perfect, but never think he didn't love you."

He fell against her and let the tears fall. When he stopped crying, he looked at Maggie. "Thank you for this. Thank you for everything."

Becca had made her decision; the only problem was it would prove to be more challenging than she first thought. Going back to medical school after a three-year absence required that she take the MCAT once again and would have to reapply hoping for admission to Tufts Medical School. Her frustration grew when she learned that the two years she had already devoted to her studies were lost.

She could try for another school that might not have as strict a requirement for entry, but Tufts was the school she had always dreamed of attending. She'd come so far and gone through so much; it wouldn't make sense to give up her dream now. If she'd learned anything from her mother's fearlessness, she wouldn't let anything stop her from achieving her goals.

Taking the MCAT again after all this time would require preparation. She searched her books and notes for anything that would help her. Studying in between her working hours would be difficult. She had no choice but to confide in her father. Hopefully, he'd give her the time she needed to study and let her brothers handle most of the work in the store.

Crawford hovered over the engine of his car when she found him in the garage.

"Hey, Dad. Marilyn giving you trouble?"

Her father named the car Marilyn after Marilyn Monroe because she was, in his opinion, the best actress "back in the day."

Becca figured it had more to do with her legs than her acting, but she never questioned him about it.

"Nope, I'm just checking the oil. What's up?"

"I'm going to go back to school."

Her father came out from under the hood and grabbed the cloth hanging from his belt. Wiping his hands, he smiled. "I think that's great, honey. What made you decide to go back?"

"A lot of things I guess. Gran had a lot to do with it."

"No one else?"

"Why do you ask?"

"Oh, I don't know. I just wondered if anyone else helped you decide?"

She kept her feelings about Christopher to herself, but Becca sensed that her father knew more than he was letting on.

"A number of people have influenced me recently, you included."

"Me? What did I do?"

"You let me be me. You let me take my time to figure out what I wanted to do and never pushed me."

"Well, I'm happy if you're happy. So, what's the next step?"

"I called admissions and talked to someone there. Seems the two years I spent in medical school are lost. Too many years have passed so I've got to start over. That means taking the MCAT again and apply just like I did before."

"Are you disappointed?"

"It's an uphill climb that I wasn't expecting, but it's not so terrible. Those two years weren't wasted. I'm sure what I learned back then will help me get through my studies."

"It'll all come back to you. I'm proud of you, Becca. I've always been proud of you and would continue to be no matter your decision."

"The thing is, Dad, that I'm going to need time to study. I can take the test again in a few weeks, and I've got to do everything I can to pass. It means I won't be able to work in the store as much."

"Don't worry about that. You do what you have to do. Your brothers and I will move the schedule around. We'll be fine."

Becca smiled. "Nice to know you all can get along without me."

Crawford put his hand on Becca's face. "Never."

CHAPTER TWENTY-THREE

Paperwork laid out over the conference table, Beth, Heather, and Alice worked their strategy. A timeline of events on the wall board helped to follow the movements of Tyler, Kaitlin, and their father the night of the murder.

Mitchell Glassman stood at the door.

"Whatever you're working on, you can stop."

Beth turned to look at him.

"What?"

"Andresen hung himself in his cell. I just got the call. They found him this morning. Bed sheet tied to the bars."

Beth sunk into a chair and threw her pen on the table.

"How is that possible? Why wasn't he watched?"

"I don't know. I guess they didn't see him as a possible suicide threat. Do you remember his threat to his kids? He said his plan was to turn the gun on himself after he shot them. We should have caught that. He should have been on suicide watch from the start."

Heather and Alice started to collect the files and untack items off the wall board.

"Listen, the guy won't hurt anyone ever again. It's not the way we wanted to get him, but at least he's gone. And look, I know you're disappointed kiddo, but you'll get your chance to prove what you can do."

Mitchell walked out of the conference room, and Beth felt the sting of his words. No mention of Kaitlin and the trauma she'd been through. Beth didn't care that she'd missed her chance to be a star in the eyes of her peers. What mattered most to her was that Kaitlin was only one child in a million who fall victim to violent abuse every year. Beth was more determined than ever to put the abusers away for life, and she didn't care if she got one minute of attention for it.

Sarah had her blood drawn earlier in the day, and now sat in the waiting room of her doctor's office. She didn't tell Trevor about the appointment because she didn't want to worry him. Everything was finally going so well for them, the last thing they needed was another problem to overcome.

"Ms. Hutchins. Come with me."

Sarah followed the nurse into the doctor's office. Once again, she sat on the medical exam table, and waited. Dr. Phelan was new to Sarah. Since moving to Florida, she'd put off finding a new doctor.

"Ms. Hutchins. Hello, I'm Doctor Phelan. Nice to meet you."

The doctor had a lovely demeanor and made Sarah feel relaxed instantly.

"Nice to meet you as well. Although, not necessarily in this way."

"I understand you've been feeling under the weather. How long?"

"Oh, just the last week. We've had a lot going on in our family and I think I'm just a bit run down. Did you get the results of my blood test?"

"Yes. Of course, since you haven't had a physical in a while, we should schedule you for one before you leave today. As far as I can see from your bloodwork, everything looks fine. There is one thing, however, that could be causing you to feel tired. It seems that you're pregnant."

The doctor smiled when she delivered the news, but her face changed when she saw Sarah's reaction.

Sarah's eyes grew wide. Thinking the doctor was making a joke, she laughed out loud. They were both laughing when the doctor continued, "So, this is good news?"

Sarah stopped laughing. "What? You're not joking?"

"No. No joke. You're really pregnant."

Sarah started to laugh again and then tears began to flow. She must have appeared hysterical because the doctor looked concerned.

"Are you all right? Why don't you take a deep breath and lay back on the table. I'll close the blinds and turn the lights down and we can talk."

Sarah couldn't believe this news. She was pregnant. She was a new mother to a two-year-old and a six-year-old, and now she was going to have another in nine months. When she calmed down and felt better she told the doctor everything that had happened in the last two years. Sarah thought it might be more than the doctor was prepared for. Dr. Phelan wasn't a psychiatrist after all.

"Not to worry. I'm glad you told me what you've been going through. You've had a lot of major changes in such a short amount of time. It's no wonder you feel overwhelmed. How do you think your husband will react to the pregnancy?"

"I don't know. We haven't really talked about growing our family. We've pretty much been enjoying what we have. I guess I'm about to find out when I get home."

"Sarah, I'm more than happy to be your family physician, but we have an excellent OB-GYN group here who you'll need to make an appointment with."

Sarah nodded. "I'll do that on my way out. Thank you for being so understanding and comforting. I think I was just in shock at the news. I need time to just live with this before I talk to Trevor. I'm thinking an ice cream cone and a walk along the beach might be in order."

"You're very welcome, and that sounds wonderful. If I wasn't working, I'd join you. Seriously, I'm here anytime if you need to talk. And, congratulations, Mom, on all your children."

Sarah took her time getting home. She played the words over in her mind, and each time laughed at herself for thinking she could control Trevor's reaction. In the span of one year, their lives had been turned upside down with so many changes it was head-spinning. As a couple they had handled everything thrown at them and grew stronger for it. She had every reason to believe they'd handle this news just the same, as a loving family.

No one was home when she got there, and she decided to follow through with her idea of having an ice cream cone. She went into the kitchen and got out the Cherry Garcia and cones. She made herself a small one and sat out on the porch looking out at the people walking along the beach. She rubbed her belly and talked to her baby.

"Listen, they're going to be home any minute, and I'm going to tell your father all about you. But, before I do that, I might as well tell you a little bit about us. You've got a big brother and a big sister. I have a couple of those myself. They tend to boss you around now and then, but don't ever think that's because they don't like you. They do. As a matter of fact, they love you to pieces. Just like I do."

She thought about this moment in a way she hadn't earlier.

When she left the doctor's office, she wanted time to herself. She needed to get used to the idea.

The pregnancy obviously wasn't planned, and so the news was unbelievable at first. Now, sitting on her porch eating her favorite ice cream, she loved the time alone with her baby. By the time Trevor, Sophia and Noah came through the door, Sarah was deeply in love with her unborn child.

"Hey, Sarah, where are you?"

"Out here on the porch."

Trevor had Sophia in his arms and Noah jumped onto her lap.

"Mommy, can I have some ice cream too."

Sarah looked at Trevor and she tried not to cry. They knew something wonderful had just happened and although Noah probably didn't give it one bit of thought, the fact that he called her mommy changed her life forever.

"You sure can. As a matter of fact, I think we all should have ice cream. It's just one of those ice cream kind of days."

Trevor put Sophia in her pack-n-play and hugged Sarah. "It is a good day, isn't it?"

Sarah laughed to herself.

"You have no idea."

The rest of the afternoon was spent on the beach and when it was dinner time, Sarah went inside and prepared the pasta and meatballs that Trevor requested.

After dinner, Trevor gave Noah a bath and Sarah put Sophia to bed. By eight o'clock, the kids were asleep, and Trevor and Sarah went outside onto the deck to enjoy the night air and some alone time.

Trevor got up from his chair. "I'm going to have some white wine. Would you like one?"

"No. Thanks. Nothing for me."

Sarah hadn't thought much about the physical changes to her body or the things she needed to think about to keep a safe pregnancy. It was the first of many adjustments she'd have to make.

Trevor returned with his wine. "Today was a long one. We had tons of meetings and for a minute I didn't think I'd get out in time to pick up the kids from Ciara's. How was your day?"

Sarah smiled, "Eventful. I finally went to the doctor to see what's been going on with me lately."

"What? Why didn't you tell me? I would have gone with you."

"Normally, I'd disagree. But this time, I would have loved to have you there."

Trevor put his glass down and moved to Sarah's cushioned lounge chair. "Is everything all right? What did the doctor say?"

"Well, she wants to do more tests because it's time for me to get a physical. You know the usual mammogram and annual physical stuff they put you through. This wasn't that kind of appointment. All they did today was take my blood and urine. I spent quite a bit of time with the doctor. I like her. Her name is Dr. Phelan. I think you'd like her too."

"Sarah, you're scaring me. Did they get results from the blood test?"

"Yes. It doesn't look like I'm sick."

"That's great news."

"Yes. I have more great news. At least, I hope you'll think it's great news. I'm pregnant."

For the first time in their relationship, it was Trevor who looked like he might faint.

"Do you want to lie down? Are you ok?"

"Pregnant? As in a baby?"

Sarah laughed. "Um, yup. That's what they're calling them."

"Is it a girl or a boy?"

"Sweetie, I think you're in a bit of shock. It's too soon to know the sex of the baby. Are you happy?"

Trevor was as shocked as Sarah was, but his face lit up when he realized she was waiting for a response.

"Happy? You better believe it. Our baby. You and me."

Sarah nodded. "You and me."

He put his arms around her, pulled her close, and then kissed her. Their family had grown with this new child, and Sarah smiled, thinking that she didn't pursue any of it. Her family was a gift, one she'd hold close to her heart forever.

CHAPTER TWENTY-FOUR

As much as Becca enjoyed her time working at the Key Lime Garden Inn, she knew it was time to leave. There was too much tension between her and Christopher. Maybe she could fool him once that she felt only friendship toward him, but she'd never be able to keep up the pretense. Besides, getting back to Tufts was her main focus and she didn't need any distractions.

So far this morning, she hadn't crossed paths with him. As soon as her work was done, she looked for Maggie. Waving to Paolo, she walked into the garden.

"Hey, Paolo, I'm looking for Maggie. Is she around?"

"She's upstairs in the carriage house. Go on up."

"Really?"

"Of course. It's not off limits you know."

Becca laughed. "Sorry, I've just never been up there. Thanks, Paolo."

Becca climbed the stairs leading up to the second floor of the carriage house. She called out before entering the large great room.

"Hello? Maggie?"

"Becca. Come on in."

"I'm sorry to bother you like this, but I need to talk to you about something."

"Don't be silly. You can come up here any time you like. Is everything all right? How is your family doing since Lillian passed?"

"We're all doing fine. Thank you for asking."

Becca felt guilty for what she was about to say, but there was no turning back now.

"Maggie, I'm afraid I'm going to have to quit working here."

"Oh, I'm so sorry to hear that. Is there a problem?"

"No. Not at all. I've loved working here. It's just that I've decided to go back to Boston. I'm not exactly sure when, but most likely at the end of summer. I know that's several months away, but I've got to prepare to take the MCAT. I'm going to go back to medical school."

Maggie seemed as excited as she was. "This is fantastic news. I'm so happy for you. Your father must be thrilled."

Becca nodded.

"He is. I told him the same thing I'm telling you. My brothers are going to run the place and I don't have to work unless it's an emergency. I guess I could say the same for the inn. If you have an emergency and you really need me, just call my cell. I'm thinking of going up to Boston at some point to find a place to live, but I'll still be on the island here and there."

Maggie hugged her. "Have you told Christopher?"

Becca was surprised she asked her that. She didn't want to be rude, so she kept her answer vague.

"No. I've not told anyone but you and my father."

"Well, I guess I can tell him for you if you want."

"No!"

Becca hated that she sounded so desperate, but she wasn't sure how she'd tell Christopher and needed time to think.

"I'm sorry, Maggie. I didn't mean to be so abrupt. I'll tell him when I see him next."

Maggie walked to the window and looked down at the inn's porch.

"I'd say you have your opportunity right now. There he is."

Becca stood next to Maggie and saw Christopher on the porch reading a book.

Why exactly Maggie thought Becca needed to tell her son she didn't know, but the more Becca resisted going anywhere near Christopher, the more suspicion she would draw. She had no choice but to tell him.

"Good luck, Becca. I know everything will work out exactly as it should."

Becca nodded and smiled at Maggie. "Thank you. I hope so."

Walking across the driveway Becca took a deep breath and ignored the tightness in her stomach. In that moment she realized that this might be the last time she'd walk up these stairs.

"Hey, Chris. How's the book?"

"I'm still trying to decide, actually. Check with me in a few days and I'll let you know."

A few days. In a few days she'd be deep in the study of anatomy.

"Becca, before you say anything I wanted to tell you how sorry I was to hear of your great-grandmother's passing. I understand she was well loved by everyone on the island."

She smiled. "Thank you. She was a very important person in my life. I'm sorry you never got to meet her."

After a long silence, he changed the subject.

"I see you've been visiting my mother."

"Yes. The carriage house turned out really nice. I'd never been up there before."

She leaned against the railing trying to find the right words.

"I told your mother that I had to quit working here."

He closed the book and placed it on his lap.

"Why would you do that?"

"I've decided to go back to medical school. I've got to take the MCAT again and I've lots of studying before that. I've even cut out my work at the store. If I don't put all my effort into studying, I'll never pass. It's been three years. I know this is going to be difficult but…"

Christopher stopped her.

"Do you remember how inseparable we were when we were kids?"

There wasn't anything about their past that she didn't remember, right down to the way he chewed his bubble gum.

She smiled and nodded. "I remember."

"I used to wait for you when you were helping out in the store. You'd come running down to the beach and into my arms, and we'd fall on the sand. I laughed so hard my stomach hurt."

She suddenly felt sad and wished they were back ten years ago, secure in their innocence without a care in the world.

"It looks like the planets aligned at just the right time so that you and I could cross paths on Captiva these last few months. I have to believe we'll see each other again. No matter what, I am happy you're going back to school. I'm going to miss you though."

"Are you?"

"We all will, Becca."

They stayed like that for what seemed like an eternity. There wasn't anything more to say, and so, she bent down and kissed his cheek.

"I'll miss you too."

She didn't wait for him to say anything else. Instead, she ran down the stairs, grabbed her bike and sped off, leaving the Key Lime Garden Inn behind her.

"You're an idiot."

Christopher looked up as his mother came up onto the porch. She sat on the swing and stared at her son.

"I'm sorry, are you the same woman who's been telling me how wonderful I am?"

"That was yesterday. Today, you're an idiot."

"Do you mind explaining that to me? What are you so upset about?"

"Becca Powell, that's what. There isn't one person around here who doesn't know that you and Becca are in love."

"What? That's ridiculous. I care very much about Becca, but we're just friends. It sounds to me like the island gossips are still going strong."

Maggie moved off the swing and pulled up a chair close to him.

"I've told you before that you can't lie to me. I know you're in love with her. What I don't know is why you refuse to tell her. That girl is going to go back to Boston and who knows where she'll end up doing her residency. You may not get another chance."

"I can't."

"Why Chris? Tell me why?"

"I don't want her treating me like a patient. You don't understand what it's like sitting in this chair. Sure, I'll make the best of it and do what I have to do to carve out some sort of life for myself, but I'm not going to drag her into it. She's about to start her life. I want her to have the best chance for success. Being tied to me will make that much harder."

Maggie sat back in her chair and looked out over the garden.

"Maybe I don't know what it's like to be sitting in a wheelchair or to have my leg cut off. But I know what love is. I know that it's staying up all night for days listening to your child's cough and praying that he doesn't stop breathing. I know what it's like to take care of someone you love. I also know that if the roles were reversed and Becca was in that chair instead of you, that you'd do everything you could to love her through it. Don't tell me that you don't know what love is, because I've watched you talk about your love of country, and of your fellow soldiers. I know what you are capable of. I know my son."

He tried to keep his voice steady, "Let me do this my way, please. I love you for caring, but I know what I'm doing."

There wasn't anything more Maggie could say or do. She had to give up and let him live his life the way she'd done for all her children.

"Ok. I won't bring this up again. But promise me you'll think about what I've said?"

He didn't say a word but nodded his head.

She walked into the house and let him sit with his thoughts. She knew that he hadn't made this choice lightly. In fact, she was certain that every night when he shut the door to his room, he thought about Becca Powell and what it meant to let her go.

Chelsea answered her cell phone.

"Hey, what's going on?"

"Do you feel like a walk on the beach?"

"Can we get a drink with an umbrella in it after?"

"At least one."

"I'm in. I'll see you on the beach in ten minutes."

Maggie grabbed her sweater and walked out the front door to avoid another confrontation with Christopher. Chelsea met her just outside the inn's property line.

"Hey there. This isn't your usual walk on the beach time. Something must be on your mind."

"Chelsea, I promise you I do not regret having children, but there are days..."

"Uh-oh. Which one is it this time?"

"Guess."

"Must be Chris. He's been a handful for the last few months. I'm guessing he's got you riled up again?"

"You know Becca Powell, right?"

"Yeah, the young woman who's been working at your place. Her family owns Powell's Water Sports."

"Did you know that Christopher and Becca are in love with each other?"

"No. Really? That is so cool. I knew that boy had it in him. He does remind me of my Sebastian. I think Chris is a romantic at heart. He always feels things so deeply. I remember one time he and I were talking about…"

"Chelsea. Focus. I need to talk about this."

"Oh, sorry. Can we skip the walk and go straight to the Straw Hut? I really want a Piña Colada."

"Fine. We can talk when we get there."

Chelsea walked so fast; Maggie was out of breath by the time they found stools at the bar.

"You know, Maggie. I think you're not getting enough cardio. You shouldn't be out of breath like that."

Maggie couldn't do much talking, and it didn't matter anyway. She couldn't get a word in.

"Sebastian and I come to this place all the time. You've got to get the Piña Colada. Things are going really well with us. I never imagined that his kids would accept me, but they have. It's not like we're super close and go shopping or anything, but at least they're not actively trying to sabotage our relationship. Anyway, you wanted to talk about Christopher, right?"

Maggie reached for her drink and took a sip before continuing.

"You're right, these are delicious. Yes, Chris won't tell Becca that he's in love with her and she's about to go off to medical school without knowing. At least I think she doesn't know."

"What's his problem?"

"He doesn't want her to become his caretaker."

"Oh, for heaven's sake. Why? Is he planning on being an invalid?"

"That's just it, isn't it? Even though he plans to have a prosthetic device made for his leg, he still can't see himself as a complete human being. I hate that he thinks he's 'less than' everyone else."

"He needs more than a prosthetic leg, Maggie. He needs to talk to a professional. I've said that to you before. No fake leg is going to fix what ails that boy. Trust me on this."

Maggie knew Chelsea was right. Christopher had made progress, but he was a long way from being whole. How to mend what was broken was something beyond her capabilities. If loving him wasn't enough, she had no idea what the next step was. Not even Becca could help her son, and that frightened her more than anything.

CHAPTER TWENTY-FIVE

The next few weeks were filled with doctor's appointments and physical therapy. Getting a prosthetic device wasn't a certainty for Christopher. He needed mobility training to determine range of motion and he was frustrated with the constant reminder that discontinuing inpatient rehabilitation care month earlier had been a mistake.

There was a prosthetic lab in Cape Coral which made it easier to get to his appointments. Although he expected a physical evaluation, he never anticipated a mental one. It felt good to talk to someone about what he'd been through. The experience encouraged him to continue with therapy, and he promised himself not to hold anything back in those meetings.

After several appointments with the prosthetist, his functional level was determined to be K4 which made him an excellent candidate to begin his prosthetic fittings. He loved his doctor and felt confident that his life was about to change significantly. What he loved most about Dr. Hensley was that he never talked down to Christopher and had a can-do attitude.

"How long do you think it will be before I'm able to have

some fun with my sister's kids? She's got a six-year-old that can't wait for me to get on two feet."

"I'm afraid we're talking months. There's plenty of shrinking and forming of your limb before we can start the next step. You've got a way to go with the physical and occupational therapists. Can I ask you what your plans are?"

"What do you mean?"

"It's important to think beyond getting the prosthetic device. What does your life look like two years from now?"

Christopher shrugged. "I don't know, Doc. I hadn't thought that far."

He smiled, "I thought so. I understand your family is from Massachusetts."

"Yes, Andover. My mother moved to Captiva almost two years ago now."

"Are you planning on staying in Florida or will you be moving back north?"

He thought about Becca and her plans to move to Boston soon. "I'm not sure. There's a girl…"

The doctor smiled. "There always is. Is she here in Florida?"

"She lives on Captiva but is going back to Boston soon. She's going to Tufts Medical School."

The doctor took his glasses off and leaned against the cabinet.

"Good school. Listen, Christopher, I don't know if you plan to follow this girl, but if you do, there's an organization up there that's doing amazing work. I've got the paperwork around here somewhere."

He rummaged through the files on his desk and found what he was looking for.

"Here it is. Summit Dreams. They connect pediatric cancer patients and their families with vets who've had limb amputation. I go up to visit them occasionally. Check out these photos. I love the kids climbing the rock wall. The folks up there have found a way to give these children the motivation to push through and fight. It benefits the vets as well because they're making a real difference in these kids' lives. Just something to think about."

Christopher looked through the information and wondered whether he could see himself working there. It had been a long time since he felt that he could inspire anyone. He looked at the doctor who was busy on his computer.

"I bet I'm a long way from being able to do something like this, huh?"

"If you think a few months is a long time then you'd be right."

"A few months? I'd love to be walking by Christmas, but that's seven months away."

"How does four to six months sound?"

Christopher smiled and nodded his head. Feeling empowered he asked one more question.

"Any chance I can get a prosthetic blade? I think I'd like to run the Boston Marathon next year."

Beth's hours at work picked up after the Andresen case, but she was no more than a glorified gofer. Her frustration building, she wondered if taking this job had been the right decision. There were plenty of ways to be of service to the community. Working for the Assistant District Attorney wasn't all she thought it would be.

She last envisioned herself as a trial lawyer over a month ago. There were moments since when she'd walk into an empty courtroom and sit imagining herself at the front of the room making her closing argument. She loved everything about the law, but she didn't want to wait years before getting another opportunity to prove herself.

Several of the friends that had graduated with her were now

working in prestigious law firms. A high-paying corporate law firm had never been attractive to Beth, however, lately, she wondered if she'd made a mistake. No matter the struggles to get to the top, at least the money made every step along the ladder, a profitable one.

Beth looked at her watch.

"Oh, man. I'm going to be late."

She promised Lauren that she'd stop by and have dinner with her and Jeff one night when the girls were sleeping over at friends. Lauren said that she needed adult conversation, but Beth felt there was more to it than what she was willing to say over the phone.

Unfortunately, twice before she'd promised Lauren that she'd join them, and both times she had to cancel at the last minute. Beth called Lauren's phone as she ran to the elevator.

Lauren answered and sighed.

"Don't tell me. You're cancelling again."

"Nope. I'm not. I'm just running late. I should be there in forty-five minutes."

"I'll believe that when you walk through the door."

"Very funny. I'm on my way."

Before Beth reached Lauren's front door, she could hear voices coming from inside. When she rang the doorbell, the talking stopped, and Lauren answered the door.

"What's with the locked door? I don't think I've ever had to ring the doorbell before."

Beth hugged Lauren and carried two bottles of wine to the kitchen where Jeff was leaning up against the sink.

"Hey, Jeff. I brought one red and one white."

He reached for the corkscrew and began to open the bottle of Pinot Noir without so much as a hello. The tension in the room was palpable and she wondered if the reason for the dinner invite was more of a referee operation.

Lauren came into the kitchen and held out her glass.

"I've been looking forward to this for a while. I miss my little sister. How's work?"

"Work? You mean that place I go every day to feel small and insignificant?"

"Whoa. I think I regret asking."

"I'm sorry, I shouldn't complain. I sound like a whiney spoiled child, but isn't my big sister's shoulder the right place to cry? You always know how to make me feel better. So, make me feel better."

Jeff's body language was hard to ignore.

"Your sister has all the time in the world to help you. She's good at being there for everyone. Well, not everyone."

He gulped his wine and poured another.

Beth felt uncomfortable and looked at him and then Lauren.

"I'm sorry guys, but is something going on? Why do I feel like I've just stepped into a boxing ring?"

It was Jeff who didn't hold back. He finished his wine, walked to the front door, and took his coat off the rack.

"I think the two of you need time alone. If you don't mind, I'll sit this one out."

He started the car and sped out onto the street.

"Should he be driving?"

Lauren shrugged. "Probably not, and not because he's drunk, because I don't think he is. He's probably more sober than I am, but he's angry, and no one who's angry should be driving."

"What is he angry about?"

"He's angry at me for everything these days, but specifically, he's upset that my job is consuming so much of my time. He doesn't understand that I'm working so hard for him and the girls. I mean, what does he think I'm doing every day-having a party? Starting a real estate business takes work and time to get established. He knew that when we agreed he'd be a stay-at-home dad."

Beth put her arm around Lauren.

"I don't think either of you realized at the time that this would be harder than you imagined."

"It's awful for everyone involved. I try to be home to see him and the girls, but sometimes it's not possible."

Beth laughed. "You're talking to me about working long hours? I get it. Gabriel's been a sweetheart about it all, but I know sometimes he's disappointed when I have to cancel. It's not easy. Have you tried a marriage counselor?"

"We're seeing someone now but spend most of the time blaming each other for our problems instead of trying to fix what's not working."

"How about a weekly date night? Gabriel and I make sure we have one night a week where we don't let anything get in the way of our time together. There have been moments when we've had to miss a date, but most of the time we make it happen. We don't have children so it's easier. Speaking of the girls, how are they handling this? They must sense something isn't right."

Lauren nodded. "We try not to have these disagreements around the girls, but the tension is still there. If we don't get our act together soon, I'm worried where this all will lead."

"Are you talking about divorce?"

Lauren didn't answer Beth but instead, sipped her wine, and looked down at the kitchen island.

"Come on, Lauren. You can't let that happen. You guys have to do everything you can to work things out. I know you both still love each other."

Lauren's inability to say more worried Beth.

"There isn't anyone else in the picture is there? I mean, neither of you are seeing someone else, right?"

Lauren took a deep breath and answered her. "I can only speak for myself, and the answer is absolutely not. I love Jeff but

I'm not sure he still feels the same way about me. I have a feeling that he's been crying on Cynthia Frawley's shoulder these days."

Beth's eyes grew wide. "Who is Cynthia Frawley?"

"She's a divorcee and mother of one of Olivia's friends. You should see the way she dresses. Tight clothes and exposing cleavage every time we run into her. You should see the way she flirts with Jeff. The way she dresses, I don't think there's a man in town who doesn't look at her."

"Lauren, looking isn't the same as doing. There's no crime in that."

"I know that, but how do I compete with her? Jeff's a new stay-at-home dad and there are plenty of women in town who'd love to help the clueless father of two girls. You should see how Christy Michaels ran to Jeff when Olivia wanted her hair in a French braid. Christy was all too willing to teach Jeff how to do it. And don't get me started on Jillian Krensky."

"What's the deal with Jillian?"

"She actually told Jeff that she'd come over and walk him through cutting coupons if he needed help. I mean, for heaven's sake does she really think my husband doesn't know how to handle scissors?"

Beth tried not to laugh. As ridiculous as these complaints sounded, Lauren was seriously worried about losing her husband. She couldn't see Jeff falling into the arms of any of these desperate women, but Lauren could, and that was all that mattered.

Panicked, Lauren ran to the oven.

"Oh, thank goodness it didn't burn. Looks like the roast chicken is done. I guess it's going to be just the two of us for dinner. I'm sorry this night isn't turning out the way you planned, but I'm still glad to see you. Is work really that terrible?"

"It's not terrible, my attitude is what's terrible. I'm in a funk and I've got to find my way out of it."

"That doesn't sound like my Bethy."

"I've been wracking my brain trying to understand what my problem is, and all I can come up with is that I've lost confidence."

"Confidence at work?"

"Confidence at everything."

Lauren carved the chicken and put the sliced meat on a platter.

"Do you think Dad has anything to do with this?"

"Dad? What do you mean?"

"Well, you and I both know how accomplished he was, not to mention, ambitious. I often think the three of us girls inherited those same qualities. I don't think anyone is as hard on us as we are on ourselves. Sarah has made peace with it. I'm still a work in progress, and I think you are too. Maybe that's your problem."

Beth never made the connection to her father's ambition because it was always tied to money, and she didn't care a bit about that. It didn't occur to her that ambition came in many forms, and her competitive spirit, although the strength she had relied upon thus far, might be the driving factor in her disappointments. She'd set the bar so high for herself that it was near impossible to reach.

"You know, Lauren. Every time I think about Dad I'm always reminded that he's still here with us."

"I believe that, but why do you?"

"Because we have mirrors. I'm reminded of him every time I look at myself."

Lauren put her knife down and reached for her wine.

"I'll drink to that. To Dad."

"To Dad."

CHAPTER TWENTY-SIX

*P*assing the MCAT was much easier than Becca thought it would be. She reapplied to Tufts and was waiting for an answer on whether she got in. The waiting was hard, so she focused on helping out at the store.

She'd occasionally receive a text from Christopher, but they were always the same.

"Wishing you good luck on the MCAT." "Hope you get into Tufts." "It's been quiet around here without you, but I'm getting much more reading done."

If it wouldn't look like she was mad at him, she'd block his cell phone number. As it was she often deleted the text before opening it. Once she finally acknowledged her feelings for him, she had no interest in being Christopher Wheeler's BFF.

As she checked on the store's inventory, her brothers came out back to join her. Surrounding her, she knew something was up.

"Hey, Becca, I know it's last minute, but Kat can't make it tonight for the cruise. I know we said you didn't have to do the boat, but we really need you tonight."

"What was Kat's reason this time?"

"She's not feeling well. I think she's got an ear infection which makes going out on the water a problem."

Becca nodded. "Fine. I'll do it."

Joshua hugged her. "You're the best." Looking over at Luke and Finn. "What did I tell you? Isn't our sister the best ever?"

Becca threw a towel at them and, laughing, chased them out to the front of the store. "Get out of here. You guys are such losers."

Waving at Becca, Maggie Wheeler came through the front door of the store.

"Hi Becca."

"Maggie. It's good to see you. You don't usually shop in here, so I have to assume you've come to see me?"

Maggie nodded. "You're right, although I could probably use a few new floats for the pool."

Becca smiled at Maggie's attempt at pretense.

"How have you been?"

"I'm doing well, thanks. I passed the MCATs."

"That's great. What's next?"

"Just waiting for Tufts admissions to tell me if I'm in or not. I should hear any day."

"Oh, you'll get in. I have no doubt. Becca, I don't want to take up too much of your time, but I wanted to talk to you about Christopher."

Becca wasn't surprised by her comment. She knew almost the minute Maggie walked into the store why she came to see her.

"I hope you'll forgive me for sticking my nose in where it probably doesn't belong, but I know how the two of you feel about each other."

"How we feel about each other? I'm sorry, but I don't understand."

"I know you love him."

Becca felt uncomfortable talking to Christopher's mother

about her feelings. She'd never said a word to Maggie or anyone else for that matter, but somehow she knew.

"How I feel about your son doesn't have any bearing on my future. We're friends and that's all we are."

"My son is in love with you."

"And you know this, how? Did he tell you that?"

"He doesn't need to."

"I see. Maggie, I appreciate what you're trying to do, but honestly, Chris has had plenty of opportunity to tell me himself. The only thing he's said to me is that we are good friends. I can live with that. We're on different paths anyway. What good would it do to start something we can't finish?"

Maggie came closer to Becca and put her hand on Becca's arm.

"I know you're going back to Boston soon. You have a promising future ahead of you. The only reason my son hasn't told you how he truly feels about you, is because he doesn't want to slow you down. He doesn't want to be a burden to you."

"Did he say those exact words to you?"

Maggie nodded. "All I'm asking is that you don't give up on him…please."

Becca was stunned. Maggie hugged her and then walked out of the store, leaving Becca unsteady on her feet.

How could Chris think he'd be a burden to me?

She didn't know what to do. She was certain that Chris didn't know about his mother's visit to the store. She knew that confronting him about his true feelings would only force him into something he wasn't ready for. If they had a future, he'd have to come to terms with his need for her. The one thing she would do was to fulfill Maggie's wish that she wouldn't give up on him.

Her brother Finn called out to her from outside.

"We're heading down to the dock. Can you help get the food and drink into the kitchen?"

"I'll be right there."

She ran to the boat and helped carry several boxes on board. Stocking the shelves, she moved as quickly as she could before the passengers arrived.

Once everyone was seated and she made the safety announcements, she gave her brother Joshua a thumbs up to push off.

She'd pretended to be upset that she had to help out with the sunset cruise. The truth was that nothing made her happier than to be out on the water. For Becca, watching the shores of Captiva Island as they pulled away from the dock, was far better than any sunset. It was her home. Knowing how much she would miss it once away at school, tugged at her heart. She wiped the tear that fell and turned her face into the wind, and to the ocean ahead.

Maggie crossed her legs on the blanket and waited for Paolo to join her. Carrying a bottle of white wine in an ice bucket, along with two glasses and a sweater under his arm made her feel guilty that she hadn't helped him carry the items down to the water.

"I'm a bad wife."

"Well, you're a gorgeously, beautiful bad wife."

"OK. I'll take that."

"Looks like a lovely sunset tonight."

She looked at Paolo and smiled. "Do you realize how lucky we are to have this little stretch of beach to ourselves?"

"I know. This way, we get the wine all to ourselves."

"Oh, you. That's not what I meant."

"I know. We are truly blessed, my love. Here, let's toast to our good fortune."

They clinked their glasses and tasted their wine. She leaned against Paolo, staying quiet in his arms. The first year on Captiva, Maggie saw the pace of her life slow down, and she felt happy and at peace. The last few months had brought so much change, she had a hard time keeping up.

"Do you ever feel like life is just spinning so much that you lose your balance and have to hold on tight?"

Paolo smiled. "Only every day."

"I'm serious. Everything is moving too fast."

"Maybe you're just feeling old. I have those moments. Half the time I don't have a clue what younger people are saying. It's like they're speaking a language I can't understand. For instance, Ciara told me the other day that she's thinking of becoming a Death Doula. I didn't know what she was talking about, so I asked her."

"And?"

"It's a new career. A Death Doula helps you die."

"Helps you? As in assisted death?"

"No. No. Nothing like that. It's like what a mid-wife does only in reverse."

"What in the world?"

"Ok, maybe I'm not saying this right."

"You think?"

"They stay with you and comfort you as you pass away. She said ever since Sharon died, she's been thinking about doing it. It's something she'd do part-time. I guess Sharon's death really had an impact on her."

"It's not the same thing as Hospice?"

"I don't think so."

They didn't say anything for a few minutes until Maggie spoke.

"Anyway, what does this have to do with what I was talking about?"

Paolo thought for a moment and scratched his head.

"You know, I'm not sure."

"Let's just enjoy the sunset and stop trying to make sense of things."

"Sounds like a good idea to me."

The alarm went off at exactly six o'clock, but it didn't matter. Becca turned it off and rolled over pulling the covers over her head. For the first time in weeks, she had no desire to go for her morning run. A fitful night, she couldn't stop thinking about what Maggie had told her.

All through the sunset cruise she watched couples in love cuddle up against each other and she wondered why she'd subjected herself to such torture. She imagined herself in Chris's arms, and she touched her lips, remembering his kiss.

His mother presented her with new information. *What if she was right? What if Chris was in love with her? Would it change anything?*

Soon, the letter from Tufts would arrive and she'd begin making plans to find an apartment in Boston. Thinking about Chris could only make her question her decision.

She got out of bed and went to the kitchen, hoping her energy would return. She made a pot of coffee and sat at the kitchen table waiting for it to brew. Her father never slept past seven o'clock, and so she decided to make scrambled eggs for everyone. Finn still lived at home, but Joshua and Luke shared a house on the island. Most mornings they had breakfast together before heading next door to the store.

Becca loved the quiet just before everyone came looking for food. It was her one chance to listen to the birds and the ocean waves in the far-off distance. As soon as she splashed water on her face and brushed her teeth, she'd greet the morning this time by staying close to home.

"Hey, sweetie," her dad whispered. "That smell of the coffee reached all the way upstairs into my room and under my nose."

He gave her a quick hug and poured himself a cup of coffee.

"No running this morning?"

"My bathrobe gave me away. I didn't sleep very well last night."

"Waiting for the acceptance letter probably is what's keeping you awake."

Becca nodded. Talking about Chris would only make things worse. "I'm sure that's it."

"You know, Becca, if there's anything you want to talk about, I'm here for you."

She usually loved how her father could read her mind. This time, she didn't know how to respond to him. Not once did she tell her father about her feelings for Chris, and yet, she felt certain that he knew anyway.

"I know that Dad."

She turned back to the stove. "Let me get your eggs. The toast should be ready in a minute."

"He came to see me."

"Who?"

"Your young man, Christopher Wheeler."

Her mind spinning, she buttered his toast.

"He wanted me to convince you to go back to medical school. I guess the two of you had a fight and you both said some things about hiding out on Captiva because you were scared to move on with your life. Do you think he was right?"

Becca sat in the chair across from her father. As much as she didn't want to talk about this, she needed to, especially before her brothers descended upon them.

"Yes. He was, and I told him so. We apologized to each other and that was that."

"Is he the reason you decided to reapply to school?"

"Dad, I told you before, there were many converging reasons. Gran, you, Chris, and even Mom. I had a lot of thinking to do and remembered how much I've wanted to be a doctor my whole life. Why would I give up something that meant so much to me?

Mom and I talked about it, and she encouraged me to live my dream no matter what was happening at home."

"She knew she was dying."

Becca nodded. "Yes, and her only thought was for me and the rest of her family. I think she wanted to know that everyone was happy and on their chosen path. I got sidetracked for a bit, but that's ok because I needed the time to understand who I am and what I want."

"And Christopher Wheeler doesn't factor into that? That boy loves you, you do know that, right?"

Becca's anger started to show, and she wanted her father to know how strongly she felt about the situation.

"Did Chris tell you that he was in love with me?"

"No. Not in so many words."

"It's interesting, that's pretty much what his mother told me yesterday."

"When?"

"She came into the store to tell me that she was certain that Chris was in love with me and asked me not to give up on him."

"What did you tell her?"

"I didn't promise her anything because the truth is that everyone keeps telling me that he's in love with me…everyone but Chris."

She reached across the table and took her father's hand in hers. "Dad, you haven't asked me if I'm in love with Chris."

He smiled. "I don't have to. I already know the answer."

"Then, understand this. If Chris and I have a future, then he's going to have to come to me when he's ready. I want him to need me more than anything or anyone. He can't do that right now because he has to focus on getting better. Not just his leg, but his mind and his heart. When he can finally heal and let me in, I promise you, I'll be waiting."

Just then, Joshua came into the kitchen.

"Morning guys. Breakfast ready?"

Becca got up from the table and continued getting breakfast ready for her brothers. Finn and Luke joined them, and for once, Becca was grateful for her brothers' interruption. She hadn't intended it but was glad that her father now knew how she felt about Chris. For so long she'd kept her thoughts to herself, Now, even though talking about it wouldn't change a thing, her father's support would help her get through whatever she had to face in the coming weeks.

CHAPTER TWENTY-SEVEN

Beth watched the mulch drop out of the truck and onto the driveway. She'd already been up for hours pulling weeds and cutting back the fruit trees, and now, with this delivery, she'd be able to put the finishing touches on the front yard. Forsythia, tulips, and lilac bushes had already gone by, and the business of garden tending was in full swing.

She couldn't be certain but thought the woodchuck had already poked his head out of the ground just beyond the fence. Soon, the two of them would become friends once again. She was glad for his company as she needed someone to talk to who wouldn't talk back.

The delivery man closed his truck and waited for the hydraulics to lower the bed in place.

"That should do it. I'm off to pick up another order for this neighborhood. Did you know the people in Andover make up the majority of our deliveries?"

Not wanting to insult him, she had to state the obvious.

"Well, your company is the only one in town."

"Good point. Have a nice day."

He got back in his truck and backed out of the driveway.

As the truck was leaving, Gabriel's truck arrived.

"Hey, I didn't know you were coming down."

"I thought I'd take the day off and surprise my girl. I see you've been working in the garden."

He wiped the dirt smudge off her face and planted a kiss on her lips.

"You want some iced tea? I made a pitcher this morning. I even put mint leaves from the greenhouse in it."

"Sounds delicious."

They walked into the house, and Beth pulled off her garden gloves.

"This must be the first Saturday in months that you haven't been working in the shop. And a surprise visit to boot. What gives?"

Gabriel looked like he was stalling. Taking a few sips of his tea, he shrugged.

"I just wanted to see you. Is that such a crime?"

"No."

She knew there was something on his mind, and she also knew that Gabriel's method for addressing the elephant in the room required slow, deliberate thinking.

"I'm a little worried about you."

Beth looked at him and smirked. "You're joking, right?"

He shook his head. "No. I'm not. Something's going on with you and since you're not talking to me about it, I thought one of us should bring it up."

"What's to talk about? So, I'm feeling a little out of sorts. I don't need to examine it."

"Beth…"

She stopped what she was doing long enough to face him and be serious. "Welcome to the Wheeler family where we avoid confrontation at every opportunity. In Florida, we call that sticking our heads in the sand. Up here in Massachusetts, it's dirt. Pass me that bag of soil please."

He carried the bag into the greenhouse, and she couldn't ignore the fact that she was running out of excuses for her behavior. He stopped her before she reached for the spade.

"This isn't funny. I'm really worried. Talk to me."

His sincere request melted her resolve and she walked toward him and planted her head in his chest. He wrapped his arms around her and waited for her to speak.

"For the first time in my life, I'm afraid that I'm not good enough. That's never happened before."

He took her arm and walked her to the sofa.

"At some point in every person's life, we all feel the same way. Doubt has a way of keeping you down and afraid. Everyone goes through it."

She shook her head. "Not me."

"What do you mean, 'not you?'"

"What I said. I've never been afraid of anything. I mean, sure there have been times when I knew I needed to think things through and take my time before jumping in. In general, though, I can't think of a single time when I thought I couldn't do something."

Gabriel seemed skeptical, so she explained.

"For example, one year when we were vacationing on Captiva, we stayed at this hotel/motel kind of place. It had a pool. I was eight years old. I sat by the side of the pool and watched everyone dive in from the diving board. I mean some of these people were doing really cool swan-like diving. I wanted to do the same thing, so I watched them for about fifteen minutes, and then I marched up onto the diving board and lifted my arms to the front, pointing my fingers straight ahead. I did one bounce on the diving board and then dove right in, headfirst."

"Yeah, ok. So, you're a quick study. Nothing wrong with that."

"Right, except I couldn't swim. I'd never had a lesson. No one had taught me what to do so it never occurred to me that I might drown."

"Seriously? What happened?"

"After coming up to the surface a few times and consuming several gulps of water, not to mention my yelling for help, someone jumped in and pulled me out of the water. Everyone said my dive was really awesome and I looked so professional. They just assumed I was a really good swimmer."

"Beth. That's crazy. What would make you do such a thing?"

She smiled and shrugged.

"Because I thought I could do anything I set my mind to. All the skill I thought I needed to dive into the water like everyone else, was the desire and determination to show off. I'm a master at that. I've been showing off my whole life…and now I'm drowning."

He went to hold her, but she got up from the sofa so quickly, he couldn't reach her. She started for the front door.

"So, are you coming?"

"Where?"

"To help me spread this mulch. If you've come all this way to make my day better, then I suggest you get a shovel."

The first time Becca received her acceptance letter from Tufts Medical School, the celebration with her family turned into a major party, with decorations and a cake. This time she didn't expect or even want any fanfare. The unopened envelope in her hands had the power to change her life forever, and because of that, she stood frozen, unable to look inside.

Her father leaned against the kitchen sink and waited for Becca to make a move.

"It won't open itself you know."

Becca smiled at her father and nodded.

"Here goes."

Her hands shook and she had to sit for fear of passing out from the stress.

She opened the letter and read aloud.

"Dear Rebecca Powell, Congratulations! It is my honor and distinct pleasure to inform you that the Committee on Admissions has accepted you for admission to the traditional M.D. program/regular track at Tufts University School of Medicine for the class of 2024.

She couldn't help but cry if for no other reason than to relieve the tension from her body. She ran to her father and fell into his arms.

"Dad, I did it. I can't believe this. I really did it."

"Congratulations sweetheart. I knew you'd get in. We've got to celebrate. How about I get us some champagne and maybe your favorite take-out from the Mexican restaurant? We need to toast to this good news. I'll go tell your brothers and be back in a bit."

Becca nodded and quietly read the letter again. She wiped the tears from her cheeks and ran to the garage. Opening the box of Gran's belongings, she searched for the photo. She found it and then closed the box.

She ran to her room and closed the door. Placing the photo next to her bed, she ran her fingers over the image. She knew who was responsible for her success and wanted to celebrate with the three most important women in her life.

Her mother, grandmother, and precious Gran gave her the courage to be the best version of herself. Without them, she'd never have the strength and hope to see a better future. This was only the beginning. She'd take this photo of them with her to Boston and it would always serve as a reminder of where she came from.

~

From the moment Becca received her acceptance to Tufts Medical School, she went into overdrive to get everything done before leaving for orientation in mid-July. The building that she lived in before had a studio apartment available, and she wasted no time in signing the lease.

When the day finally came to leave Captiva, her excitement was replaced by an overwhelming sadness. It wasn't her first time living in another state, but this time it hurt knowing that she'd be leaving more than her family behind.

There were several things to buy for her apartment, but since it was already furnished, she had little furniture to purchase. A new bed was a must, so it was one of the first things to do on her list.

Her father put her luggage in the car, as Finn, Joshua and Luke stood on the sidewalk ready to see her off.

"What am I going to do without you guys irritating me every day?"

"We can always fly up and visit if you need us to bother you."

"Very funny. Maybe come up for a visit anyway. Leave the attitude down here."

She got into the car, and as her father pulled away from the curb, she stuck her arm out the window and waved goodbye.

They drove to the airport in silence, and it wasn't until they were almost at the JetBlue terminal when her father spoke.

"Do you remember how you used to try to punch me in the stomach when you were little?"

Becca laughed. "No. When did I do that?"

"Oh, you were about six years old. You wanted to show me how tough you were. You'd start swinging and I'd have my hand on your head keeping you at arm's length. Of course, you were too little to reach me from that distance, but that didn't stop you from using every ounce of your power to try. Eventually, you'd give up because you exhausted yourself trying so hard."

"It sounds like me, that's for sure."

"You were always like that, even when you were a toddler trying to figure things out."

He pulled the car up to the JetBlue doors and turned to look at her.

"Becca, you always give two hundred percent no matter what you're trying to accomplish. Don't ever change. Keep swinging for the fences, sweetheart. You're going to be an amazing doctor."

She could see her father trying to hold back tears, and she threw herself into his arms.

"I'll try, Daddy. I promise, I'll try."

Christopher wheeled out to the kitchen and waited for his mother to notice him.

"Mom, got a minute?"

"Sure, what's up?"

"I thought maybe you'd want to make us a pot of tea first."

She stopped cleaning the sink and turned to face him.

"It's that serious? You know a cup of my tea is reserved only for important discussions."

Christopher didn't smile at her and that had her concerned.

"Ok then, one pot of tea coming up."

She placed two teacups on the table and filled the teapot with water and added tea leaves to the strainer. She felt an anxious pull in her stomach and hoped whatever it was that he wanted to tell her was good news.

"Mom, you know that I've been working with my therapists and I'm making real progress. I think I've got a lot to look forward to, and I have you to thank for that. I don't know what I would have done if you didn't let me sulk and brood in my room these last months."

They both laughed at that, even though she still felt like there was something more he wanted to share.

"But?"

"But it's time for me to start planning my return to Massachusetts."

Nothing had prepared her for this talk. She didn't know what to expect, but this news surprised her.

"I guess I should be happy for you, but I'm selfish. I want you here with me."

"I'm going to continue for a couple more months here in Florida, because they said I'm adjusting so well I can expect to be fully ready by end of September. The thing is that I want to use the prosthetic blade to train for the Boston Marathon. I'll have six months to get ready. I need to be up there to prepare. Not only that, but I've also already had a few video appointments with a therapist to deal with the trauma stuff. Veteran's Affairs is helping me transition."

The whistle from the teapot startled her. Elated as she was, she hated that another of her children was leaving her once again. She poured their tea and placed the milk and sugar on the table. Forcing herself not to cry, she hugged her son.

"I'm going to miss you like crazy, but I know this is the right thing. You do realize that every single family member will be cheering you on next April, right?"

"I hope so, but first things first. I've got to learn how not to fall down walking across a room."

She placed the sugar and milk into her tea and stirred the liquid. She decided to give up being coy. The time for dancing around the subject of Becca was over.

"Will you look for her when you move back to Massachusetts?"

He smiled and nodded.

"I've never admitted this to anyone before, not even to myself I think. Yes. As long as I can stand on my own two legs, I'll tell her what everyone's been insisting for months."

"What's that?"

"That I love her, and I can't live without her."

CHAPTER TWENTY-EIGHT

*B*eth stared out the window and admired the changing color of the leaves. Working in the city there were few trees along the road, and she was lucky to have a couple just outside her office. She loved this time of year. Something about September reminded her of new beginnings. She looked forward to apple picking with Gabriel in a few days and pictured them sitting by the fire at his home.

Mitchell Glassman walked into Beth's office and sat on the chair in front of her desk.

"Hey, Mitchell. What's up?"

He threw a copy of the Boston Globe on her desk. The front page showed a mug shot of a woman.

"Who's this?"

"Cara Blessing. She's been arrested for child neglect in the past. But now she's in for murder. It seems one of the kids in her care died day before yesterday. As soon as this story hit the papers, we've been getting calls all morning from other parents who've left their kids with her in the past. One of them died last year from what the police said was an allergic reaction to peanuts. Now, the kid's mother is not so sure. The day care is shut down of course. I think sending her away for the rest of her life shouldn't be too difficult. The problem is, we need to chase down these other complaints. I think there might be more kids who've either died or have been abused."

Beth nodded. "Sounds good. I assume you're telling me this because you want my help?"

"Nope. I'm telling you this because this is yours. You can request anyone you'd like to be on the team. However, you want to run this is your call."

She'd been waiting for this chance for months, and now that it was here, she didn't know how to react. She looked at the woman's face.

"It says here that she has children of her own."

Mitchell nodded. "Yeah, two boys and a girl. They've been removed from the house and have been placed into good foster homes. Doesn't appear there are any family members coming forward."

Beth looked at him for any signs of ambivalence.

"Does everyone in the office know you're giving me this case?"

"Yup. I've already made the announcement. This is all yours."

It gave her no pleasure to come face to face once again with evil. For the sake of the children and their parents, she'd do whatever she could to give them the support they needed.

She didn't want to make a big deal about this news, so she simply said, "Thank you."

He got up from his chair and headed for the door.

"Go get 'em kiddo."

When she got home later that day, Beth called Lauren to see how she was doing.

"Hey, Bethy. What's new?"

"I've just been given a big case, and I thought I'd call my big sister for support. Tell me these exact words. 'You got this.'"

"You got this."

"Thank you."

"Is that it? I didn't know I had so much power. It's a shame no one asks me for my opinion around here."

"I'm sorry, Lauren. Is there anything I can do?"

"Nah. Unless you want to have a girls' weekend somewhere."

"I'd love to, but now with this case…"

"I'm just teasing. I know you're going to be busy. I'm really happy for you Bethy. You're going to be great."

Beth's cell phone buzzed, and she could see it was Christopher on the other line.

"Lauren, I've got to run, Chris is on the phone."

"Tell him I said hello."

"Will do. I'll call you later."

She hung up and answered her brother's call.

"Hey you. I'm glad you called. I was going to call you in a bit."

"Like minds sis. I'm good. I have some news and want to run it by you. Do you have a minute?"

"Sure. What's going on?"

"I'm coming home to Massachusetts."

"No way! Chris, that's great. When?"

"I've already got my plane ticket for October 7th. I thought maybe my favorite sister could pick me up at the airport."

"I'm your favorite because you need a ride and Lauren is probably too busy."

Christopher laughed. She loved hearing his voice and couldn't wait to see him.

"So, what's the plan? Where are you staying?"

"That's why I'm calling. Can I stay with you at your house?"

"Oh, Chris, I'd love it, but it's not my house, it's our house and you know it. You've as much right to live here as any one of us. I think it's a great idea."

Beth took a chance that he might talk to her about Becca but decided not to bring it up just now. There would be plenty of time for them to talk when he returned home.

"You've really made my day, Chris. I can't wait to see you."

"Me too, Bethy. I'll call you before I leave."

"Wait. Chris, how did Mom take your leaving?"

"At first she was sad, but she's come a long way since I told her I was leaving. She's happy for me. You know Mom."

"I certainly do. I'll give her a call tomorrow. Thanks for calling little brother. I love you."

"Love you, too, Bethy."

Sarah got to the inn as early as she could. When she walked into the kitchen she found her mother taking something out of the oven.

"Something smells delicious."

"Hey, Sarah. I wasn't expecting you this morning. How are you, honey?"

"I'm doing great. I just wanted to see my mother, that's all. What's this-no scones?"

"Nope, this morning I was in the mood to make my favorite, heirloom tomato corn leek quiche. Doesn't it look gorgeous?"

Sarah had kept her pregnancy a secret from everyone for the first couple of months. When the first trimester was almost over, she felt comfortable with sharing her good news.

"I assume the quiche is for the guests?"

Maggie laughed. "Is that your way of asking for a slice?"

"Yup."

"No problem, I've made two. Have a seat and I'll cut you a slice. So, what's been going on over at your house these days? How are Trevor and the kids?"

"Oh, everyone's fine."

"And work?"

"We've been really busy. We have a benefit coming up in a couple of months, and so we've already started the preparations."

"When is it?"

"The first week in November. If you can believe it, there will be Christmas decorations all around. It should be fun. The money goes toward the women's shelter I told you about last year."

"Oh, right. I remember that. Sounds like fun and it's for a good cause."

"Yeah, I'm looking forward to it. I hear the second trimester is when you have the most energy."

Sarah waited for her mother to realize what she'd said. It didn't take long.

"Sarah! You're pregnant?"

Sarah smiled and nodded. "I am."

She knew that her mother would be excited, but she didn't expect her to scream when she heard the news.

"Shh, Mom. You're going to wake up the whole neighborhood."

"Sarah, this is the best news."

Just then, Chelsea came through the back door.

"What news?"

"Sarah's pregnant."

"Oh, my goodness, congratulations. You are going to have your hands full my dear."

Rubbing her stomach, she smiled. "I know. I'm sure I can handle it though. Can you believe it, Mom? Me, a mother of three."

Maggie handed Sarah her plate, and Chelsea hovered over the stove top. "Is there some for your best friend in the world?"

Sarah and Maggie laughed. Chelsea never missed a breakfast opportunity at the inn. Maggie cut her a slice and then one for herself.

"Maybe I should have made three of these."

While they enjoyed their quiche, Christopher cleared his throat to get their attention. He walked out of his room and stood in the doorway. Standing on two legs, his prosthetic device in place, he stood tall and smiled at them.

With a lump in her throat, his mother got up from the table and began to walk to her son. Christopher stopped her.

"Stay there. I want to walk to you."

He took slow, deliberate steps, careful not to walk into anything along the way. When he reached his mother he took her hand.

"I did it."

Maggie smiled and nodded, letting the tears flow.

"You certainly did."

Still overcome with emotion from the events at the inn, Chelsea sat on her lanai looking out beyond her property to the sea. She didn't want to cry in front of Maggie and her family, but if ever there was a good reason to let the tears fall, it was watching Christopher standing in their kitchen.

Chelsea was moved beyond anything she'd seen since her husband Carl's battle with cancer, and it gave her hope that Christopher would be just fine.

She looked at her latest painting and then looked over at Jacqui's. Her student had finished her work and would be there soon to get her materials and possibly bring another blank canvas for their next project.

Chelsea had left the front door unlocked and looked at the clock. Jacqui was late again, but nothing could upset Chelsea today, not after what she'd witnessed this morning.

Jacqui called out to Chelsea from the front foyer.

"Hey, I'm here. Sorry I'm late again, but I had lots to do this morning."

"You know, Jacqui, I think I'm giving up trying to get through to you about getting here on time. You win. You've worn me down."

Jacqui laughed and handed Chelsea a piece of paper.

"What's this?"

"It's my acceptance into the New York Academy of Art's Graduate Program."

Chelsea couldn't believe what she was reading. Jacqui hadn't said a word to her about applying to art school.

"Honestly, Jacqui, I didn't think you'd finished your undergraduate degree. This is quite the accomplishment."

"College for me was just a party, even though I did get good grades, heaven knows how. But the point is that it's because of you that I decided to take this artist career seriously. I didn't really believe in myself the way you did…at least I didn't before. I do now."

"You do realize that you'll need to get to the classes on time?"

Jacqui smiled at Chelsea's last admonishment.

"Yes, ma'am. I won't be late, I promise."

Chelsea nodded. "Good. I'm glad to hear it. Well, I guess you're going to want to take your painting. It's quite good. You'll want to show it to your professors."

Jacqui shook her head. "Nah. I figure I'll give it to you. Something to remember me by."

"Oh, you know, Jacqui. I don't think I'll ever forget you. How about a mimosa to celebrate?"

"No. Thanks, I haven't had a drink in weeks. I'll take an iced tea though."

Chelsea poured two glasses, one for herself, and one for her student. Jacqui Hutchins had become more than her protégé. She was her friend and, dare she admit it, the daughter she never had.

CHAPTER TWENTY-NINE

Christopher walked into Powell Water Sports and found Crawford Powell at the register. Wearing long pants to cover his prosthetic leg, he waited for his reaction.

"Chris. Nice to see you."

Crawford came around from the counter and scanned Christopher's body.

"What's this?"

Christopher pulled up his pant leg to unveil his new leg. "Not bad, huh?"

"Wow. Not bad at all."

"I'm having a prosthetic blade made as well. I'm thinking of getting back into running again."

Crawford knew exactly what Christopher was referring to.

"You're going to run the Boston Marathon, aren't you?"

He smiled and shrugged. "I've already done it twice, and my time was decent. Why not try it again?"

Christopher didn't want to take up too much of his time, so he got right to the point.

"I'm going home to Massachusetts tomorrow. I thought you should know."

"You're going to see Becca?"

"I plan to. I'm going to be staying in the house I grew up in with my sister Beth. I don't know when I'll see her, but I wanted you to know that I'm going to tell her everything. I'm not sure why, but for some reason I felt like I needed to get your permission."

Crawford smiled. "I appreciate that. You don't need my blessing, but you have it. You've always had it."

He nodded and smiled. "Thank you."

"Understand that Becca might still push you away. She's been through a lot. Don't let that dissuade you. Hang in there. She'll come around. She can be stubborn."

Christopher laughed at that. "I'm counting on it."

The six of them stood in the driveway waiting for the Uber. Christopher insisted that no one drive him to the airport. There'd been enough goodbyes in his life, but this one was bittersweet. He didn't want to leave Captiva, nor did he want to leave his mother, but his life needed to begin, and it couldn't happen here.

The Uber driver pulled up close to them, and then got out of the car to help with the luggage. A carry-on was all Christopher wanted to take, and along with his backpack, he had everything he needed.

The wheelchair would stay on the island. He would buy another in Massachusetts. For now, he felt strong enough to stand on his new leg, but had a cane, just in case.

As usual, Chelsea had to make light of the situation.

"Don't forget about us poor, sad people struggling to get through every day by sitting on the beach drinking Lime-tinis."

He laughed. "I feel sorry for you already."

Paolo reached out to shake Christopher's hand, but instead pulled him close into a hug. "Take care of yourself and stay in touch often."

After Ciara and Chelsea hugged him, Sarah threw her arms around her brother. Teasing she said, "I guess I'm down one babysitter now."

Christopher squeezed her tight and then pulled back looking into her eyes. "You're a wonderful mother, Sarah."

He touched her stomach. "This is one lucky baby."

He looked at his mother and pulled a tissue out of his pocket to wipe her eyes. "I knew you would do this. Everything is going to be ok, Mom. All your children are doing great. You don't need to worry."

He hugged her, stroked her hair, and whispered, "Thank you for everything, Mom. I love you."

"I love you too. Call me, don't text. I want to hear everything that's going on in your life. Do you understand?"

He laughed. "I promise to call."

He pulled away from her and Maggie held his hand as long as she could before they separated.

He got in the car and as they drove away from the Key Lime Garden Inn, Christopher looked out the back window and waved one last time.

The flight to Boston was only three hours, and it gave him plenty of time to think. He pulled his father's wallet from the backpack, now filled with his own license and credit cards, and one photo. He looked at Becca's face and marveled those ten years hadn't changed a thing. She looked exactly the same after all these years.

He didn't know exactly when he would look for her, but he knew he couldn't go much longer without seeing her. Text messages and emails wouldn't do. He needed to see her in person, or more to the point, he needed her to see him.

Christopher thought about Crawford's description of his daughter and smiled. He relied on Becca's tenacity and stubbornness. Without it, they might not have come this far. All he could do now, was pray she hadn't finally thrown in the towel.

He loved landing in Boston. Planes always appeared to skirt the Boston harbor before reaching the runway. He used his cell phone to capture the landing on video, and as they taxied to the gate, he breathed a sigh of relief that he was finally home.

He sent Beth a text.

"Just landed. No checked bags so I should be outside shortly."

He stood and reached for his carry-on in the overhead compartment. With a full plane, Christopher struggled to maneuver his way down the aisle. There would be many situations like this where he'd have to learn how best to move. He was tired and walked slowly, pulling his luggage behind him, and using his cane for support. Once outside the baggage claim doors, he saw his sister by the curb.

"Hey, Bethy."

Beth ran to help him. They hugged and she took his suitcase from him.

"How are you doing? Is it hard walking?"

"I'm fine, but do me a favor? Help me get this jacket on? It's cold."

"It's sixty-five degrees. That must be freezing for you, coming from Florida."

She helped him put his jacket on and made their way to the car. The security guard looked at her impatiently and told her to move along."

"It feels good to be home."

"So, what are your plans?"

Christopher kept his desire to see Becca to himself.

"I've got a couple of appointments this week. I'm meeting

with a therapist I've been working with through video. He's in Boston so now I'll be able to meet with him in person. I'm having a prosthetic blade created. So, I've got appointments with doctors there."

"What's a prosthetic blade?"

"It's a device that replaces the leg I'm wearing so that I can start running again."

Beth almost jumped out of her seat.

"Seriously? You're going to run the Boston Marathon?"

"That's the plan. I've been doing a lot of research on the blade. It's not the same as the leg I've got now. Since my amputation was above the knee, I've got choices of using a running foot by adding a straight pylon or a running foot with a knee joint. There are different advantages using either one, so I've got to decide what I want to do."

"This is so exciting, Chris. Maybe I can run with you in the mornings. I could use more exercise in my life."

"I need more information on the Boston Marathon Para Olympics Division. I'm not sure of eligibility. Besides, I have no idea if I'll have enough time to prepare. I've got to have the device made, get it fitted etc., then I'll need time to get used to it and train. It's already October. The race is in a little over five months."

"You'll do it, Chris. I have no doubt. I'll help you get ready."

They reached the Andover house and Christopher couldn't wait to get inside, but first he needed to tell Beth what had been on his mind for weeks.

"Maybe you can help me do more than train. I want to run the marathon for Erin. What do you say to us creating that foundation we talked about in Florida? There are lots of kids like Erin. Let's do something for them."

"Oh, Chris. I think that's a wonderful idea. I say, let's do it."

He grabbed her hand. "Thank you, Bethy."

Beth opened the front door and Chris followed her inside. He walked through the house, looking in every room.

"I feel like it's been forever since I've been home."

"Two years, I think. The Christmas before Mom left for Captiva."

"I couldn't wait to get here, but now that I am, it feels weird that it's so quiet. How has it been for you living here alone?"

Beth opened the refrigerator. "I have mixed feelings about that. You want something to drink?"

"Any chance you've got a beer in there?"

"As it happens, I do. I'll join you."

She opened the bottles and they moved to the living room sofa.

They clinked bottles and drank their beer. Beth answered his question.

"There are days when I feel so sad that everyone's lives have taken them away from this house. We're all so scattered. I've thought about getting everyone to come here for Christmas, but the truth is that I think mom is so busy with the inn, especially during the holidays, that would make it impossible. Other times, I enjoy the quiet, I love the garden and continuing with what we all started here. My family is still here in this house."

Christopher smiled. "I get that. I hope my living here will help you on those lonely days. Why don't we plan a dinner with Michael and Lauren and the kids? I'd love to see everyone."

"That sounds wonderful. We should have Thanksgiving here too. I know Mom and Sarah won't be joining us in person, but I'm sure we can Zoom them in on that day. Having some of the family together is better than none. Although I should warn you that Jeff and Lauren are having problems."

"What does that mean?"

"They fight all the time. They're seeing a marriage counselor, but it doesn't seem to be working. She's even told me there's a possibility of divorce."

"You're kidding me?"

"I wish I were. I've been over there for dinner a few times, and nothing seems to improve. It's awkward but I have to be there for Lauren, no matter what."

"I hope they can work it out. I'd hate to see them divorce, not just for the kids but for all of us. I love Jeff. He's been a part of this family for years, long before they got married."

"I agree."

"So, I've told you about me. Tell me what's been going on with you."

Beth took another gulp of her beer. "Oh, you don't want to go there."

"Why not? Are things not good between you and Gabriel?"

"We're doing great. Nothing wrong there, although I'm sure I'm driving him crazy with my insecurities."

Christopher almost spit out his beer.

"You? Insecure? Since when?"

"It started when I took this job. It's one thing to want to help people and to feel like you're making a difference in the world. It's a completely different issue when you realize the responsibility you have. If I screw up, bad people get to go free."

"You're only human. Since we were kids you always acted like you had this incredible power and there wasn't anything you couldn't do. I always admired that. But there comes a point when you have to admit that you're just like the rest of us mortals."

Beth laughed. "You make me sound like a character in a comic book. But I know what you're saying."

"Everyone fails, and everyone makes mistakes, Bethy. Think of it this way. Be happy you're not a surgeon. Imagine making a mistake in an operating room."

Beth's eyes widened. "You certainly know how to change my perspective."

Christopher finished his beer and looked down at the cushion.

"Hey, do you have a dog?"

"Oh that? That's Charlie, Gabriel's dog. He brings him over here on occasion. I hope that's not a problem."

"Nope. I love dogs. Just don't tell mom he's been sitting on her furniture."

CHAPTER THIRTY

The Director of Summit Compass, Duncan O'Connor, met Christopher at the reception desk.

"Christopher, or should I call you Chris?"

"Either is fine."

"It's good to meet you. Dr. Hensley shared a little about your story with me, but I'd like to hear from you why you're here. First, why don't I give you a tour of the place?"

"Lead on."

They passed rooms filled with children and adults sharing stories and engaging in physical activities. They stopped at a rock wall at the far end of the building and watched as an amputee in a wheelchair encouraged a child to keep climbing.

"You've got this Aiden. Keep going. You can do it. You're a warrior remember?"

The young boy continued his climb until he reached the top. The others in the room clapped and called out his name. "Way to go, Aiden. Woohoo. You did it."

Christopher and Duncan clapped as well.

"It's hard not to be inspired by these kids. Some are in remission, but not all. I've got to say that it feels pretty darn awesome to know you're making a real difference in these kids' lives. It's not always a good day. Some days we get bad news and it's tough, but they don't give up, so neither do we. Let's go into my office so we can talk privately."

Duncan's office was little more than an extension of a gym.

"Can I get you anything to drink?"

"No. Thanks, I'm fine."

"So, Chris, I know about the bombing, and what happened to your leg, my question is what has happened since the day of your surgery?"

He was glad that Duncan hadn't described it as the day he lost his leg, as if he'd misplaced it somewhere.

"It's been a journey. I went through every emotion you can imagine. Something similar to the stages of grief. The only thing is when you go through an experience like this, you don't realize how you take those who love you along for the ride. It's not fair. Collateral damage I think they call it."

Duncan nodded. "I hear stories like yours every day."

"I've been lucky. I have an amazing family and people who love me, but sooner or later you have to come to terms with your situation and decide whether you want to live or die. I hate to say it, but for a while I chose death."

"And now?"

He smiled. "I want to live, and I want to help others who want the same."

Duncan leaned forward and stuck out his hand.

"Well then, welcome to the land of the living. What do you think? Can you see yourself working here? You won't find a better reason to get up in the morning."

The words were music to Christopher's ears. He had much to be grateful for. Paying it forward brought passion back into his life.

He had only one answer for Duncan.

"This is where I belong."

A white coat, green scrubs and purple latex gloves were part of Becca's new wardrobe, and she loved it. She'd just finished her cardio/pulmonary class and was headed to anatomy next. Looking around the classroom she thought how strange it was that while several of these students were her friends now, they'd be her competition if any of them shared the same first year residency program with her.

Studying molecules, tissues, microbes, infectious diseases, and the immune system wasn't as difficult as it was years ago. Grateful for her previous two years at medical school, Becca could enjoy the experience without stress. She assumed she'd retain much more the second time around but would have to wait for her mid-terms to prove that point.

When she wasn't studying, she rode her bike along the city streets, making her way down Summer St. toward South Boston and Castle Island. She enjoyed the food and activity in Chinatown but getting to the ocean as often as she could soothed her soul. She couldn't shake the need to be on the water but would have to wait for school breaks to return to Captiva. Boston Harbor was too cold this time of year, and so the best she could do was enjoy breathing in the salt air and watching it from the shore.

Becca always carried her schoolbooks with her. She gently placed her bike on the ground and sat on the grassy area, watching people walk by. Soon the snow would cover everything, and she'd be forced to abandon her bike-riding.

The seagulls didn't care what time of year it was. They swooped down and surrounded the trash barrels looking for discarded food. Occasionally, someone would pass by walking their dog. She'd encourage each one to come visit her. Crossing her legs, a small cocker spaniel climbed on top of her, trying to lick her face.

The owner pulled the puppy away. "Sorry about that."

"Oh, that's ok. I don't mind. I love dogs."

"Do you have one?"

"No. Maybe one day I'll get one."

"Have a nice day."

"You, too."

The man and his dog continued along the path. Becca watched the dog stop often to investigate the smallest item. Reaching for her anatomy notebook she opened it to review the latest lecture. She pulled her hair into a messy bun keeping her hair from her face.

Looking up, she saw a man walking toward her, and she couldn't help but notice how much he looked like Christopher. She'd thought about him often and missed him terribly.

The man's features coming into view, she stood, her hand reaching for her throat. It was Chris. Her Chris.

"Hello, Becca."

Her heart racing, she could barely speak.

"What?...How?"

Lifting his pant leg, he exposed the prosthetic device.

He laughed and said, "I'm bionic now."

Becca walked down the hill toward him. It felt impossible to believe that he was standing in front of her. If she didn't know better, she'd think maybe all of this was a dream. He looked as handsome as ever, and her heart leaped in her chest at the sight of him. He put his hand on her face.

"My beautiful Becca. I've waited so long to tell you what you mean to me. I've loved you since we were kids. I've never stopped. The world spun out of control, and I lost my way for a while, but you were always with me. I should have told you this before, but pride and stupidity got in my way. I let you go because I wanted you to have the best life that you could…"

Her voice returning to her, she stopped him.

"And you thought my being away from you would give me the best life? You're right, that's stupid."

"My mother called me an idiot."

"I love your mother."

He smiled at that.

"My pride got in the way. After you left, I promised myself that as soon as I could stand on two legs, I'd find you again."

"Chris…"

He stopped her. "I know. You didn't need me to have two legs to be with me. You've loved me unconditionally since we first met. But *I* needed it, so I could stand in front of you like this, face-to-face and tell you that I can't live without you. I need you Becca, not as my caretaker, but as my partner in life. Sitting or standing I don't want one more day on this journey without you by my side."

Christopher took her hands in his and leaned in to kiss her gently on the lips. Wrapping his arms around her, he pulled her close. They held each other for several minutes before she spoke again.

Becca whispered in his ear, "I don't care what you say. You still lost that volleyball game."

Maggie carried her bucket of seashells as she walked along the beach in the early morning. She didn't feel like baking a thing which was unusual for her. Instead, all she wanted was to listen to the seagulls as they passed overhead, and the waves as they crashed onto the shore. She even asked Paolo to stay behind. She had some thinking to do. Her husband always gave her the space she needed whenever she asked, and this morning was no different.

She walked up to her blanket and pushed the bucket deep into the sand to hold it in place. Her ever-present journal by her side, she wasn't sure what to write in it today. So much had happened in the last six months. She'd chronicled each event in her leather-bound book, but she felt introspective and unsure if she'd be able to capture her thoughts adequately.

Was she happy? Was she content? Was she confused about life?

All of those emotions played out in her mind, and she tried to remember Rose's words about riding the wave. Learning to let go had been her most important lesson, and each day was another reminder of how little she had control over. Anything worth anything took time, so she was gentle with herself and held on to her belief that patience solved almost every problem.

Maggie reached for the bucket and looked over her new collection. She recognized a Double-Sunrise shell. It had two, delicate identical sides, a golden hinge keeping them attached. Anne Morrow Lindbergh talked about this very seashell in her book. Not usually found on Captiva, the find was special.

Maggie kept a copy of Gift from the Sea on her iPhone. She searched the Kindle app and pulled up the information on the shell.

"The double sunrise shell has the eternal validity of all beautiful and fleeting things."

Maggie's life, from its beginnings, had been beautiful, but it was only with the passing of each year did she fully understand just how fleeting it was.

Like this rare shell, it stood at the center of her family's life and no matter where each member traveled, the hinge that kept them perfectly connected would not break.

Nothing held more value in her eyes than that.

THE END

For a sneak peek at the next book in this series, check out the Prologue for Captiva Christmas on the next page.

CAPTIVA CHRISTMAS

PROLOGUE

*L*auren Phillips panicked as she stood at the top of the escalator. Descending into the throng of Christmas shoppers, she pulled a tissue from her coat pocket and blew her nose. She'd been fighting a cold for several days, but now, just when she needed her strength the most, she melted into the crowd with little energy and a red nose.

Christmas music played over the store's speakers as she pushed through the crowd. The line leaving the building was as long as the line for the lady's room. Eyeing a chair near the entrance, she sat and waited for the strength to walk to the mall garage.

Bundled up against the cold, she regretted her selection of layered clothing that she was unable to remove in the store. She watched the line continue to move like a conveyer belt. As people entered the revolving door, more were added to the line. She'd have to get up and attack this situation with all the courage she could muster. It was, in fact, the only way out.

She walked to the end of the line and suddenly wondered if she'd be able to get through the doors with all her shopping bags. As she approached the front of the line, a man carrying nothing, but a briefcase directed her to another door that had just been unlocked.

He held the door open for her. "Please, come this way."

Lauren turned sideways to get through and laughed at her predicament. She suddenly saw the humor in her situation and wondered if the man had thought she was crazy and took pity on her.

His British accent, startling blue eyes, and pleasing demeanor made her wish that she looked more appealing. As it was, all she could do was thank him for his help.

"Thank you so much. For a minute, I didn't think I'd get out of there alive."

"You did look a bit frazzled. I'm happy to be of service. I guess you could say that I was in the right place at the right time. Will you be all right now, or do you need help getting to your car? The snow is coming down quite heavily."

Lauren looked past him and searched for the garage.

"I parked my car in the garage across the street. At least I think it's across the street. This snow is blinding."

He took a couple of her bags and then her elbow and together they walked toward the garage. Once inside, they shook the snow off their coats and tried to find her car.

"I have one of those little alarms on my key. It's supposed to help me find the car. I've never used it before so I've no idea if it works."

"Let's give it a try, shall we?"

Lauren placed the remaining bags on the ground and looked inside her handbag, searching for her keys. When she found them, she pressed the alarm button, and her car flashed its headlights and the alarm beeped on and off.

"There it is."

They gathered the bags and walked to the car. Lauren couldn't help but wonder who this man was. She had no right to ask him anything, but her curiosity got the better of her.

"So, am I allowed to ask a little about the man who rescued me?"

He laughed. "Oh, hardly a rescue, but forgive me. My name is Callum Foster. I'm headed to my hotel after a business meeting. Silly me, I thought I'd make a stop into the store to pick up a few Christmas gifts for family. I changed my mind when I saw the crowd. Perhaps another day. I'm very pleased to meet you."

Lauren put her bags inside the car and then closed the door.

"Lauren Phillips, it's nice to meet you as well." She extended her hand, and they shook. He didn't let go and seemed to want more time with her.

"I'm sure after all this you want to get home, but I wonder if you might be interested in having a drink or something, tea perhaps?"

She wanted nothing more in that moment but thought better of it. She could tell that he seemed embarrassed by the offer.

"I'm sorry, that was rather forward of me. It's just that I don't know anyone here, at least not yet, and I could use a friend."

"I don't understand."

"My firm is sending me to our Boston office and so I'm in the process of looking for a place to buy and well, all that moving to America entails."

Lauren saw the opportunity.

"What kind of place are you looking for? Is it just you or do you have a family?"

"It's just me. It's hard to make a long-term commitment with someone when you travel so often. I'll be working out of the Boston location but will continue traveling back and forth to the UK. I'm not sure what I'm looking for exactly except to say that it shouldn't be a place that needs work. I need something I can move into right away."

Lauren reached into her wallet and pulled out her business card.

"It just so happens that I own a real estate company. I'd be happy to help you find something that will work for your situation."

He looked at the card. "Lauren Phillips. Brilliant. It looks like you might have saved my life as well today. What shall we do to celebrate?"

Lauren didn't want to hurt his feelings, but she had to get back to her husband and two daughters who were waiting for her at home.

"My husband will be worried about me, especially in this weather. Thank you so much for helping me, and for the offer to have tea, but I must decline."

"Right. Of course, you must get home. Well then, thank you again for giving me your card. I'll be ringing you first thing Monday morning if that's all right with you. We can talk about the details then. Would you be willing to meet over coffee on Monday?"

After turning him down once, she didn't have the heart to say no. It wasn't official, but he more than likely would be her client by then. There was nothing inappropriate about having coffee with a client, after all.

"Of course. That will be fine."

"I'll see you then, Lauren. Be careful driving home."

She waved to him as she pulled out of the garage and onto the road. The snowflakes were large and coming down at a steady pace.

With four inches on the ground, it bothered Lauren that Jeff hadn't at least called her cell phone to see if she was all right. She'd been gone for hours, and if she wasn't careful, she might easily skid off the road. Driving slowly, the only sound she could hear was the wiper blades streaking across the window. Watching the brake lights in front of her, she used them as a guide to stay in her lane. Lauren tried not to be upset at her husband's lack of concern for her safety and focused on the ride home. She knew what she'd find as soon as she walked in the front door. No one would great her or even say hello. Everyone would be busy with their own interests and odds were she'd find Jeff laying on the sofa watching a Bruins game.

Maybe turning down tea with Callum Foster was a mistake.

At least he'd be someone interested in her. She wouldn't be invisible to him. He'd make her feel that her real estate business success was something to feel proud of instead of ashamed. Whatever awaited her at home, there was always Monday morning, and the intriguing life of a British gentleman to look forward to.

ALSO BY ANNIE CABOT

THE CAPTIVA ISLAND SERIES

Book One: KEY LIME GARDEN INN
Book Two: A CAPTIVA WEDDING
Book Four: CAPTIVA CHRISTMAS
Book Five: CAPTIVA NIGHTS
Book Six: CAPTIVA HEARTS
Book Seven: CAPTIVA EVER AFTER

THE PERIWINKLE SHORES SERIES
Book One: CHRISTMAS ON THE CAPE
Book Two: THE SEA GLASS GIRLS

For a **FREE** copy of the Prequel to the Captiva Island Series, **CAPTIVA SUNSET** - Join my newsletter HERE.

ACKNOWLEDGMENTS

A huge thank you to Lisa Lee of Lisa Lee Proofreading and Editing. Even with all the computer and software issues, we managed to get this done. Thank you so much for your patience and sense of humor, and for putting up with my constant emails.

To Michele Connolly and Anne Marie Page Cooke, thank you for agreeing to read and reread my books. You've truly helped me add scenes that I know have made it a much better book.

To Marianne Nowicki of Premade Ebook Cover Shop. The cover of Captiva Memories is stunning and as always it is a joy to work with you.

To my friends and family who have supported me and cheered me on from the beginning. I love you all.

To my readers: Here we are on book three - can you believe it? Without your feedback, kind reviews, and encouragement, I'd be lost. I'm thrilled that you have enjoyed this series. Hang on because there is so much more to come.

Blessings dear friends,
Annie

ABOUT THE AUTHOR

Annie Cabot is the author of contemporary women's fiction and family sagas. Annie writes about friendships and family relationships, that bring inspiration and hope to others.

Annie Cabot is the pen name for the writer Patricia Pauletti (Patti) who, for the last seven years, has been the co-author of several paranormal mystery books under the pen name Juliette Harper. A lover of all things happily ever after, it was only a matter of time before she began to write what was in her heart, and so, the pen name Annie Cabot was born.

When she's not writing, Annie and her husband like to travel. Winters always involve time away on Captiva Island, Florida where she continues to get inspiration for her novels.

Annie lives in Massachusetts with her husband and adorable new puppy, Willa.

For more information visit anniecabot.com

Made in United States
Troutdale, OR
02/29/2024